The Wallflower

Linda Francis Lee

 JOVE BOOKS, NEW YORK

THE WALLFLOWER

A Jove Book / published by arrangement
with the author

PRINTING HISTORY
Jove edition / August 1995

ISBN: 0-515-11683-1

A JOVE BOOK®
Jove Books are published by The Berkley Publishing Group,
200 Madison Avenue, New York, New York 10016.
JOVE and the "J" design are trademarks
belonging to Jove Publications, Inc.

PRINTED IN THE UNITED STATES OF AMERICA

10 9 8 7 6 5 4 3 2 1

For my father-in-law,
Tony Lee,
who has accepted me into
the family like a daughter

And of course, as always,
for Michael

One

THE HOUSE WAS IN AN UPROAR. ONE OF THE DALTRY CHILDREN was turning twenty. And everyone in the family in this small town of Paradise Plains, Texas—Paradise as it was frequently called—knew what that meant: the birthday child was assigned the "labor" their grandmother, Minerva, a woman who loved mythology as much as she loved her family, had chosen for them to improve their character.

It was a Daltry tradition. No Daltry had ever escaped. And no Daltry had ever failed.

Persephone Daltry paced back and forth across the floor of her and her sisters' bedroom high up in the attic of their lifelong home. Persy had lived twenty years to see this day and learn what her labor would be. Her grandmother had been crooning that simple word into every one of the Daltry children's ears since birth. She was certain that unlike most children whose first word was "mama" or "papa," the Daltry clan's first word was "labor."

Part of Persy was excited beyond belief to learn what her task would be. Her older brother Hercules, Lee to everyone who knew him, had already performed his labor. Despite the fact that he had been assigned the task of teaching school—Lee with a bunch of screaming, snot-nosed children gathered around his feet had been a scary thought—he had sailed through the assignment with flying colors, acquitting himself famously; met his loving wife, Meredith; and had a library built in his name for his efforts. Everyone knew that a special prize was the reward for a job done well.

But another part of Persy, the saner part, she reasoned, was scared out of her wits. There was not a story to be found about an aunt or uncle, her father or now even her brother, who had ever failed at their assigned task. As a result no one knew what happened if someone did. Heavens above, Persy pleaded silently, please don't let me be the first one to muck things up.

From praying she went on to wondering, torturous wondering, as she had been wondering since the moment she flipped the calendar page over from September to October, announcing that the assignment of her labor was only days away. What could her labor be? she wondered. But she wouldn't have to wonder for long. The answer was nearly at hand. The day had finally arrived.

October 7, 1879. Persephone Daltry's twentieth birthday.

Pressing her eyes closed, she took a deep breath, trying to calm her racing heart and churning mind. Gradually she became aware of the sounds that wafted up two flights of stairs to the attic. Rugs were being beaten within an inch of their lives, floors swept and scrubbed, and, more importantly, pots and pans scraped and banged against the stove, sounding more like mentally incompetent musicians attempting to make music than anyone trying to produce something edible in the kitchen.

Ahh, the kitchen. The warm, newly modernized kitchen. And her domain. Many years ago the Daltrys had employed a cook named Mrs. Wilcox. Minerva had never been very good in the kitchen and Minerva's daughter-in-law, Jane, Persy's mother, wasn't much better. But Persy had taken to cooking like a duck takes to water, and when Mrs. Wilcox had retired, Persy stepped into her shoes and hadn't kicked them off in the intervening eight years.

But today was the day of Persephone's birth, and it was part of the twentieth birthday tradition that the birthday child not do a thing other than enjoy. But just the thought of her family down there trying to cook made Persy's mind reel. Someone could be killed for all any one of them knew about culinary skills. And even if nothing that dire happened, she knew the kitchen would never be the same after the day was done and she was back in her favorite place, preparing the meals as she always did.

She grimaced at the thought of the mess that was undoubtedly being made and the heat that was most assuredly scorching the room from the stove that was temperamental at best and had to be monitored continuously in order to keep the temperature just right.

And then, as if to confirm her fears, she heard a loud bang and a "Doggone it!" rush up the stairs. She recognized the voice as Lee's, and recognized as well that he was none too pleased.

Persy scowled but made herself stay put. She had promised her family that no matter what she heard, she would keep out of their way and let them prepare her birthday feast. But when another pot banged, only this time louder, and the curse that followed would have made a cowpoke blush, she raced toward the stairs, promises forgotten, determined to save her precious domain.

"Out of this kitchen, Hercules Daltry!" Minerva Daltry exclaimed. Her normal loving demeanor was being pushed to the limit by one mishap after the next as she tried to prepare her darling Persephone's special day. "You, too,

Venus and Atalanta! And, Cupid, quit being so dramatic. Unrequited love never killed anyone. If you have to lament, do it somewhere else. This place is enough of a mess without the four of you trying to help. Help! Good Lord, this bunch is worthless when it comes to the kitchen! Give this lot a pot or a broom and they wouldn't know which was for cooking! Well, let me tell you, it's about time each and every one of you learned. What would happen if Persephone wasn't here to cook your meals?"

"But Persy's always here, and she loves to cook," the blond-haired, blue-eyed Venus stated from just outside the kitchen, all too ready to make her escape. "Besides, she doesn't like us to get in her way."

"And Persy would never leave," Atalanta exclaimed, ready to follow her sister to safer climes. Allie, as she was known, had silvery-gray eyes and short, curly brown hair that stamped her as a hoyden more clearly than words. "Where would she go? This is her home!"

Minerva grumbled. "Of course it's her home. But that doesn't mean that she, or any one of you for that matter, won't leave at some point." Her gray eyes grew pensive, her brow furrowing gently as she stared at the long set of stairs that led to the floors above.

"Grandma, what is it?" Lee asked, his voice laced with genuine concern.

The words startled her, but when she finally returned her attention to her grandchildren, the faraway look was gone as if it had never been there at all. "What's wrong is that every one of you needs to learn how to cook."

Her grandchildren sighed.

"All right," Allie grumbled, heading back toward the kitchen. "Where do we start?"

"Not today, you don't," Minerva countered. "I was simply making a point. You can learn another day!" She turned away, distracted. "Where is Atlas, I want to know.

He's supposed to be bringing more firewood for the stove! Burning hot or freezing cold that thing is. I do declare, it was easier to cook over an open fire with a cast-iron skillet than on this newfangled monstrosity."

Just then Atlas, nicknamed Bub, the twelve-year-old and youngest Daltry sibling, walked into the house, a perfect pyramid of wood in his arms, his father Odysseus on his heels.

"There you are, you little scamp!" Minerva said, though her smile belied her harsh tone. "You were probably out there counting each log, measuring even, to put them in order. Good Lord, how such an orderly child was born into this household I'll never know. Well, hurry up, the fire's almost out."

Bub only smiled, then pushed through the swinging door to the kitchen. Odysseus started to follow, a hammer and toolbox in his hands.

"And where do you think you're going, Odysseus?" Minerva asked, eyeing her son.

Odysseus Daltry was as tall as his mother was short. He was big and burly with laughing blue eyes and wiry brown hair. "I'm going into the kitchen, Ma," he said, the corners of his eyes crinkling when he bent over and kissed her on the cheek.

"You have no business in the kitchen, Odysseus Daltry. Not today, at least. Your wife and I are having enough problems trying to cook Persephone's special birthday meal without the likes of you getting in our way."

"I have faith you and Jane can do anything you put your mind to," he said, his voice teasing, as Minerva was the first to give her clan the very same advice whenever anyone mentioned a problem.

"Next you'll be saying that I'm being hoisted by my own petard!" she muttered.

"Good God, Mother!" he exclaimed, his eyes wide and

teasing. "Hopefully you're serving something better than that!"

Minerva stared at him for one long second before his meaning became clear. In the next second she blew up like a blowfish, gathered her long skirt in her fists, and took out after him. But he only laughed and skipped just out of reach and into the kitchen, his tools rattling in their box, Minerva ranting and raving close behind, leaving Hercules, Cupid, Atalanta, and Venus standing in the entry hall shaking their heads at the all-too-familiar sight.

"What are you doing, Odie?" Jane Daltry stood at the stove, flour covering just about every inch of her apron-clad body.

Odie stopped in his tracks, tilting his head, then smiled at his wife. Seconds later Minerva plunged through the door and cannoned into the back of him.

"The two of you are at it again, I see," Jane said, turning back to the stove. "The children, even at their youngest and most outrageous, weren't as bad as the two of you." Jane shook her head, blond wisps of hair curling about her face, and ran her finger down a page that was marked in a recipe book. "Sometimes I'd swear I married into a crazy family," she grumbled as she peered more closely at the book.

"Crazy or not," Odie teased from close behind her, "you'd have us no other way."

Jane laughed in spite of herself. "True. But today, husband, I would appreciate a slight reprieve. At the rate I'm going, we'll be serving Persy boiled water and day-old bread for her birthday meal, and how special do you think that will be?"

Odie laughed. "I find that hard to believe. My beautiful wife and sainted mother can't come up with something better than bread and water? Never." But then he looked over her shoulder and nearly groaned at the sight of the page his wife had returned her attention to—a page that

was nearly destroyed with grease, flour, and clumps of
. . . something, though who knew what.

"Is that one tablespoon of flour for the gravy or one
cup?" she wondered out loud, forgetting her husband for
the moment.

Odie stepped closer until he stood scant inches behind
her. "Can't tell, darlin'. But I can tell that you look good
enough to eat," he said, wrapping his arms around her
waist.

"Mind your manners, husband," she said, slapping at
his hands, leaving a powdery-white handprint on his arm.

Odie, however, didn't let go. He turned her around,
slowly, pretending to study her with great intensity.

"What are you doing, Odie Daltry?" she asked, the recipe, for the moment, forgotten as heat rose in her cheeks.

"Why, darlin', I'm looking for a clear spot where I can
give you a kiss."

And before she could protest he leaned down and
kissed her right on the lips. After a moment's hesitation
Jane melted in his arms, hardly aware of the hoots and
whistles that came from the doorway when several of their
children pushed through the door and began to cheer
them on.

Minerva shook her head and tried to stifle the smile
that threatened. "The two of you are going to be my age,
hobbling around, walking with canes, and still kissing like
a couple of lovebirds."

Odie pulled away. "We can only hope."

Jane's cheeks reddened even further before she turned
away and tried to concentrate on the recipe before her,
while everyone began talking all at once.

Unable to read the recipe and with her thoughts mud-
dled to boot, Jane determined that if she wanted enough
gravy for a family of nine, she'd best use a *cup* of flour.
With that she measured out the amount, then started to
pour it into the huge pot on the stove.

"Oh, my stars!"

Everyone stopped and swung around toward the door. "Persy!" they cried in unison.

"Oh, my heavens!" Persy exclaimed, her porcelain features marked with disbelief. And then her eyes found the cup of flour being poured into what she could best determine was supposed to be gravy. She stifled a groan.

The Daltrys glanced back and forth between themselves. Persy shifted her attention from the gravy that would undoubtedly be more suited to repairing a wall than enhancing a slice of meat, and looked about the kitchen. Flour covered not only her mother but the floor and tables as well. "What is going on here?"

"We're cooking," Venus replied as if she spoke to a dimwit.

"For your birthday," Allie added, as if there was a need.

"But don't you worry, love," Jane said, bustling over to her eldest daughter and giving her a quick hug. "You are going to have the very best meal. I promise."

For one very quiet second, every Daltry there glanced about the kitchen, realizing in unison that a small miracle —no, a large miracle, they amended—would have to occur for Jane's statement to prove true.

Minerva shrugged her shoulders, then came up on her granddaughter's other side. "Just the kind of meal you would have made had you been the one cooking. Just you wait and see. We've only gotten off to a rough start is all."

Persy blinked, then blinked again. She wouldn't have had a speck of flour on anything but the inside of the flour canister. From the looks of things now, there was more flour covering the kitchen than in whatever it was they were cooking, or trying to cook, she amended when she watched her mother return to the cookbook and wrinkle her nose at whatever it was that she was reading.

But then Persy smiled. It was her birthday. For a change she wasn't going to worry about kitchens and cooking or even cleaning up the mess. She was going to enjoy whatever the day and the meal might bring.

A loud bang captured their attention. Everyone turned to find Odie installing the brand-new oak wood kitchen cabinets he had built in his work shed.

"Not today!" Jane screeched, egg yolk from a newly broken egg flying through her fingers at her sudden turn.

Venus and Allie groaned their disgust over the yolk that spattered the wall. Atlas thought it quite funny. Meredith, Lee's wife, who had just walked in, turned her head into Lee's shoulder to hide a smile. Persy headed for her bedroom. Her kitchen, she confirmed, would never be the same.

Back upstairs, Persy tried to keep her mind occupied. But try as she might she could not keep the big question at bay.

"What in the world has Grandma chosen as my labor?" she whispered to the mirror that stood in the corner. "What part of my personality needs to be improved?" She could make a list a mile long out of all she needed to do to improve her character. But what, she wondered, was that one trait that stuck out?

She studied herself in the silvered frame for a long while. Though she couldn't put her finger on it, somehow she felt different. Her long brown hair that was pulled up and away from her face was the same. The color hadn't changed and it was pulled up the same way. She still looked more like her grandmother than anyone else in the family. And like her grandmother, her eyes were the same dark gray, and she was still just as short. But where her grandmother longed to be tall and regal, Persy had always felt comfortable with her petite frame.

Yes, she concluded, she looked no different today than yesterday or the day before. But still she felt she had changed. Was it that when the magical year of twenty had been set as some sort of demarcation point in her life, that upon reaching it she was bound to feel different by sheer expectation? Maybe. Maybe not.

She looked around the room she had slept in her whole life. She smiled when her eyes strayed to the beds that came out of the wall. They, like just about everything else in the house, were one of her father's many inventions. She loved those beds, but . . .

She pressed her eyes closed against the sudden, nearly painful insight. That was it. That's what was different. Lately there always seemed to be a *but* attached to everything she did or thought. She loved Paradise, but . . . She loved her home, but . . . She loved cooking, but . . . She loved her family, more than anything, but . . . Too many buts, all adding up to the same persistent idea that had been plaguing her more and more every day.

She wanted more out of life, or more accurately, she wanted something different. She wanted to live, to feel, to do more than live vicariously through the books she read.

She glanced over at a long-cherished picture made from a woodcut of what she had always called "The Sophisticated Life." Long, flowing ball gowns, orchestras, top hats, and canes. She could no more imagine her father, or even Lee, wearing a top hat or carrying a cane than she could imagine running naked down the only street in Paradise Plains, Texas.

Persephone longed to sip tea and eat crumpets, though not in the family parlor with her siblings bellyaching about how they would prefer cookies and milk. She wanted polite conversation about art exhibits and famous museums. She wanted to eat at a table with long lines of utensils lined up like sentinels surrounding her plate. She, unlike anyone else in her family, would know what each extra knife, spoon, and fork was for. Her books had taught her such things.

But that, she knew, was tantamount to sedition. Besides, how could she ever possibly find a way to leave?

Certainly she couldn't expect her grandmother to send her away to some exciting place to complete her labor. The labor was designed to improve one's character, was meant to be a hardship—after which a prize was rewarded. How would her character be improved if the very thing she wanted was handed to her on a silver platter?

And as far as being sent someplace special as her reward for completing the labor, she was certain no one knew about her desire to be gone. She had hardly been aware of the fact herself until just moments before. And certainly she would never hurt her family's feelings by telling them. As much as she loved the idea of going away, she loved her family even more.

Besides which, Persy had no idea where she would go even if she had the chance. She had never gotten much past the ball gowns and museums in all her daydreams. She had never pictured the actual city, never put a name to that place where she would live this sophisticated life.

"New York City."

"New York City!?"

The Daltrys sat around the dining-room table, mouths agape, staring at Minerva with looks that said as clearly as words that at fifty-eight years of age she had finally gone mad—stark raving mad. Only Persephone's mouth was firmly shut. She pressed her back against her chair, her heart suddenly pounding in her chest, afraid to believe what she felt was happening.

"What are you talking about, Grandma?" Lee asked, leaning forward, his elbows planted aggressively on the table.

"Oh, I just wanted to know what you all thought about that great huge city called New York." She took a sip of wine and surreptitiously studied her clan.

At length, Odie cleared his throat and said, "Well, from all I've heard, it's a hellish place."

"A person can't hear the name of that city without hearing about crime and filth in the same breath," Lee added, his tension fading slightly as he leaned back.

"Yes, a hellish place," Odie said once again. "Not a bit like our Paradise."

Meredith laughed. "All of that's true, I'm sure, but I could see how a person could want to go there."

Most every Daltry turned accusing eyes on the newest member of the family. Persy glanced down at her hands.

"For a visit," Meredith quickly added. "There is more to New York City than crime and filth. There are fancy stores, museums, mind-boggling architecture . . ."

"How do you know so much about it?" Cupid wanted to know.

"I'm from Boston, remember, C.J., and I've seen pictures of New York in books and magazine pictorials. All from our wonderful new library," she added, reaching over to squeeze Lee's hand.

"Enough about this New York City nonsense, Grandma," Venus interjected. "When are you going to tell us what Persy's labor is going to be?"

Minerva glanced down the table at Persephone. Their nearly matching gray eyes locked and held. "Soon, family," she said, though she looked only at Persephone. "Very soon."

The table grew quiet. An uneasy ripple ran down the length. Last year when Lee became the first of the grandchildren to turn twenty there had been talk and speculation about what his labor might be. With Persy's there had been none of that. No one could imagine how Persy could be improved. She was smart and kind, she knew more about cooking than anyone around. She was polite and well mannered, and always well groomed. She was the first to help someone in need and the last to ask for anything for herself. What, everyone secretly wondered, could Minerva possibly come up with to improve their perfect Persy?

"But today's the day!" Allie exclaimed impatiently. "If you don't hurry the day will be over. Today is her special day with her special meal."

As if on cue, every Daltry at the table glanced down at their plates. The roast was charred, the potatoes still hard, the gravy solid, the string beans stringy.

"Oh, dear," Jane said, her brow furrowed. "I tried, really I did. But look at this meal."

Everyone avoided everyone else's eyes.

Jane's voice grew tight. "This meal is about as special as hog slop."

Bub chuckled. "Hog slop might have been better."

Odie reached over and firmly took hold of his youngest son's shoulder.

Bub cringed. Odie rarely got angry.

"You've hurt your mother's feelings, Bub."

"I'm sorry, Mama."

Jane's eyes burned with tears. "No, son, don't apologize. You are absolutely right. Hog slop would have been better."

Persy forgot her burgeoning excitement. She forgot all her dreams and desires. "Oh, Mama," she said. "I know you tried. And I love it all the more because you care so much. I know how much you wanted this to be special, and it is."

C.J. snorted, then grimaced when his father turned a baleful gaze in his direction.

"I'm serious," Persy continued. "I've loved every minute of today. From Venus's appetizers—"

"Breakfast sausage," Allie explained with disdain.

"To Allie's fruit punch—"

"A knuckle punch would have been easier to get down," Venus retorted.

Persy scowled at them both. "And Lee and Meredith's vegetable soup—"

Bub's mouth opened to comment, but Lee glared at him. "Don't you dare," he said, which snapped his younger brother's mouth shut as quickly and efficiently as if Lee had reached over and snapped his lips together himself.

"Everything is wonderful," Persy continued "because my family cares enough about me to try."

Jane sniffed into her napkin and sent her daughter a grateful look. "Thank you, dear."

"No, thank all of you for spending your day doing the very task that each of you hates. Cooking."

"Here, here," Odie cheered, holding up his glass of wine. "To Persephone Daltry, a wonderful daughter, who on her special day makes everyone else feel special, too."

"Here, here," came the response.

And for the first time all day, Persy felt truly happy and completely content, and not plagued by the need to escape the limited life she led in Paradise.

"Now for dessert," Minerva announced.

She brought in a cake that tilted precariously to one side. The icing barely covered the cake on its high side and must have been a good three quarters of an inch thick on the low side.

The family eyed first the cake, then Persy.

"It looks perfect to me," Persy pronounced emphatically.

C.J.'s chortle was cut short by another meaningful look from his father.

"Really," Persephone said, reaching over to ruffle C.J.'s hair. "It *is* perfect to me. And I'm sure it's going to taste even better."

"It couldn't taste any worse than it looks," Atlas added.

And with that, meaningful looks from their father no longer did any good, and resounding laughter rang out from around the table. Even Minerva, the proud baker of the confection, had trouble keeping back her smile.

The supper dishes were cleared away. Jane brought a stack of plates over for the cake. Bub left the table and sat Indian style on the floor to arrange Persephone's gifts from smallest to largest, ever concerned about the order of things. It was growing dark and hurricane lamps had been lighted. Jane poured coffee while Minerva cut the cake.

"The twins from town said they would stop by to wish you a happy birthday, Persy," Lee said as everyone took up their forks to take a bite.

"And the sheriff, too," Meredith added.

"Oh, dear. I don't know if we'll have enough cake," Minerva said.

"They can have mine," Lee, C.J., and Allie responded together.

Minerva scowled, but only picked at her cake as conversation resumed all around.

No one noticed when Venus slipped away from the table and up the stairs. And no one took any particular notice when only a few minutes later she returned and kept her head down, concentrating on her dessert.

"Now," Minerva announced, standing up from her seat. "On to my oldest, darling granddaughter's twentieth birthday labor."

"Venus!" Jane screeched abruptly.

All heads turned first to Jane, then to Venus. Eyes opened wide in surprise, and even a few people gasped at the sight.

"Paint!" Bub announced. "Venus painted her face!"

"It's only rouge, you fool," Venus snapped. She turned to her family, her chin coming up defiantly. "What's wrong with the way I look? I want to look my best when company arrives."

"Your best! You look like a harlot, young lady," Odie stated.

"Harlot!"

Everyone started talking at once, some half out of their chairs, others shaking their fingers to emphasize their point, though for all the good it did them since it was impossible for anyone to hear anyone else. The sound was enough to deafen a mule. Only Persy sat back and shook her head. She loved her family, she did. And she truly loved them even more for the very meal that had turned out so abysmally. Truly she meant it when she said the meal was perfect. It was, because they had made it all for her. They had to think about what she liked to eat, and while not a single item had turned out well, it was the fact that someone had spent time thinking about her that made her feel loved and special.

But still, as the verbal warfare raged on over first Venus's painted face, and then surprisingly took a turn toward Allie and her desire to wear britches constantly, Persephone felt that disconcerting feeling of earlier return. She wanted intelligent, sedate conversation over a fine wine and a lovely meal. She wanted sophistication. She wanted the kind of life, she suddenly knew without a doubt, that she wouldn't find here in Paradise.

"Enough!" Minerva commanded.

Instantly everyone stopped talking. Eight bodies seemed to freeze in place.

"Sit down! Sit down this instant!" Minerva demanded.

Everyone settled down into their seats, but not without a few choice muttered complaints.

"Go ahead, grumble all you like. But this family," Minerva admonished, "myself included, should be ashamed of itself."

Lee and Odie shifted uncomfortably in their seats.

"It's Persephone's birthday and not only couldn't we give her a meal that even the hogs would eat, we can't seem to carry on like anything but a bunch of disgruntled schoolchildren. And just when I'm on the verge of announcing her labor! A sacred event in the history of this family if ever there was one!"

Then Minerva straightened her person, trying to become dignified and regal. "As I was saying before I was so rudely interrupted . . ." She took a deep breath, forced a smile, then turned her attention back to Persephone.

Persy sat in her chair, thoughts of everything else evaporating from her mind in the face of what she was about to find out, about to learn she would be spending the next year of her life doing to improve her character. Her heart pounded. Her palms grew moist. What could it possibly be? she wondered again.

Jane reached over and took her eldest daughter's hand. Odie glanced across the table and offered her a smile.

Minerva took a deep breath before plunging ahead. "I am sending Persephone away."

Silence. Confused silence. Until at length Lee asked, "Away?"

"Yes, away to have a debut with her cousin."

The group became perfectly still as if everyone had stopped breathing.

"Cousin?" Allie finally asked.

"Debut?" Venus asked next.

Jane's hand tightened its grip as Persy scoured her brain trying to remember a cousin.

"Yes, a debut with her somewhat distant cousin." Minerva felt a small part of herself revolt against the words —her own words, words that she had spent years formulating. Suddenly she found herself weighing the wisdom of her decision. Perhaps she could take it all back, she thought. Perhaps she could tell her precious Persephone to dig ditches for a year instead. Minerva didn't want to send Persephone away. The very idea broke her heart. But it had to be done. Persephone had to leave Paradise Plains to find her way—to find the path that she needed to take. Minerva knew that, had known it for years. But only God knew what the result would be. Minerva had to believe she was doing the right thing. She could only hope they wouldn't lose her forever.

"What cousin are you talking about?" Bub demanded.

Jane's hand tightened still further. "It has to be your Aunt Margaret and Uncle John's daughter, Betty," she said, her voice barely a whisper.

Allie sucked in her breath.

"Oh, my heavens!" Venus exclaimed softly.

Persephone looked between her sisters before she turned with a start to her mother. Jane quickly dropped her head and began to stroke Persy's hand with her thumb.

"Aunt Margaret and Uncle John!" Lee sat back in his chair, stunned.

"Mother!" Odie began, but no other words followed.

"What's wrong with Aunt Margaret and Uncle John?" Bub asked, his brow furrowed with concern. "Are they criminals or something?" His brow suddenly wavered between concern for his sister and excitement at the prospect that there might be an outlaw on the family tree.

"Nothing's wrong with them, Atlas. They are from my late husband's side of the family," Minerva stated.

"Nothing, that is," Odie practically whispered, "if you don't count the fact that they live in New York City."

"New York City!" C.J. exclaimed. "That's clear on the other side of the world!"

"Not exactly," Lee stated.

"But close enough," Jane responded.

Silence wrapped around the Daltry family. Amber light flooded the room. Every person there was either too stunned to speak or waiting with bated breath to see what someone else would finally say. But silence reigned.

The clock on the mantel ticked the minutes away. At

length Bub squirmed in his seat, toying with his slice of uneaten cake, before he tossed his fork aside and asked, "If Persy goes to New York, who's going to do the cooking around here?"

"Atlas!" Jane admonished, before all at once, everyone was talking again, the cacophony of sound filling the room.

The sounds echoed in Persephone's mind. Her heart pounded. Her breath grew short. New York City. A big sophisticated city. It was perfect. She could hardly believe it. Her dreams were coming true.

Two

PERSEPHONE COULDN'T BELIEVE IT. NEITHER DURING THE LONG weeks of preparations nor during the interminable stage-coach ride, then the train ride that had followed after leaving Paradise Plains, could she believe it. Even now with the conductor announcing their arrival into the Jersey City, New Jersey, train station, it was still hard to believe. She was almost there.

New York City.

She was finally on the verge of entering a place of muse-ums and symphonies. Knowledge and sophistication. She could hardly wait to board the ferry that would take her across the Hudson River to the shores of New York City. She could hardly wait to plunge into her new life—her destiny.

Of course always at the back of her mind was the both-ersome question: Why had her grandmother sent her away? Sure she had explained that Persephone was to make her debut, but that hardly seemed like a "labor." It seemed more like a gift—a present come down from the gods on Mount Olympus. But never in all the years of the "labors" had anyone simply received a gift. Which meant, her mind circled, there was more to this excursion to the East than met the eye.

But what, she wondered for the thousandth time, could it be?

On top of everything was the plain and simple truth that she missed her family a great deal more than she had anticipated she would. There was not a single brother or sister, her grandmother or parents, whom she did not start to say something to as she traveled across the country, only belatedly to realize that they weren't there, wouldn't be there until she traveled back that great distance to Paradise. And that she wasn't sure would happen anytime soon—if ever, the thought wafted traitorously through her brain.

When the rest of her family had sat dumbfounded around the table trying to comprehend Minerva's words, Persy had barely kept down her excitement at the prospect. Even though she had hated her teary departure from Texas, she had wanted to go to New York from the moment she heard the words.

The image of her mother's stoic face as she tried not to cry was etched in Persy's mind. There had been Lee and Meredith, C.J., Atlas, Venus, and Allie, standing close together, watching and waving as the stagecoach pulled away. Grandma had been there, too, looking worried and uncertain, Persy had thought at the time, making her suspect all the more that there was more to this excursion than met the eye.

And of course her father had been there as well. She loved her mother dearly, but she had always had a special bond with her father. An understanding. An ease they shared whenever they were in each other's company. A bond that seemed to make them closer than she was to any other. A bond that she would miss more than anything else while she was gone. Her father had been the only one in the family who had seemed to understand that it was not a fate worse than death to travel to New York as the rest of them believed. A rueful grimace pulled at Persy's lips as she wondered if the fact that he understood hurt him all the more.

But none of that had changed the fact that she wanted to get away from the suffocating confines of a small town where everyone knew everything about everybody else since the day they were born. No secrets. No ambiguity. No mystery. Life was laid out for a person as clearly as her father's detailed sketches of his many inventions were, starting with birth and ending with death. Talking and visiting with the same people for a lifetime. Working and living the same life that their ancestors had lived before them. Hoping some stranger would happen through town for a little diversion, since it was only strangers they didn't know anything about. And Persephone wanted more than that.

She pressed back against her seat as the winter landscape passed by. Guilt and excitement mixed together inside her, nearly making her sick. She didn't know how she could go back to Paradise Plains, nor could she see how she could not.

But then the train hissed one last gasping breath before they came to a halt and she caught sight of a man and a woman with a young woman about her age that she knew just had to be her relatives, standing on the platform, waiting for her. Concerns about her future vanished from her head. She was here. And she was going to love it. She would deal with the future as it arrived.

"Persephone Daltry!"

Persy smiled as she stepped down from the train and was immediately swept up in her aunt's embrace.

"My, how you have grown into a beautiful woman," Aunt Margaret exclaimed, holding Persy at arm's length to look the length of her. "What has it been, ten, twelve years since last we saw you? And look, John, she is the exact replica of Minerva," she said to her husband. "You remember your Uncle John don't you, dear? And your Cousin Betty," she added with a smile toward her daughter.

"It's been a long time," Persy agreed.

"Too long." Margaret turned back to Persy and looked her over once again. "Already with Betty, beaux have given us no rest for all their calls and flowers and boxes of candy . . ."

"Mother!" Betty admonished.

"Nothing but the truth, darling. And now with Persephone here we'll have to hire a secretary just to keep track of all the gifts. My, my, my, we'll be beating back the fellows this year!"

At this Persy blushed a painful shade of red. Just one look at her stunning cousin, who stood just to the side with her silky blond hair and cornflower-blue eyes, told a person all they needed to know about for whom "fellows" would be beating down the door.

"Welcome to the East, my dear," Uncle John said, the tips of his fingers wedged between the buttons of his heavy black coat as he stepped forward. "We're glad you've traveled all this way, and we hope you will feel at home during your stay with us."

And then her cousin Betty stepped forward. Persy didn't know what to expect. Betty was only eighteen years old and Persy had no idea if Betty was interested in sharing her home, family, and debut with a virtual stranger.

But any concerns Persy had were banished when Betty reached out and took her hand. A genuinely kind smile lit her eyes. "You and I will be just like sisters, I just know it."

Persy was nearly overwhelmed by such a kind welcome and truly genuine delight at her arrival. "Thank you so much for having me." She returned Betty's gaze and squeezed her hand. "And I look forward to being just like sisters, too. It will make being apart from my own sisters not so difficult."

"Oh, that's right. You have a whole gaggle of siblings back in Texas."

"Betty!" her mother admonished. "They're not geese, for mercy's sake."

"I know that, Mother," Betty snorted, before turning back to Persy. "And I will do my very best to fill their shoes while you are here."

"That's an awful lot of shoes to fill," Persy said, her tone teasing.

"Oh, this is grand," Betty exclaimed. "We'll shop . . ."

"And go to museums," Persy said, getting caught up in Betty's excitement.

"And gossip . . ."

"And attend plays! Yes, this is grand," Persy added as the girls walked with arms linked toward the family carriage.

When they stopped at a maroon enameled landau with large plate-glass windows and liveried footmen waiting expectantly, Persy felt the need to pinch herself for fear it was all a dream. Never in all her life had she imagined there were such means of transportation. Maroon, indeed!

The carriage weaved its way through carts and wagons until they came to the ferry that would convey them across the river. The women talked incessantly during the whole long smooth ride across the water. They spoke of plans and people and all they would see and do.

But then suddenly Persy's mouth snapped shut when she became aware of sounds that interrupted the quiet of the river ride. Peering out the window of the carriage, her heart beat excitedly at the sight that greeted her. New York City. She was finally there.

The sounds only got louder as they neared the dock. The noise at the Pennsylvania terminus in Jersey City had been significant. But it had been overshadowed by the great groaning and hissing of the train. Here there was no single noise that attracted the attention, but many. Horses, carriages, people. Good heavens, she hadn't heard so much noise in one place since Herb Miller got drunk, set up tin cans in the town hall, and proceeded to take target practice right there in the empty bastion of community justice, the tin flying and pinging, bullets ricocheting off tables and walls, and only minutes later children laughing, women screaming, and men bumping into one another in the vain attempts to "bring Herb in." Thank goodness he had finally run out of bullets or he might still be in there today, shooting and carrying on, giving the town a fit.

Persy's mind reeled. New York City. At last. And Lord, how she loved it! She felt the pulse of the city mix with her own. The place was alive. Thriving.

It was all she could do to hold herself still and not jump out of the carriage onto the deck of the ferry boat, spread her arms and twirl around in circles. New York City. So far away, so foreign. But strangely she felt as if she had come home.

Within days, Persy was settled into her relatives' elegant three-story home of brick and gray stone, and was treated as if she were one of the immediate family, a cherished member certainly, but with an ease that made her feel as if she belonged.

"We're going to the dressmakers today," Betty announced as she flung herself down on Persy's bed the following week.

Persy sat before a mirror brushing her hair. "The dressmaker? Sounds interesting. What are you planning to have made?"

Betty laughed. "A dress, silly. What else does a woman have made at a dressmaker's."

Persy shook her head and gave her cousin a sly smile in

the mirror. "My sister, Allie, would have preferred to have britches made."

"Britches! Tell me it's not true!"

"True as the wind, I'm afraid. Thankfully my mother put her foot down."

"Thankfully! And thankfully you didn't get off the train wearing britches yourself. Though truthfully I have to admit the thought had crossed my mind. We talked of little else on the ferry ride over to get you."

Persy turned around at that. "No!"

"Yes," Betty said. "We hear things about you Westerners."

"What kind of things?"

"Nothing, nothing," Betty said, rolling over onto her back and studying her nails. "None of it's important."

"You can't dismiss the topic after saying something like that!" Persy demanded, intrigued despite herself.

"Well, if you must know," she said, eyes wide with excitement as she rolled right back over. "It's commonly thought that Texans are . . . a little on the rough side."

"Rough side? Go on."

"Well," Betty said with a shrug of her shoulders, "you know."

"No, Betty, I don't know. What do you mean, 'a little on the rough side'?"

"Mannerless, loud, loutish." Betty raised her brow. "Enough?"

"Yes, enough." Persy stared at her cousin in disbelief.

"But rest assured, Persy, Mother set me straight. She said that Minerva Daltry would not raise a bunch of heathens, no matter how far out in the wild you live."

"Heathens! The wild! Good Lord, you don't know the first thing about Texans or Texas."

"Well, I'm sure over the next months you'll set me straight about your cherished homeland."

Persy looked at her cousin. Cherished homeland, she

wondered. Only days before she had been glad to see it
behind her. Suddenly she was confused, she didn't understand what she felt. She wanted to be far away from the
rustic nature of Texas. But she was disgruntled over someone else implying the very same thing.

"But again, that's not important," Betty said, breaking
into Persy's thoughts. "What *is* important, however, is that
we are going to the dressmaker to have a dress made for
you!"

Persy's hand stopped in midstroke as it descended the
length of her hair. "For me?"

"Yes, for you. Mother and I both agree. You need the
perfect dress for your debut." Betty's eyes widened. "Not
that what you brought isn't lovely. All your clothes are
. . . nice."

The minute Persy had arrived—well, perhaps the minute is an exaggeration since she was so caught up in her
arrival—but soon after arriving she had become painfully
aware that her wardrobe was adequate at best. Her
dresses were well made, certainly, but plain just the same.
But she didn't dare write home for more money. One, it
would never arrive in time, and two, she knew that this
trip was costing a fortune as it was. Her grandmother had
hired a seamstress from St. Louis to make her an entirely
new wardrobe. Unfortunately that wardrobe had very little in common with her cousin's. But there was no help for
it until now, and she wasn't sure if she could possibly accept such generosity.

Aunt Margaret walked in just then. "Hurry, hurry, girls.
We don't want to be late to see Madame Gullierre."

"Oh, Aunt Margaret. Betty just told me, and really I
couldn't let you buy me a dress."

"Nonsense, love. We want you to have something
lovely." Her eyes opened wide much as Betty's had earlier. "Not that what you have isn't beautiful. It's just that

here in New York . . . we have rigid dress prescriptions for every kind of event."

"You dress one way for the theater," Betty explained, "and another for the races, and something else again for the opera, et cetera, et cetera. It can be really very boring at times."

"Unfortunately," Margaret said, eyeing the ball gown Persy had brought with her, "while your dress is absolutely gorgeous"—she hesitated, seeming to search for the right words—"well, plain and simple, bustles are out of fashion this year. Of course they will probably be back in next year, but for now . . ." She shrugged her shoulders. "We should have thought to write to tell you before now."

"Out?" Persy asked. "Bustles are out of fashion?"

"Yes," Betty replied. "Most definitely out this year."

"Capricious, this fashion business is," Aunt Margaret said. "And New York is always right on top of what is de rigueur. So off to the Ladies Mile and the seamstress we go to, to ensure you have the grandest of debuts."

Persy threw back her head and laughed. "If we must! Take me to Madame Gullierre's!"

They took the landau down the narrow, cobbled length of Fifth Avenue to Madison Square, which sat squarely at the intersection of Fifth, Twenty-third Street, and Broadway, where the Ladies Mile began, then extended down the length of Broadway to Eighth Street. The Ladies Mile was lined with every type of shop imaginable. Yard goods, hats, and even gloves came from separate shops, which coexisted with shops for cigars, and photographers, and even great hotels. Anything anyone could possibly want or need could be found on this fashionable stretch.

At Madame Gullierre's establishment Persy was measured and draped with laces and satins, silks and chiffons, every type of material they had in white. Only after hours of Madame Gullierre and Aunt Margaret discussing the dress and Persy as if she weren't there was the decision made. As best as Persy could tell, she was going to be wrapped within an inch of her life, in a double skirted, pleated, flounced, hobbled, lined semiprincess gown that would rustle on the ground behind her as she walked. She couldn't imagine for the life of her what this dress was going to look like when it was all said and done. Though when Persy, Betty, and Aunt Margaret departed, Persy seemed to be the only one who wasn't sure what she would end up with when they picked up the dress the following week.

"It's going to be perfect on you," Betty enthused.

But Persy wasn't so sure.

As they traveled through the streets on their way home Betty and her mother discussed a gown Betty wanted.

"I saw it in the latest issue of Mr. Fogel's Fashion Guide. It was divine, Mother, simply divine."

"Mr. Fogel doesn't know the first thing about fashion for young ladies. With his reds and oranges and cuts below the neckline, mercy, he'd have every woman in town looking like trollops if he had his way."

"Mother!" Betty moaned.

Persy turned away. Apparently, whether a person was an only child or one of many, conversations between mothers and daughters were generally the same.

Persy looked out of the landau. It was all she could do not to hang out the window and gawk at all she saw. Never in her life had she seen so many buildings and people and carriages. There were vendors hawking their wares and teamsters shouting at pedestrians to get out of their way. Flat-bedded and low-sided drays hauling barrels and boxes competed with shiny carriages and two-wheeled hansom cabs for right-of-way on the not so broad width of Broadway. But suddenly, with hordes of people everywhere she looked, Persy realized with amazement that she didn't recognize a single face she saw. She knew no one here, and no one knew her! The realization jolted her, then filled her with an amazing sense of freedom. No one knew her here! She could do as she pleased! She could walk the street and by noon everyone in town wouldn't know. She could dance the jig and no one would care.

She took a deep breath and relished the feel. Freedom. Anonymity. A whole new life.

And it was as she was reveling in her sense of newness that she saw him. A man who virtually leapt out at her from a throng of meaningless faces, startling every other thought from her mind.

He stood very still, that in itself was enough to make him stand out in a crowd of constantly moving people. His chin was raised slightly. His body looked hard, as if chiseled from stone. He faced the west, his eyes intent. She had the sudden thought that he looked as if he was searching, but not for someone. He seemed to search for something, something distant that he could not attain. He seemed to be yearning. Yes, yearning, she concluded, for some distant land.

But then his chin lowered and he began to walk, moving with the crowd, not swept up in it as most were, but apart from it. A man who lived by rules of his own making. He walked with an uncanny grace, especially for such a large man. He looked predatory. Dangerous, she thought suddenly. And she smiled at the prospect. How strange to find a man in this civilized, sophisticated city who looked as if he belonged in the corner of a saloon in Texas, surveying the room with cautiously narrowed eyes, and a six-shooter on his hip. The vision was so perfect that it was a moment before she remembered that she was in a maroon enameled carriage in New York City. But the feelings of danger and Texas didn't leave her.

As he continued people seemed to give him space, as if he deserved more of the walkway on which they trod.

They must have sensed that he was dangerous, too, for not a single person met his eye.

He had dark curly hair and, as best Persy could tell from the distance, either blue eyes or green. He was tall, taller than the people surrounding him on the street. The crowd around him parted for a moment and she could see the rest of him. Yes, chiseled from stone with broad shoulders tapering down into a narrow waist. A ray of sun caught the gold of a ring on his small finger. She had never seen such a thing. She took a deep breath.

He was well dressed if one liked unrelieved black. Persy had the unexpected thought that the man would look out of place in any other color. She couldn't imagine him in blues or reds or even browns or tans. He was a man who belonged in black as sure as the devil belonged in the underworld. But when a slight breeze caught the flap of his unbuttoned coat, a vest as purple as a king's robe was revealed from beneath, and she nearly laughed out loud. He might be refined on the outside, but he was devilish good fun on the inside.

Just then he stopped and turned toward their carriage as if sensing her gaze. She sucked in her breath when, even at this distance, their eyes met and held. He seemed confused, as if he should know her, though common sense told her that based on the distance he only appeared to be looking at her, in fact didn't see her at all. In spite of that logical thought, she felt the need to draw back into the carriage as a proper maiden would do, press back against the velvet seat, and not look again until they were well on their way. She felt the need to find safety in what felt suddenly like an unsafe world. Propriety bade that she do just that, but something else that she could not name, stronger than propriety, made her stay.

Never in her twenty years had she experienced such a feeling. Hot and cold all at once. Her heart beating hard against her chest. Certainly she had been ill before, making her alternately hot, then cold, and sometimes both. And certainly she had been excited before, on her way to New York most recently. But what she was feeling now was different.

"Who is that man?" she asked her cousin and aunt without thinking.

"Who?" Betty leaned forward to peer out the carriage window.

"Over there," Persy said, pointing as unnoticeably as she could. "The tall man with the dark hair."

"Heavens, Persy, there are hundreds of men out there who are tall and have dark hair." And then suddenly she saw him. "Oh, him!" Betty exclaimed, her blue eyes widening as she clasped her hands to her breast. "Oh, my stars, it's him! The Prince of Prince Street!"

Betty flung herself back against the plush seat, slightly out of breath as if the movement had entailed a good deal more effort than it actually had. Her eyelids grew heavy and a slight half smile tilted her lips. "I can't believe we saw him. In person. Too bad we weren't closer."

Her mother's brow knitted as she glanced between her daughter and niece. "Who are you talking about, Betty? Who have you seen?"

"Jake Devlin!" she breathed.

"The Prince of Prince Street?" Persy questioned.

"Yes, that's what they call him. He's practically famous."

"Infamous," Aunt Margaret muttered, her knitted brow knitting even farther and her mouth turning down into a scowl. She glanced once again between Betty and Persy before she pursed her lips, then leaned her considerable form forward and peered out the carriage window.

They had broken through a knot of traffic and had moved some distance away. But it didn't take long before Margaret's eyes landed on what she was instantly certain was the man in question.

"Jake Devlin," she confirmed as she jerked back from the sight. "Right there plain as day, like nobody's business."

"Who's Jake Devlin?" Persy asked, further intrigued by her relatives' dramatic responses.

"Why only one of the most well-known men in town," Betty explained with a knowing look.

"Will I meet him at my debut?" Persy asked, trying to sound nonchalant rather than hopeful.

Aunt Margaret's eyes bulged and her face turned a violent shade of red.

Betty laughed out loud. "Mother wants everyone to talk about our debut for weeks afterward, and certainly," she said with a teasing smile, "Jake Devlin would be cause for talk. What do you think, Mother? Shall we invite him?"

"He most certainly will not be invited," Margaret snapped, "as well you know, Betty Olson."

Persy glanced between the women. "Why not? What's wrong with him?" Persy asked, her eyes straying toward the window.

"What's wrong?!" Aunt Margaret demanded. "He's . . . he's . . . not acceptable."

"But you said he was well known."

"There are a great many people in this city who are known but are not . . . acceptable, Persy," Margaret said with importance. "Moreover, he is known for his . . . sinful ways, not for charitable contributions! Heavens above, he owns a gambling house!"

"Sinful or not," Betty breathed, "he's devilishly good-looking."

"He's a devil, I'll agree," her mother countered.

Betty only laughed. "I've heard he has the manners of the finest of gentlemen."

"Manners, my foot!" Margaret stated. "Are you going to sit there and tell me he says 'please' and 'thank you' when he lures men into his den of iniquity?"

Persy's head bobbed back and forth between her aunt and cousin.

"Maybe, I haven't heard," Betty replied. "But I have heard that he woos the women with sweet words and they fall at his feet, begging for his . . . attentions," Betty stated, her eyes wide with drama. "Then he whisks them away to places unknown."

"And returns them without a shred of reputation left to be salvaged," her mother responded heatedly. "As well you should remember, young lady, and you as well," she added for Persy.

Betty turned her attention to Persy. "He is seen with rich women . . ."

"And soiled women," her mother added.

"It is said important men seek his advice . . ."

"But those same men wouldn't have him at their dinner tables if their lives depended on it! He's no good, young ladies," Aunt Margaret said in a stern voice. "He owns a saloon, for mercy's sake. With dancing girls and who knows what all going on upstairs. And I'll have no daughter or niece of mine hanging out windows gawking at a man like that. Good heavens, what would your parents say, Persy, if they thought I was introducing you to the likes of him?"

Betty laughed. "You were hardly making introductions, Mother, or inviting him over for supper. Though I can't say that I'd mind."

Margaret's head jerked back at the mere thought.

"And our reputations are safe," Betty continued. "Even you have to admit that we'd have to get a little closer than thirty yards to have our virtues . . . breached."

Margaret's eyes opened wide. "Betty!"

Betty stifled her amusement and reached over and patted her mother's hand. "Just playing, Mother dear. Not to worry."

"Well, I never." Margaret sniffed and turned her head

away. "I just don't know where you ever got it in your head to speak to me in such a way. When I was a girl—"

"Yes, yes, Mother," Betty said gently, patting her mother's hand, "I've heard it all before. I'm not nearly as good a daughter as you had hoped for."

"That's not what . . ." Margaret took a deep breath, sighed, then turned away in defeat.

The women grew quiet then, and the sounds of New York faded in Persy's mind. The carriage swayed gently, rocking the silent occupants as they continued on their way, turning onto Fifth Avenue, away from the Ladies Mile and the dressmaker. Persy leaned back, Betty's and Aunt Margaret's conversation twirling in her head.

The man was obviously someone a person would do well to steer clear of. Every book on propriety she had ever read, and there had been many, said so. As the owner of a saloon with fancy dancing girls he was a man she should detest. But try as she might, his dark handsomeness plagued her mind. The waves of hair were like creamy swirls of dark chocolate, his eyes light and startling with their contrast. And his lips, so full that she longed to . . .

Persy took a deep breath and shook her head as if to shake the thoughts from her mind. Good Lord, what had she been thinking! Kiss. Kissing. That man. Who owned a saloon and whom she had not seen for more than a handful of seconds at a respectable distance, to boot. The Prince of Prince Street, she thought with a shake of her head. She was daft, she was convinced. What else could explain her reaction to the man. For even if he were a prince, he was the Prince of Darkness if ever she had seen one.

But try as she might the forbidden images persisted. Filling her mind. Making her lean toward the door. And she had a fleeting understanding of how women could actually drop at that devil man's feet.

Three

JAKE DEVLIN CAME THROUGH THE FRONT DOOR OF THE DUSTY Rose Saloon. Not the black, solid oak door of the respectable-looking town house on the side street that was connected to the saloon, but the red door with etched glass panes that led directly to the drinking establishment that was as popular for its friendly faces and easy way as it was for its fine whiskey and even finer dancing girls. A place to forget one's cares, he had always said. But this day Jake sighed. A place to spend one's money and drown in drink. God, how he had come to hate owning a saloon.

He ran his long, strong hand through his dark hair, leaving ridges where his fingers had passed. The discontent had grown over the years, slowly so that at first he hadn't been aware of its presence. But then one day, for no particular reason that he knew of, it hit him. Hard. And he wanted out.

After that, as days had passed, he began to feel closed in by the laughter that grew louder as the evenings progressed, and sickened by the smell of liquor that he made sure was scrubbed away at the end of the night. Even the city made him feel hemmed in, the buildings looming everywhere he looked.

And the people. New York had the richest and the poorest, and the city reflected that fact. Beggars huddled in doorways, their dirty hands extended to the passing impervious industrialists who spent more on a single meal than the poor saw in a lifetime.

Jake had never thought much about it before. Having been born and raised in the city, the sights, good and bad, became a blur, nothing in particular standing out. But now he found himself longing for wide-open spaces, for a place where a man could see forever, a place where a man could breathe. No longer was it enough to ride up to Central Park, or to gallop dangerously through the night as if demons were on his heels. He wanted a new life. Far, far away.

He had worked tirelessly to build his empire. And his efforts had paid off—in spades, as they say in the gambling world—his world. Yes, it was the spades and hearts, the diamonds and clubs that had paid, and still paid, in the back room of his saloon.

When he had been young the thought of owning a saloon with dancing women in the front and gambling in the back had appealed to him. It was the type of life of which stories were told, that the young boys he had known and grown up with talked and dreamed about. But it captivated him no longer. He wanted something else. He wanted to move on. But to what he had no idea.

Frequently he found himself with his face turned toward the west when the sun was setting in the sky, imagining. He saw a new life as clearly as if it were real. He didn't know the name of the place or exactly where it was. But he saw it nonetheless. The friendly faces. The quaint line of shops and stores off a main street in town. He could almost smell the sun-dried long grasses and the green fields after a summer rain.

But then he turned away from the images in his mind. For that was all they were. Imaginings. Dreams. Longings. And Jake Devlin was not a man to waste time wishing for things he couldn't have. His life was here, in New York, as it always had been. He was damn lucky he had made it up from the gutters to become as successful as he was after his father ran off and his mother died when he was no more than four years old. And the saloon had been the key to his success. The saloon and Harold Harvey, that is.

Jake took a deep breath. Harold Harvey had been the father he had never known. He had taught Jake everything he knew, and when Jake had been ready Harold had financed the saloon. Over the years, Jake had paid his mentor back tenfold. He had even helped Harold after the tables had turned. When things had gone bad for the older man and he needed to get out of town Jake had taken care of everything and moved Harold and his family to Chicago. But even though the tables had long since turned, Jake still respected Harold Harvey a great deal. More importantly, he owed him, and in some elemental way he always would.

If only the man didn't have a daughter.

Jake stiffened involuntarily at the image that came to mind. An intolerable daughter. Beautiful, admittedly, but intolerable all the same. Velda. Whom Harold wanted Jake to marry.

Jake stifled a shudder of distaste.

He had only managed to avoid the tangle of matrimony to the woman by convincing Harold that he wanted a simple, quiet girl who knew a woman's place. The fact of the matter was that Jake didn't want to marry any kind of woman, quiet or not, at this point in his life. He had no understanding of the word "husband" or of the commitment and obligation that word entailed. He neither understood nor wanted to understand, especially when the words were in any way associated with Velda Harvey. And he'd had to convince her father of that without revealing his true feelings for Velda.

Jake remembered the conversation well. He had thought long and hard to come up with just the right words to describe an entirely different type of woman from Velda without insulting her. No easy task. In the end, Jake had talked about a woman who only wanted to bake cookies, iron clothes, and wipe babies' noses. Not that he had ever thought about such things. He simply knew that Velda Harvey was about as suited to docile wifely ways as he was.

With a grumble, Harold had been left with no alternative but to concede that his daughter wasn't the woman for Jake. Harold had taught his daughter to stand up for what she believed in. She was a strong woman who knew what she wanted and went after it, regardless of how she appeared to others. But Harold had only grudgingly conceded defeat.

A lesser man would have told Harold he wanted no part of his pushy daughter. But Jake was not a lesser man. He was a man who paid his debts and lived with honor, and would never dream of insulting a man who had virtually saved his life.

Once Harold and his family had moved away, Jake had thought he was in the clear. But once a year like clockwork, the Harveys came to town to see loved ones, Jake included.

And as the years had passed and Jake had produced no wife, Harold had begun to press his case again. "Perhaps a passive wife isn't what you want after all," Harvey had said on his last trip to New York, his thick cigar clamped between his teeth. "With just about everything in a skirt trying to gain your attention—docile, aggressive, and everything in between—perhaps you can't find this perfect woman because you don't really want her. You want a fireball, Jake. Someone to match you step for step. Someone like my Velda."

Jake stiffened just remembering the conversation.

And now, like the inevitability of a snowstorm in winter, the Harveys were back in town for six weeks. Thank God they had decided to stay at a hotel instead of in the upper rooms over the saloon as they had in years past. That arrangement had never failed to provide the surprise of Velda in Jake's bed at least one night of the stay, and him having to cajole her back to her room, which was like luring a ravenous dog away from a bowl of fresh meat. Jake didn't like to be compared to fresh meat.

Thankfully he would be spared that hardship, or so he hoped. But still Jake wasn't sure how he was going to survive this trip without ending up engaged. He had received letter after letter from Harold over the months extolling Velda's virtues. Jake knew, with a sense of impending doom, that Harold would broach the subject again.

The knowledge irritated him. He was beholden to no one—no one, that is, except Harold Harvey. Why, he wondered once again, did the man have to have a daughter?

The bar was quiet so early in the day. The rich-grained wood wall bespoke a fine library more than a saloon. The brass railings were polished to a high shine. But by the end of the night they would be dulled from mud-covered boots. Jake walked to his study without seeing any one of the members who made up the live-in staff of the Dusty Rose. There was Mr. Bills who dealt with the day-to-day workings of the establishment, Howie who kept all would-be troublemakers in line, and Lola and May, two of the finest dancing girls anywhere in the city.

His family.

The hard lines of his countenance eased as he sat down in the high-backed leather chair of his office. Yes, next to Harold, the four people who lived in the rooms that lined the top floor of the building were the closest thing he had ever known to a family. And just like a family, they depended on him for their welfare. He hadn't liked the responsibility at first. But he had grown used to it. He also conceded that they were part of the reason he felt trapped —unable to move away to the wide-open spaces that he longed for. What would they do if he left? Come with him? He wasn't sure how he would support himself much less others. All his money was tied up in the Dusty Rose. The only thing he knew how to do was run a saloon. And that was the very thing he was trying to get away from. Which led him back to where he started. New York City and the Dusty Rose. That, unfortunately, was where he belonged.

Suddenly, seemingly out of nowhere, commotion interrupted the silence. Before Jake could stand the door burst open, bringing a short wiry man in its wake, his eyes wide, panting as if he had run for miles.

"What is it, Mr. Bills?" Jake asked, knowing that something must be terribly wrong for the man to have burst in without knocking.

Slamming the door behind him, Mr. Bills plastered his back against the hard plank as if his puny weight could block out intruders. And intruders it seemed to be, Jake thought, based on the sounds he suddenly heard coming down the hallway.

"It's her!" Mr. Bills panted. "She's here. I couldn't stop her."

"Who's here?" Jake asked, his dark countenance darkening even further for he had a sinking feeling that he knew.

"Miss Velda!"

Jake groaned.

And sure enough, in the next second, the door burst open, sending Mr. Bills practically flying across the room,

Miss Velda Harvey entering on its wake, Howie trailing behind her like an uncertain hound dog.

"Jake! Darling!" Her voice was deep and smoky, her ample bosom heaving as she came around the desk and wrapped her arms around him.

Jake Devlin was a big man, tall and strong, with a broad, heavily muscled chest. He had scared more than one man by doing nothing more than standing up and looking down at him with a hard stare. He had broken his share of jaws and bones in his long journey from the gutters of New York to the position of successful saloon-keeper. But every time Velda Harvey enveloped him in a hug he felt as if every bone in his body were being crushed into tiny bits.

"Velda," he said, carefully unwrapping himself and putting her at arm's length. "Don't you look . . . just like you." His smile was forced and everyone in the room knew it, everyone except Velda, of course, who preened at his words.

"Don't I," she purred, running her hand provocatively down her side. "How do you like my new hairstyle?"

Jake studied her tresses and wondered what was different.

"It's a beautiful shade of red," Mr. Bills interjected, casting the helpful hint toward Jake.

Velda turned a shrewish eye on the smaller man. Jake hated to think what would happen to poor little Mr. Bills if Velda ever got it into her head to hug him. Bone dust for certain.

"I wasn't asking you," she hissed at Jake's manager, her face contorting unbecomingly. "And why is it that every time I turn around you are butting yourself into my business?"

At first Mr. Bills looked like a stricken rat. But then he puffed out his wiry chest and pulled back his shoulders. "Somebody's got to," he stated angrily.

Velda's eyes opened wide as her face worked even harder. Jake looked about as stunned by Mr. Bills's comment as both Howie and Velda appeared to be. Never had any of them witnessed anyone standing up to Velda Harvey. It was both comical and amusing. And dangerous for a puny man like Mr. Bills.

But Mr. Bills didn't have to worry for long about the consequences of his outburst when she turned away with a huff and looked at Jake, her smile magically returning.

"What do you think, Jake darling?" she purred.

Jake glanced between Mr. Bills, who had slumped back against the wall as if unable to believe what he had just done, and Velda, who was running her palm lightly over her colored tresses. Red, brown, or green—Jake would have hated it as long as it was on Velda. "I think it's . . . festive, Velda. Where's your father?" he asked. He had no interest in further discussions of her person or things personal. He had learned from experience that to talk too much about her led her to believe that he cared.

Velda, however, was not so easily dissuaded. "Did you miss me?"

She batted her eyelashes, an action that looked absurd on such a large woman. Mr. Bills had obviously recovered himself and grumbled in the corner.

"Jaaake," Velda said, drawing the word out like a complaint.

Jake hesitated. "What, Velda?"

She stomped her foot and the floorboards shook. "Have you missed me?"

"Oh, yes. Of course I've missed you, just like I missed your father. Where is he anyway?"

Howie stepped forward. "He's on his way, sir."

With teeth virtually bared she turned on Howie this time. "He wasn't talking to you, you nitwit!" She looked the length of the huge man. "Howie!" she said with a sneer. "What grown-up, respectable man goes around being called Howie, anyway?"

Howie's massive face fell. Jake knew that Howie was a sensitive man for all his girth. Sensitive and caring and hated being called Howie as much as Velda obviously hated it.

But just when Jake stepped forward to defend his offended friend, Mr. Bills puffed up once again. "Howie is a damn fine name," he snapped, pulling his scrawny shoulders back and stepping forward. He had to look up a good bit to meet Velda's eyes but look up he did. "Didn't anyone ever teach you manners, missy?"

Her eyes opened wide and for the first time since Jake had met her, he realized she was at a loss for words. Now there was no telling what she would do.

"Mr. Bills," Jake warned.

But both Mr. Bills and Velda ignored him. Mr. Bills seemed to forget that Harold Harvey lurked somewhere near and still had enough connections to put him in harm's way. Mr. Bills was only aware of the woman who stood before him. But just when Mr. Bills was about to say something more, surely causing the situation to degenerate further, Jake said, "How about lunch? I'm starved."

Velda stared down at Mr. Bills for one more long, hard moment before turning around to Jake. "Where are we going?" she asked a little quietly for Velda.

"Downstairs," Jake answered simply.

"That's right," Mr. Bills barked. "Right here! A person would be hard-pressed to find better fare than what they can find here at the Dusty Rose."

She glared at Mr. Bills, then moved closer to Jake. Mr. Bills scowled. "Jake, honey. I'd just love to go to The Willow Room." She stepped closer and took his upper arm between her hands. "Caviar and champagne," she added in a sultry voice, her breasts pressed to his triceps.

Jake shifted uncomfortably. Why him? he wondered.

Why did she have to want him? His mentor's daughter. For a second he nearly damned them all and told Velda, father or no, to leave. But then, as always, he remembered the little lost waif in the gutters and the debt of gratitude he owed. So he merely forced a smile and said, "The Willow Room it is."

Velda squealed her delight and pressed herself still closer.

"Just as soon as your father gets here," Jake added, his voice dry as he glanced at the clock that ticked slowly against the wall.

Velda's squeal turned to a snort of impatience and Jake had to force himself not to shake his head in disgust. Good God what a mess, he thought to himself.

Fortunately, no sooner had Mr. Bills and Howie departed than Harold Harvey arrived.

"Jake, my boy!" the older man stated from the doorway, extending his arms.

Jake crossed the room. The two men embraced, and where Velda had nearly crushed Jake, her father seemed frail and very breakable. This wasn't how Jake remembered the man. Jake stepped back, suddenly concerned. Despite his perfectly and expensively tailored suit and freshly barbered hair and face, Harold didn't look well.

"Harold, it's good to see you. Come sit down."

Jake ushered him to a seat next to his daughter. Harold sighed when the soft leather touched his back. For a moment he closed his eyes and didn't move.

"Daddy?" Velda said, concern etching her voice.

Harold smiled, then opened his eyes. "I see you have already found my Velda." He reached out and ran a loving hand down her cheek. "Isn't she beautiful, Jake? More beautiful, I think, with each passing day."

Velda's concern evaporated as quickly as it came and she preened.

"What do you think, Jake?" Harold asked.

"Of course, Harold. She's lovely," he replied, trying, for Harold's sake, to sound sincere.

Harold basked in his daughter's beauty for a moment before he turned his attention to other things. "Tell me, how is everything here?" Harold asked as he shifted his weight in the chair.

"Fine, everything is fine. How about Chicago?"

Harold tilted his head and shrugged. "The same. Always the same. Chicago is Chicago, not New York." He smiled a distant smile. "I remember the good old days—"

"Daddy! You can talk about all that later."

"So true, so true. Nothing worse than the ramblings of an old man."

"Daddy, that's not what I meant."

"I know, my darling. Don't fret your pretty head." He turned to Jake. "From what I hear you're making more money than ever with a smoother operation than anyone around." He looked pointedly at Jake. "A perfect time for a man of your advanced age to be seriously considering marriage."

Jake's fingers froze on the desktop. He was to be given no reprieve. "I wouldn't say thirty is such an advanced age, Harold," he said tightly. "But enough about age and business. It's time for lunch."

But if either Velda or Harold noticed Jake's rising anger, they didn't let on.

"Jake is taking us to The Willow Room." Velda said the words as if she had won some sort of a prize.

"Really?" Harold replied, one bushy gray eyebrow raised. "The Willow Room. Must be a special occasion if you want to take us there."

Jake leaned forward. "It was—"

"A perfect idea," Velda interjected. "Don't you think so, Daddy? He obviously missed us."

"Yes, maybe he has missed us more than usual," he said

with a considering look. "What without a family or wife to care for him. Probably hasn't had a decent meal in ages."

"If we don't hurry," Jake interjected, refusing to get into a discussion regarding the fact that the Dusty Rose had one of the best restaurants in town attached to it, "we'll never get a table."

With a laugh, Harold said, "You, Jake? Not get a table at The Willow Room?" He snorted. "At the Rhine House with all those snotty society types, maybe. But at The Willow Room, never."

Harold pushed up from his chair. "Let's go."

The trio was off to what Jake knew would be an interminable lunch. It was also becoming crystal clear that he had to come up with some way to once and for all get Harold to stop trying to ply him with Velda's dubious charms. The question was, how?

Four

"I STILL CAN'T BELIEVE IT!"

Persy stood alone, in front of the full-length mirror, shaking her head in disbelief.

"I've never seen such a beautiful dress in all my life," she breathed out loud to the empty bedroom, running her hands carefully over the skirt of the new gown to be worn at her debut. "And to think it belongs to me!" She lifted her arms as best as she could, and would have twirled around had the garment allowed her such freedom of movement.

When she had overheard Madame Gullierre and her aunt discussing the "hobbled skirt," Persy had thought it an interesting description. Never in her wildest imaginings, however, did she think that she would actually feel a bit like a horse that had indeed been hobbled!

She tried to take a step, to peek at the matching white pointed slippers that made her feet look dainty and stylish.

"Careful, Persy!"

Betty, dressed in a stunning day dress, came to the door just as Persy nearly toppled to the floor.

With admirable swiftness, she reached out and grabbed a chair back. "I guess I need some practice getting around in this," she said with a rueful half smile.

Betty chuckled. "At something like a debut you're not expected to walk very far or talk very much or do anything even remotely strenuous," she said with a raised brow. "You just need to look gorgeous."

Persy's brow furrowed with concern. "Just look gorgeous?" she questioned, her excitement evaporating into the sunlit room. She had been called many things in her days, but not gorgeous. Sweet, kind, caring, yes; gorgeous, never.

"Not to worry, cousin. Not only do you look gorgeous but you look divine as well. The cut of the gown is all the fashion and you are one of the few women I've seen that doesn't look like one of those hot-air balloons from the waist down."

Red crept into Persy's cheeks. She assumed her cousin's words were a compliment; but she wasn't entirely sure. Betty had been nothing but splendid since Persy's arrival, but she always sensed a tension about her cousin that made Persy wonder if beneath the smiles and gaiety there was something wrong. "Even if I don't have to do much walking, land's sakes, I've got to dance, don't I?"

Betty tilted her head and conceded Persy's point with a delicate shrug of her shoulders. "Maybe we should practice a bit at that. Perhaps I should give you a lesson or two sometime. I learned from the best dancing master. I can teach you what I learned. But not for too long or not too often. This type of dress ruins easily and Mother would just die if something happened to it."

"Nothing will happen to the dress, Betty, unless I fall in a flower arrangement or a punch bowl while trying to dance—at the debut!"

Betty looked down at the skirt that tightened around the knees, then flared out down to the floor. "Yes, I suppose you'll just have to practice. Fortunately, whether you can get around or not, the dress is perfect on you." She smiled. "For now, however, I'm off."

"Off? Where are you going?" Persy asked without thinking.

Uncle John had already left the house for his office at the oldest and finest law firm in town. Aunt Margaret had departed for Mrs. Collingswood's home where the women were preparing for the annual fund-raiser for the needy. Since Persy's arrival in New York her cousin hadn't gone much of anyplace during the day unless it was to go shopping, and she always took Persy with her for that.

Betty hesitated. "For a walk."

"In that?" Persy questioned.

Both Persy and her cousin glanced at the lace and ruffled chiffon dress that Betty wore, a dress more suited to sitting in the solarium receiving visitors and sipping tea than touring the great outdoors.

Betty shrugged her shoulders and laughed, twirling around so that the skirt belled around her ankles. "Yes, cousin love, in this. I'm off." She turned to go, then stopped. "And don't you say a word about this to Mother or Father."

Then she was gone, leaving Persy to wonder just exactly where her cousin was going to be walking that she didn't want her parents to know.

Left to her own devices Persy decided that there was no time like the present to practice moving around in the dress. Just the thought of making a complete fool of herself at her debut made her want to die of embarrassment. But surely if she practiced a little each day during the ensuing month until the debut finally took place, then she should be able to walk without falling flat on her face.

After she took one more step, however, she had to wonder.

But she persevered. She walked carefully about the room and after a bit she decided she might not fall after all. In fact, she had gotten so good at it that she decided she needed more of a challenge. Stairs, she thought to herself. She needed to practice on the stairs.

By the time she walked, with surprising grace, out of her room, then down the steps, she was feeling quite confident. Once a person got the hang of it, she reasoned, it wasn't so very difficult to move about at all. If she kept her knees close together and didn't take very large steps she walked without a hitch. Though any strenuous movement was still beyond her, but given time who knew what she would accomplish.

Just when she was about to turn back to ascend the stairs, she smelled the most delicious aroma. It had been so long since she had been in a kitchen. In Paradise she had cooked every day, three meals a day. Upon arriving in New York it had been something of a relief to relinquish the responsibility of feeding a family of nine. But eventually she had come to miss the warmth and familiarity of doing what she loved to do best.

If she could just stick her head in and look at everything, smell the aromas, and watch the cook go about her business for a few minutes, she would be content. And perhaps she could ask if the woman would mind if she joined her for an afternoon of cooking. With not a soul in the house besides the servants, who was there to object?

Taking the stairs down to the basement kitchen with the utmost care, Persy pushed open the door just as the cook let out a shriek of distress.

After that, there was no room for thought. Persy simply reacted. She flew into the kitchen, disregarding the rip that sounded when she grabbed a canister of soda and worked alongside the cook to put out the fire that had flared on the stove.

It took only minutes to douse the flames, and even less to ruin the very dress that Persy couldn't afford to destroy.

"Oh, my stars!" Persy exclaimed once she had determined the cook was all right and everything was safe. "Look at my dress!"

The cook glanced down the length of Persy. "Oh, no!" she cried, clasping her plump cheeks with her hands. "It's ruined. Your beautiful dress is ruined. The missus is going to have a fit."

Persy stood perfectly still, dumbfounded. Her mind reeled. Her stomach churned with denial. But as she stared down at the tattered remains of her debut gown, she couldn't deny for long that indeed it was ruined.

The cook's lips began to tremble. "Oh, Lordy! Lordy, Lordy! I can clean up this mess, but I cannot clean up your dress. Now Mrs. Olson is going to find out about the fire. I'm going to be fired for certain."

The cook began to cry in earnest now and Persy looked on and had no idea what to do. She hated to see the woman so distressed. "Now, Mrs. McFee, everything will be fine. Why would my aunt take your job away because of a fire? Really, she'll understand."

"No, she won't," she wailed. "She's already said as much last month when I had another . . . incident. Oh, Lordy, I'll be fired, for certain. And my Liam is sick and can't work and the money I make here is the only money I have to pay for his medicine."

"Now, now, Mrs. McFee, don't worry," Persy said, thinking only of the other woman's problems as she put an arm of her ruined dress around the cook. "You just get this kitchen cleaned up and I'll worry about the dress."

"But what will you tell Mrs. Olson?"

Persy's brow furrowed in concentration. "I won't tell my

aunt anything. Just get this place cleaned up before she returns."

"But how will you explain the fact that you won't be wearing the same dress to your fancy coming-out party? What will you tell her happened to your dress?"

Persy looked down at the garment in question. What, indeed, would she tell her aunt? Soda grit rustled underfoot as the smoke drifted out a small window near the ceiling. Birds chirped from the bushes and trees as if all was right with the world. Little did they know, Persy thought glumly, that everything was very wrong!

But then after a moment she perked up and smiled. "I'll simply go back to Madame Gullierre and have her make another one. You will keep your position here, and Liam will have his medicine. See how simple that is."

Mrs. McFee brightened at this news. "Indeed, Miss Persephone. That is a splendid idea! If the woman made one, surely she can make another."

Within the half hour, Mrs. McFee had helped Persy clean up, hide the dress, and hail a hansom cab to take her back down to the dressmaker's establishment. And within another half hour Persy was traveling back up Fifth Avenue shaking her head in despair.

How was she ever going to come up with enough money to pay to have the dress remade, she wondered. It had all seemed so simple when she made her promise to Mrs. McFee. But now, after talking to the seamstress, it wasn't so simple after all.

Persy had been stunned when Madame Gullierre told her the price of the dress. Ninety-six dollars! It seemed impossible that anyone in their right mind would spend that kind of money on something to wear, and not even something she could wear often, if ever again. She could practically see, as if she were right there in the cab with Persy, her mother shake her head in disbelief over such a

waste. If only her aunt had taken her to a place like
Macy's where she had seen in the *Times* that they advertise value. Macy's probably didn't even sell a dress for
ninety-six dollars!

Persy sighed. The fact was that they hadn't shopped at
Macy's, and whether she wore the dress again or not
hardly mattered. What mattered was replacing the gown
that her aunt and uncle had so kindly and extravagantly
purchased for her. But therein lay another dilemma. She
certainly didn't have that kind of money. And she certainly couldn't ask her aunt and uncle to lend her the
money it would take to have it remade. Heavens, they'd
want to know why she needed it, and even if she hadn't
promised to keep Mrs. McFee's disaster a secret, she
couldn't imagine telling Aunt Margaret and Uncle John
that she had ruined a dress that cost more than the entire
wardrobe she had brought with her from Texas.

"Heavens," she grumbled under her breath, so distressed that she hardly noticed the arched-roof buses, or
the wild clanging bell atop the red and brass fire engine
careening down the road. Her excitement over her new
adventure was fast paling in the face of such a calamity.
Not only couldn't she approach her relatives, but she
didn't dare write her family of her problems. She wasn't
about to be the only Daltry in history to muck up their
labor! Never in the twenty years of her life had she ever
heard of a single Daltry failing to execute their labor for
any reason, much less something as foolish as burning up
a dress. It hardly seemed to matter that in trying to help
another she had ruined the dress. She shouldn't have worn
the dress to the kitchen in the first place. Hadn't Betty
said that very thing. No, she couldn't tell anyone about her
problems. She would have to find a way out of this predic-
ament all by herself. And she would!

Confidence swelled within her. She would find an answer. There had to be a solution to her problem. It was

just a matter of giving it enough thought to sort it all out. But her confidence soon began to wane when she approached her destination and no answer had come. "What," she murmured softly into the swaying carriage, "am I going to do now?"

She stared out the window without seeing, her mind circling with possible plans as to how she could come up with enough money to pay to have the dress remade. Her head circled and swayed in cadence to the carriage until she thought she would scream. But then, just as they pulled up in front of the Olsons' home, its black-painted cast-iron hitching post and broad stone mounting block covered with a light dusting of snow that had begun to fall, inspiration struck.

Persephone sat cross-legged on her white ruffled bed, unaware that she was biting her lower lip, indecent amounts of petticoats and pantaloons showing, surrounded by copies of *The New York Times* and the *New York Tribune*. She had even found yesterday's *New York Evening Sun* and a handful of other newspapers she had never heard of before. Her concentration was intense as she ran her finger down the column of classified advertisements—classified help wanted advertisements. She was going to get a job!

She read over an assortment of the multilined missives, none of which were in the least bit appropriate. She could hardly belief the types of work people were being asked to perform—or that they needed performing at all.

Her excitement over the inspiration that had struck only minutes before was fast deserting her in the face of not being able to come up with a single job that she was qualified for. Didn't people need cooks in this city, she wondered.

She determined that she could earn enough money for her dress and then some if she were willing to dance or show certain body parts that not even she had seen since she was a child. But she'd swim naked across the width of the Hudson River on her way back to Texas before she would do something like that. Persy smiled at the incongruity of the thought. And then she laughed, rolling over on her back and staring up at the ceiling.

How had she gotten herself into such a mess, she wondered as she had been wondering ever since she had walked out the door of Madame Gullierre's front door.

Why not announce at supper that she had ruined her dress, all on her own, while attempting to cook in their kitchen? But every time she thought about that possibility she imagined the disappointed looks on Aunt Margaret's and Uncle John's faces. Betty, she was certain, would laugh out loud. And even if they allowed her to pay for the dress and loaned her the money in the meantime, eventually she would have to inform her parents of the problem so they could send her the money and then everyone would know. And that she couldn't let happen. Lee had managed to pull off his labor with great panache. Persy was determined to do the same. So she just had to find some way to make some money, and surely there was someone in this great huge city who needed a cook.

It wasn't until she reached the last column of the last page and nearly the last advertisement that she struck gold, or what she hoped would prove to be the precious metal.

"Help Wanted. Cook for large establishment. Afternoons. Some evenings possible. Experience a must. References necessary. Apply in person. 121 Thompson Street."

She read the tiny print three times before she convinced herself she was really seeing it and that her mind wasn't playing tricks on her.

"Perfect," she whispered into the room. Just what she was looking for. A cook in a restaurant. Surely she could get away in the afternoon for however long it would take her to earn the money for her dress. Her aunt and uncle had been out of the house every afternoon since she arrived and they usually didn't return until five-thirty or six. That would give her all afternoon. And she was confident she could outcook anyone if it came down to competition for the position. And as far as references went, she'd worry about those when she got there.

It took her longer to dress for her job interview than it did to outfit herself at any time in the past. She knew she had to wear just the right thing. She certainly couldn't present herself as who she was. So she had to create a new identity. Her name wasn't a problem. As she had already determined no one knew her in New York, so her name wouldn't mean a thing to anyone unless her aunt or uncle or cousin happened upon the place.

Dressed in a plain frock of light wool that she borrowed from Marie the under maid, Persy walked to the hack line, approached the first cab in line, and climbed aboard. When the bewhiskered driver opened the tiny slot above her head to ask directions, she gave him the address and hoped he knew where to go.

They traveled down Sixth Avenue for what seemed like forever. Had the cab not arrived at the indicated address just then, she would have tapped the ceiling and instructed the driver to turn around and take her home. When she was sitting in her bedroom and had come up with her plan she had been filled with confidence. Now, on her way to apply, her bravado deserted her. Good Lord, what was she doing, she wondered as she peered through the window at the building designated as 121 Thompson Street.

"Come on, lady, I don't got all day."

Persephone was startled out of her reverie when the driver leaned down and yelled at her through the slit. Forgetting for the moment what she was about to embark upon, she climbed down from the carriage, paid the driver, then stepped up onto the walkway.

The massive door was painted black and handsomely carved, up four steps from where she stood. No sign indicating that the establishment was a restaurant hung on the wall. Perhaps she had been mistaken and the position was for a cook in a private home. For a second her heart hammered in her chest. What if it was the home of someone with whom her aunt and uncle socialized?

But then she looked around her. Certainly she wasn't in the worst of neighborhoods, and she had seen a few since arriving in New York with all her desire to see everything. But neither was it one of the best. Not the type of area one of her relatives' friends would live in. If Aunt Margaret was correct and a person needed wealth and good breeding to be accepted into their circle, then someone living in this neighborhood probably didn't have enough of either.

She was safe. Or so she hoped.

Taking a deep breath, she took the steps to the door, grasped the brass knocker, and hesitated. But then the vision of her ruined dress loomed in her head and she slammed the knocker down with more force than necessary before she could turn on her heels and run.

At first nothing happened. She stood on the stoop, passersby going about their business as if she weren't even there, and waited. Just when she picked the knocker up to knock once again, the door flew open.

The sight that met her eyes nearly felled her on the spot. Gasping for breath, her mouth dropping open in astonishment, Persy stepped back at the sight of the largest, most sinister-looking man she had ever seen who greeted her with what she could only call a grunt of welcome—or at least she hoped it was welcome. Wiry red hair, pale craggy skin, and green eyes nearly the color of fresh spring grass. Only the mass of freckles covering his face made him seem a little less forbidding.

He studied her for a moment before he asked, "Are you a cook?"

"Well, I—"

"Yes or no?"

"Well, yes, I suppose—"

"Good," he said simply, then took ahold of her wrist and pulled her inside.

The door slammed shut with a resounding bang, the walls seeming to reverberate from the force, sending Persy's heart into an erratic flutter. What had she gotten herself into? she wondered with renewed dismay.

He pulled her down a long hallway that would have been dark even though it was early afternoon had it not been for the yellow glow of gas-lit scones lining the walls. She had to run every few steps to keep up with the man's long stride. Gradually she became aware of loud voices that got even louder as they walked deeper into the building.

"Mr. ah hum," she began, pulling back against his grip.

The giant, however, took no notice of what to him were obviously weak protests, and within seconds they had burst through a swinging door that led to a kitchen.

For a moment she did nothing more than stand there and stare. Never in all her days had she seen such a sight. Steam simmered up from huge black cast-iron pots on a big black coal-burning stove that steamed the few windows in the room opaque. A fire burned in a grate, casting the kitchen with an eerie netherworld light. The heat alone could have brought a strong man to his knees, though her escort did nothing more than give in to a mild sweat on his brow.

But beyond the hellish atmosphere she could see another huge stove and counters and cool boxes and every imaginable convenience a cook could possibly desire, all right there in one room. It was a cook's dream if a person could get past the devilish heat.

"A cook," the giant announced to another man, this one as small as the other one was large. "I've got a cook."

The tiny man was dressed in a suit much like the one her uncle wore when he went to his law office.

"You don't look old enough to know how to cook," the man grumbled, his face scrunched up in aggravation.

But Persy was given no opportunity to reply when the yelling she had been dimly aware of before burst forth from a pantry as two oriental women surged forth, apparently arguing over whatever it was they carried between them. Suddenly they stopped, their tone and rapid-fire language seeming to reach a crescendo, their heads jerking in cadence to their words.

Persy, the giant, and the man, all stood stock-still, unable to move, watching the women with stunned dread. And then it happened. The taller of the two women jerked one way and the shorter woman jerked the other, each failing to relinquish her burden when she moved, and suddenly the sound of ripping fabric sounded through the room. Flour fell to the floor with a whoosh, then immediately puffed up into great clouds of white powder, filling the room like fog on an early morning winter day.

The incessant fighting ceased instantaneously and both women stared dumbfounded at the mess before they turned toward the two men on either side of Persy. Persy expected the women to be filled with contrition. Instead, the rapid-fire language issued forth once again, and she had the distinct idea they were laying blame at the men's feet.

"That's the second bag of flour this week those two have ruined!" the tiny man exclaimed above the noise. "Out, I say!" he hollered, pointing toward the swinging door through which Persy had only moments before emerged. "Out this minute!"

The barrage of foreign language never ceased, this time directed solely at the man, and at twice the volume.

"Get them out of here," he told the giant, ignoring the women and their ravings.

Persy stood quietly, still dumbstruck by the events that had unfolded before her eyes.

"How old are you?" the man suddenly demanded once again.

"How old am I?" she repeated, trying to gather her composure.

"I'm asking the questions here," he snapped. "Your age. Tell me your age."

"I hardly see how that's any concern of yours," she finally responded as politely as she could, though her teeth were all but bared, after staring at him for a good long while. He really had no manners at all, she noted to herself.

He looked her in the eye for the first time. "The last thing I need is another hot-tempered female in here to make more trouble than food."

Persy's eyes opened wide. She had never been called hot-tempered in all her days.

The giant returned through the swinging door. "They're gone," he said. "But it's almost three o'clock."

The man glanced about the kitchen, then sighed before he returned his hard gaze on Persy. "Are you sure you can cook?" he muttered.

Persy pulled herself up, still uncertain how she felt about being called hot-tempered. "Of course, I'm sure."

He shook his head, then handed her an apron. "Roast beef, potatoes, green beans, and apple pie for about a hundred and fifty people." He started to turn away. "It needs to be ready by five."

Persephone blinked, then blinked again. "I can't possibly have a roast ready in two hours," she stated, as if the rest of the meal prepared in a kitchen that was not only a disaster but totally unfamiliar to her were possible!

He turned back. "I thought you said you were a cook."

"A cook, yes," she snapped, her patience drawing to an end. "A magician, no! And who said I would even take this job?" The little man brought out the very worst in her, for who was she to make demands? But that fact didn't seem to deter her as she plunged ahead. "You haven't told me the first thing about my responsibilities or my pay or anything else for that matter." She took a deep breath and tried to calm herself. Anger and impatience would get her nowhere.

She forced a smile. "If you would be so kind, sir, as to explain what the details of this position are, I would be most grateful."

A thin film of flour had settled on his glasses through which he peered at Persy, as if trying to determine how sincere she was. "You are to cook a supper for approximately one hundred and fifty patrons a day. The meal should be ready by five when the girls will take over and begin to serve. You will be paid fifty cents for each day's work, every day except Sunday. You will receive additional wages if you are called upon to work past five."

Persephone nearly staggered back at the amount. "Fifty cents a day! That's highway robbery!" She forgot about trying to be polite in light of the fact that she would have to work—her mind scrambled with calculations—good God, one hundred ninety-two days to earn enough money to pay for her dress. "I can't accept less than four dollars a day!"

"Four dollars a day!" This time he staggered back. "That's ridiculous."

One delicate dark brow raised in question. "The way I see it, you need a cook."

His eyes narrowed. "One dollar. You need a job."

"Three fifty."

"One fifty."

"Three dollars."

"Two dollars, and not a penny more."

Persy's mind churned. Two dollars a day would merely get her just over halfway there by the time her debut rolled around a month from now. But what were her choices? She sighed. Hopefully she could convince the seamstress to accept two payments for the dress. One at the end of a month when she had to pick up the dress, and the other at the end of the second month after she had finally made enough money to pay off her debt. Yes, she'd just have to work twice as long and hope the seamstress would agree. She could tell from the look on this tiny man's face that he'd not go a penny higher. "Two dollars, then."

"Good. Any more questions?" he asked.

"No," she stated. "Though I really must tell you now that working past five on any day will be impossible."

A large vein on his forehead bulged. "And why ever not?"

Persy's mind raced. She knew she wouldn't be able to get out of the house alone after five in the evening. She'd be lucky to get out unnoticed for two months during the day. "I've other obligations that cannot be broken."

He looked as if he was going to send her on her way. But then he glanced around the empty kitchen, then down at his pocket watch and said, "All right. At least for now."

Yet again he started to turn away.

"Excuse me, sir," she called after him. "What about the roast?"

He sighed. "Make whatever you can in the time allotted." He looked her straight in the eyes. "But it better be good or you'll be out the door without so much as a single cent for your efforts."

And then he was gone with the giant close behind him, leaving Persy alone in a kitchen that she didn't know the first thing about. Good heavens, she realized suddenly that she didn't even know their names. And who were these one hundred and fifty patrons she was supposed to feed? Were they guests of an important man? Or people who were paying to eat her fare?

She looked around her. There was nothing to give her any clues to the answer. But she'd do best to worry about the meal rather than who was going to eat it for now. She could worry about the rest once the meal was done.

Five

THE HEAT IN THE KITCHEN WAS ALMOST UNBEARABLE. THE flames of Hades couldn't be any hotter than this, Persy sighed under her breath as she put the last touches on the long line of Cornish game hens with cranberry cockaigne. She had gotten a deal on all the birds.

But deal or no, all she cared about was the fact that they had already been plucked, cleaned, and stuffed when she got them. All she had to do was dress and cook them. The delivery boy who had appeared in the kitchen only minutes after the man and the giant had left had told her about the hotel down the street that had a large party cancel at the last minute. She had sent the boy posthaste to the hotel to purchase the fowl without a glimmer of guilt. How else was she supposed to have a meal prepared for so many so quickly otherwise.

Stepping back from her masterpiece with a dull, blunt serving fork, she waved it with a flourish like a magician showing off his magic, rather pleased with herself for her accomplishment.

"Very nice."

The voice startled her, seeming to come out of nowhere, and Persy jumped, nearly knocking the first row of culinary delights from the counter.

"And from what I heard, accomplished in a very short period of time. Impressive."

For a second she forgot that she was in a strange kitchen with someone lurking in its depths. She forgot for a second that she should be alarmed. *Impressive,* the mysterious voice had said. She nearly preened her pleasure and agreed with what from the sounds of the voice was a man, when that very point sank in. A man. In a strange kitchen.

Holding the surge of fright at a respectable distance, she peered into the corners of the kitchen where the light didn't reach. "Who's there?"

Her surprise and concern faded, however, and her breath caught in her throat when the owner of the clearly masculine voice stepped out of the shadows and into the light.

"Oh, my God!" she cried, her eyes wide as she shook the fork at him.

He looked from her face to the utensil with amused interest. "There have been a great many who have tried to despatch me to warmer climes," he said, taking a step closer, heedless of the flour that puffed up into the air and settled on his high-polished black Hessian boots with each step he took, "but never in such an . . . ingenious manner."

Persy glanced, dumbfounded, between the fork and the man.

"Are you planning to . . . fork me to death?" he asked, his smile slow and lazy, revealing straight white teeth. "Perhaps you could use a knife instead. A sharp one preferably. Surely it would prove less painful and much quicker for the both of us if you did."

"It's you!" Persy finally managed to say, ignoring his

jests as she blinked, then blinked again as if trying to clear an unsettling sight from her eyes.

"Me?" he asked, his smile fading, his footsteps halting. "Have we met?"

Persephone took in the dark brown hair and chiseled features of the man who had stood out so clearly in the crowd of people walking along Fifth Avenue two weeks before. Jake Devlin.

She had thought him attractive from a distance, but up close he was devastatingly handsome.

Oh, my stars, she breathed silently, he was gorgeous.

He wore a loose white shirt, though the coat, purple vest, and tie she had seen him wear before were nowhere in sight. The top shirt button was undone and she caught just a glimpse of dark curling hair on his chest. Her mind started to wander down the dangerous path of wondering just where the dark hair led. But before her mind could stray beyond control, she snapped herself to attention. Her ruined dress had obviously done more to her than leave her strapped for money. It had softened her brain. For all the good that determination did, however, when in the next second she took in the dark trousers that clung to the hard lean lines of his thighs. Strong, hard thighs. Like a Greek god's. The thought popped into her head that his eyes were green, not blue, but deep, dark, mesmerizing green, the color of pine trees in Texas.

Never in her twenty years had she seen such a man. But what exactly did she feel, she wondered. Light-headed. Heart pounding in her chest. Palms alternately cold, then hot. Good heavens, she was coming down with the plague! She was sick! But then she practically rolled her eyeballs at herself. Sick, maybe, but sick with infatuation for this man, she knew without a doubt. And that was absurd. She was no schoolgirl to get schoolgirl crushes. She was a woman. A twenty-year-old woman, at that. It didn't matter that he was as handsome as sin and had a voice as smooth

as the devil's. She was too old to be going silly over this
man or any other. And her reaction, she told herself
firmly, simply had everything to do with the fact that she
had never seen a man dressed in such a way. Dark and
elegant, at ease, as if he was at home. The idea brought
her careening thoughts to heel. At home! He was dressed
as if he was in the privacy of his own home. Oh, my heavens, say it's not so! He was called the Prince of Prince
Street. Good Lord, she was on Thompson Street, she
knew it for a fact!

"What are you doing here?" she demanded, her tone
overly sharp.

His green eyes narrowed. "I own this place. Do I know
you?" he demanded once again.

Persy dropped her hand to her side, the fork dangling
from her fingers, and she groaned. Her worst nightmare
was confirmed. "I thought you were called the Prince of
Prince Street!"

His eyes opened wide for a fraction of a second before
his countenance hardened. "What is going on here?" His
voice was low and deep as he took a step closer.

Her mind raced. Regardless of the street on which this
building was placed, if this man owned this kitchen, then
he obviously owned the rooms and walls that surrounded
it. And that, she concluded dismally, could only mean one
thing. She had just cooked a meal for a saloon owner and
his hundred and fifty prospective saloon goers! She was in
the bowels of a building belonging to a notorious man.
Cooking his meal. Speaking to him this very second. She
was working in a house of ill repute! She had cooked a
veritable feast for a horde of men who undoubtedly could
care less if she served them Cornish game hens or corn
hash. They wouldn't know the difference between the two
even if the hens jumped up and pecked them in the face.
All they cared about was the liquor and the women! The

reprobates! She was providing them with the energy to do just what they shouldn't be doing!

Dear Lord, what was she going to do? It was bad enough that she had gone out and gotten a job. Her aunt and uncle would have a fit if they ever found out. But to have procured a position in a saloon, a notorious saloon at that . . . Lord have mercy, if her aunt ever learned the truth she would faint dead away, then send Persy back to Texas on the first train out of the Pennsylvania terminus in Jersey City just as soon as she was revived.

Persy groaned even louder. She would be returned to Paradise like a troublesome schoolchild not three months after she departed.

Returned in disgrace.

An embarrassment to her family.

The first Daltry to fail.

"What is going on here?" Jake demanded, breaking into her reverie.

Persy focused on the man, suddenly desperate to remember every detail of what her cousin and aunt had said about him. Perhaps if she thought hard enough she would remember some nugget of redeeming value about him. He saved young children. He secretly donated money to hospitals. Something. Anything. In fact, she thought with a sudden futile burst of hope, maybe this wasn't the man she had seen after all. This was a nice respectable headmaster who ran a private girls' school. The meal was for a hundred and fifty hungry young ladies. This man was someone altogether different, not the notorious saloon owner about whom her cousin and aunt had spoken. Surely in a city as large as New York there were hundreds upon thousands of men who had silky dark hair and devastating green eyes. She wanted to believe. She needed to believe.

"Have we met?" he asked again, his voice impatient.

He turned slightly then, though enough for her to catch sight of the gold ring that had caught a ray of sun when he was walking down the street weeks before—dashing her hopes.

"No, we haven't met," she sighed, her voice filled with defeat. "Though I saw you from a distance when I was traveling in a carriage and was struck by your good looks." She said the words as if she were telling him he had some fatal disease.

Her tone, however, went unnoticed by Jake. He had expected her to say a great many things, but to tell him so blatantly that he was good-looking surprised him speechless. And that was a very rare thing for a man who spent most of his time in control. The only time he had ever allowed his stern composure to slip was when he was in the privacy of his bedchamber, and only then when he was alone. The thought didn't sit well with him.

Persy turned away with a scowl. She tossed the fork onto the counter with a clatter and glared at the feast, her hands braced on either side of a golden brown bird.

Jake's surprise and displeasure, however, gave way to a slow lazy smile. "So you think I'm good-looking, do you?"

Persy whirled around, anger burning in the depths of her gray eyes, making them dark. But her anger wavered in the face of his disarming smile. She stared at him, and at length she shook her head. "Good-looking or not, that does not change the fact of where I am."

His smile suddenly tightened and his eyes grew leery. "And where might that be?"

She forgot his disarming smile and her anger surged with renewed force. "In a house of ill repute, that's where!"

"Ah," he said, understanding dawning bright in his green eyes, "I should have known. Not only did you see me, but others saw me as well, and they took it upon themselves to regale you with vivid descriptions of my many vices and virtues."

"Vices, yes; virtues, no!"

"Of course. How silly of me." His voice grew harsh. "I have no virtues. I keep forgetting. Very inconvenient for me, as you might imagine. And what did they tell you, my little angel? That I am beyond redemption. That I have one foot in the eternal fires of perdition? Or simply that I am the devil incarnate?"

Shifting on her feet, Persy grew a tad uncomfortable. Certainly, with the kitchen cast in a murky glow from the heat of the stoves, not to mention the spilled flour from the oriental women that had yet to be cleaned up, he looked every inch the Prince of Darkness, or at the very least, he looked as if he had one foot in that bottomless pit. But still that didn't seem to explain why she was uncomfortable.

She studied him then, from his furrowed brow to his arms held stiffly at his sides. He cared, she thought suddenly. He cared what people said about him. This dark, dangerous saloon owner cared that people talked poorly about him. He was not as dark and dangerous as he appeared to be. Or if he was, he clearly didn't want to be.

She had the sudden notion to reach out and touch his arm, to comfort him, as she took in the sight of this magnificent man. But when she took a step toward him, all signs of vulnerability vanished so quickly and thoroughly that she wondered if she had imagined them in the first place. And sure enough she must have, she concluded, when he pulled his shoulders back and looked every inch a man who indeed had one foot in nether regions.

"Do you like what you see?" he asked sardonically.

Persy cleared her throat and shook her head. Thank goodness he had broken the absurd train of thought that had run amuck in her head. She met his gaze. "I'd blush if I didn't think you said that just to be mean."

For a second she was certain that *he* blushed. The idea pleased her immensely. But then she reasoned that it had been nothing more than the eerie cast of light lending him a sheen of red when he didn't have one himself. Blushing, indeed!

"What a mess," she said with a sigh.

"And how are things a mess?"

Persy snorted aloud. "They are a mess because I need a job and this was the only one I could find that was . . . suitable." She snorted even louder. "Or at least that I thought was suitable."

"Suitable?"

"Cooking as you can see," she responded with a wave of her hand in the direction of the meal she had just prepared, "I can do. And it seemed far more acceptable than cleaning sewers, digging ditches, or"—she eyed him closely—"lifting my skirts in dance. Come to think of it, that was probably your advertisement, too!"

His hand fisted at his side. "I have no need to advertise in the classified section for dancing girls. I bring in only the best girls from all over the world. I run a respectable establishment."

"Respectable?" she scoffed. "A saloon with dancing girls, respectable? I think not, sir."

"Then quit. Walk out that door. I sure as hell won't stop you."

"Really!" Persephone pursed her lips. "There is no need for profanity."

That stopped him cold in his tracks. Jake couldn't remember the last time someone had chastened him for anything, much less for using profanity. In fact, he realized suddenly, he had become immune to it. "Hell" and "damn" came out of his mouth as frequently, or perhaps more frequently, than "please" and "thank you."

His mind drifted. Far, far away. Miles from New York. Miles from this hellish place he had come to call home. Suddenly his mind was filled with that place where he longed to be. He saw himself standing on that quaint street saying hello to friendly passersby.

He wondered suddenly why a saloon had seemed so appealing to him when he was young. Why not a mercantile or livery? Didn't young boys dream about horses and hardware? How had he become a saloon owner with dancing girls who rubbed their bodies up against his as easily as a cat purred against his leg. And with that thought he had his answer. What young man didn't long for good money and lots of women, things Jake had had a good deal of over the past years.

And then, unexpectedly, memories of his mother came to mind and he nearly smiled. Nearly. But it was dampened by a sudden tightening in his chest. His mother was long dead of consumption. Dead before he ever really knew her. She was nothing more than a faint memory that sometimes didn't seem real.

"Mr. Devlin! You're not listening to me."

Jake jerked his attention back to her, away from the memory of his mother with her sweet rounded face smiling at him in his dreams. He focused on the woman who stood before him. He took in her slight form. Her dress was that of a working girl's, light wool that had been washed and mended a great many times. But he noticed as well for the first time that the working-girl image stopped there. Her skin was too creamy and her hair too shiny. No tired circles beneath her eyes or teeth gone bad from poor nutrition. He had seen the signs too many times to keep count, enough to know the working class when he saw it.

He determined then that this woman who claimed to need a job, and he had no reason to believe she didn't, was not an average working girl. Obviously she needed the money for a very different reason than simply providing sustenance for a family.

"Sir!"

"Who are you?" he asked unexpectedly.

The question clearly startled her, as he expected it would.

"Who am I?" she repeated, running her hands down the skirt of her dress.

"I don't know." His smile was a hard, cold line. "That's what I want to know. I know your name is Persephone Daltry, you told Mr. Bills that much. But I don't know what a young girl like you needs a job for."

Persy puffed up, insulted. Why did everyone have to think she was so young. She was a woman—full grown—no longer a child. She disregarded the thought that she was acting like a child. "I'm not so very young."

He raised his eyebrow as if he didn't believe her.

"Well, I'm old enough to be married!"

"Are you?"

"Am I what?" she asked.

"Married."

She hesitated at this. "What business is it of yours?"

"As your employer I have a right to know. Are you married or not, Persephone Daltry?" he repeated.

She debated her options. If she said no, it would prove that she had implied something that was not so. If she said yes, while it suited her purposes, that would be the lie. "Of course I'm married."

He looked down at her hand. "No ring?"

"I'm widowed," she hastily responded, congratulating herself for her quick response.

"You're awfully young to be widowed."

"I started early."

"I'll need you to work nights."

"I can't."

"Why not?"

"I have a baby."

Their eyes met and held. Silence filled the kitchen. And then they laughed.

"You have a quick mind," he said.

"Thank you. I try."

"I guess we are at an impasse then. I need a cook and

you need a job. Perhaps one day you'll tell me who you really are."

"I'm exactly who I say I am," she stated.

"A widowed working woman . . ." he began, taking her hand.

The touch startled her. So firm yet gentle. Without warning she was aware of the feel of his skin on hers, and she was aware of him. She was not thinking that he was vulnerable or that he was a saloon owner, but that he was a man, a powerful man who drew her to him like a magnet, despite the fact that he shouldn't. She shouldn't. She should jerk her hand free and flee, out the door, into the street, and never turn back.

Instead, she looked up and met his eyes.

". . . with a child. Hmmm," he continued. "You don't look the part," he said quietly, turning her hand over and running his thumb against her palm.

She felt the touch all the way down to her toes. She glanced down at their hands entwined. "Why?" she whispered, hardly aware of what she was saying. "Why don't I look the part?"

He seemed to consider as he stared at his thumb rubbing slow, gentle circles around her palm. "Because you're too sweet and too pretty."

Red surged through her cheeks.

"And you blush." He tilted her chin until their eyes met once again and he smiled down at her. "I can't remember the last time I saw a woman blush."

Suddenly she became aware of his full lips, and she wondered what it would be like if he kissed her. Never in her twenty years had she been kissed, not even by the Bronson twins, and they had kissed nearly every girl in town.

"Wouldn't it be nice," he said softly, more to himself than Persephone, "to find a place where there were flowers and trees and wide expanses of earth where a person could see forever." His eyes focused on her. "A place where there were pretty girls who still blushed."

His voice wrapped around her, mesmerizing her, and without thinking she said, "A place like Paradise."

He grew very still before he laughed, deep and low, more sad, she thought, than happy.

"Yes, sweet Persephone, like paradise."

It took a moment before she realized not only that he wasn't referring to her hometown, thank goodness, but that he wasn't going to kiss her either—what a shame.

And then she chastised herself. She would have slapped him silly, she told herself, if he had even tried to press his kisses on her. He was a fiend! she added for emphasis when guilt surged in her mind over the fact that anyone with a lick of sense could figure out that she had been the only person in the room thinking of kisses.

For a second, she had lost her mind. That was the only plausible explanation. The heat had finally gotten to her. Not only did she not want his kisses, but the last thing she needed was for this devil man to learn who she was or where she was from. Though truthfully she didn't think that would prove much of a problem in a city with so many people. What were the chances that he would ever meet up with anyone who knew her aunt and uncle? Not very likely. He wasn't going to meet her relatives, nor was he going to kiss her. She bit back disappointment.

"Persephone in paradise," he said, breaking into her thoughts. "How appropriate. Our pretty Persephone in the hells of the devil's kitchen. The myth seems to be playing itself out in reality." He smiled a smile of devilish delight. "I guess I'll have to let you go home each evening just as Hades let Persephone flee the underworld for six months of the year. The world can't do without spring and summer."

"Very funny, Mr. Devlin."

"I thought so. And an apt analogy if I do say so myself."

"You're familiar with the myth, then?" she asked dryly.

"I've always loved mythology."

Persephone snorted. "Then my grandmother would love you. She is rather fond of the subject, as well."

The kitchen grew uncomfortably quiet, quiet enough that the gentle hiss of gas lights could be heard. His smile vanished, and he held her hand even tighter. "Don't fool yourself, my little goddess. I'm not the kind of man grandmothers love."

The pressure on her hand increased and before she knew what was happening, he was pulling her close. His countenance was hard and formidable. Her eyes opened wide when his other arm curled around her back and he pressed her to him.

"No," he continued, "grandmothers increasingly don't love me, as you undoubtedly learned from your friends when you saw me in the distance."

"Now, really," she said, pressing her hands against his chest, her heart fluttering in her own. "I'm sure if you gave people half a chance they would see you in a different light. Why just this day I've seen a side of you that I wouldn't have believed possible based on what my aunt said. I do believe that deep down"—she eyed him closely —"well, maybe deep, deep down, you are a very nice man."

She was trying to placate him, but only succeeded in making him angrier. And she couldn't imagine why.

Her breath caught in her though, cutting off all thought, when he dipped his head until his lips were mere inches from her own. He was going to kiss her. At last!

"Don't be a fool, my sweet," he whispered, his breath caressing her lips, "I'm not nice at all."

But she wasn't listening to his words. Her eyes had fluttered closed and she waited with bated breath for the first kiss of her life. And when he released her abruptly and started to turn away Persy nearly fell flat on her backside.

Only his quick reaction saved her when he reached back and steadied her.

And there it was, pushing all else from her mind. The unguarded look in his eyes that told her a great deal. Unmasked, unguarded, he looked vulnerable, just as he had moments before, as well as when he had stood amid the street crowd, facing west. She was correct. Deep down inside, this man was vulnerable.

He let her go unexpectedly, then turned to go. Persy had the fleeting desire yet again to comfort him. He might be a man of the underworld, but she knew suddenly without doubt that he would rather be a man of wide-open spaces and happiness. "You should move west," she blurted out without thinking.

Her words stopped him cold. Slowly, very slowly he turned back to her. "West?"

"Yes, if you hate it so much here you should move out West where a man can start new, start over in his life. A place where no man asks questions, nor is he asked."

His smile returned, though it was as cold and hard as a bitter winter night. "Don't fool yourself, Miss . . . or rather, Mrs. Daltry. This is where I belong. This is my home. A den of iniquity filled with gambling, liquor, and dancing women. A place where lurid men can appease their vulgar needs. Men like me. I am beyond redemption. And don't get it into your head to think you can do any redeeming." He reached out and grasped her chin, tilting it slightly. "And you'd do well not to forget that."

Based on the look in his eyes and the tone of his voice, Persy wasn't certain who he was trying to convince. Her or himself. Either way, she had the fleeting suspicion that neither one of them believed it.

"Understand?" he persisted.

"Yes, I think I understand a great deal."

He looked at her curiously then. For a moment she

thought he was going to question her. But then the bells from a nearby cathedral began to toll the hour.

"It's time," he said. "Five o'clock."

Persy's eyes opened wide. "Five o'clock! It's five o'clock?"

"Yes," he said, looking at her curiously. "But don't worry, the girls will be down any minute to help you get the dishes out to the dining room."

"Dishes to the dining room? I can't! I've got to go. Unc—"

Jake's eyes narrowed suspiciously.

"I've got to get home . . . because my neighbor . . . who stays with my daughter . . . has to leave." She twirled in a flurry of skirts toward the door before he could stop her.

"Your daughter?"

"Yes . . . Alberta, my daughter Alberta."

"What about tomorrow?"

"What about it?"

"Will you be coming back? Or do I need to find another cook?"

Her step faltered. She knew she should tell him to find another cook, that she would never return. But her ruined dress came to mind and she knew she had no choice. And just the thought of never seeing this man again brought a strange hammering to her chest. "Don't bother trying to find another cook, just get me some help."

He smiled a strange humorless smile. "So you'll be back?"

"Apparently so."

"Until tomorrow then," he said softly. But the words went unheard as the door swung shut, leaving Jake alone in the kitchen, oddly pleased by the turn of events.

Six

By the time Persy returned to the saloon kitchen the following day, she had convinced herself that she had experienced a moment of pure unadulterated insanity the previous day when she had made such a fool of herself over that dissolute Jake Devlin. She didn't like him. She wasn't attracted to him. And in the future, she wouldn't repeat her mistakes of yesterday.

With that, she banged the shiny brass knocker against the door of what looked to the unsuspecting eye like a respectable establishment. But she knew better. When she had fled the evening before she had found that the building was at the corner of Thompson and Prince streets. And there, on Prince Street, as bold as brass, was another door leading to the same building, with a sign embossed in gold stating The Dusty Rose. The Dusty Rose! Perhaps the dirty rose, or the devil's rose, but merely a dusty rose, she thought not!

"Hello, Miz Daltry," the giant from yesterday said, motioning her to step inside. "We didn't think you'd be coming back."

"I said I would and I never go back on a promise."

Just then someone shouted, "Howie," from somewhere deep in the building.

"Just a minute," he shouted back, before returning his attention to her.

"Your name is Howie?"

He grimaced. "Yeah."

Persy looked at him closely, realizing with a start that this giant man was sensitive about his name. So she offered him a genuine smile. "I think Howie is a fine name."

For a second he looked hopeful, but soon after the light in his eyes faded. "Ah, well," he said. "You better get started."

At first, Persy started to persist with the discussion of his name. But then she reasoned that this Howie was no business of hers, and she simply followed him down the hall and into the kitchen. The deserted kitchen. "Where is everyone?" she asked.

"Who do you mean?"

"Where are the people who are supposed to help me?"

"I didn't know anyone else was coming."

"There should be. Mr. Devlin promised."

"Mr. Devlin?" Howie asked. "You talked to Mr. Devlin?"

"I most certainly did. Didn't he tell you?"

"No, can't say that he did."

"No matter. He promised that I would have help today. Perhaps they're just late."

Howie shifted uncomfortably. "Maybe so."

"Why don't you go ask Mr. Devlin when they should arrive."

"Good idea."

Howie fled back through the swinging door and disappeared. In the meantime, Persy got right to work. She had decided during her long sleepless night that she would prepare veal cordon bleu. She couldn't depend on the nearby hotel to have large parties cancel every day. Besides, the delivery boy who had brought the other items she had needed yesterday told her he could deliver just about anything she could think up, and in a very short time. Such a pleasure.

After smoothing her plain ankle-length dress of gray wool that matched her eyes, she adjusted the cameo brooch fastening the white collar, then bent over a scrap of paper with a leaded pencil and began to make out her list. With no more than half a dozen entries written down the door swung open.

She straightened in a flash and twirled around to find not Howie but none other than Mr. Jake Devlin himself. He wore a white stand-up wing-collared shirt tucked into black trousers, without the prescribed coat and vest that should have gone with it.

"Morning, sister!" he said, his lips split with a huge smile.

Her eyes narrowed. He appeared to be in amazingly high spirits for a dissolute, she noted. She expected him to have bloodshot eyes and disheveled hair after a long, hard night of dissipation. But he didn't look any such thing. In fact, just like the day before, he looked the man at ease, and more handsome than sin. For a second she nearly forgot that he was a reprobate, and simply gawked at his good looks and charming smile. Fortunately she remembered his true nature in the nick of time.

"I am most certainly not your sister!" she snapped.

"True enough," he stated, snatching up her list and reading a few of the entries. "Though I can't say as I'd mind if you pretended that we were, and young and small at that, with our mama making us share the same bath."

Her eyes went wide and her mouth fell open. Jake simply smiled and glanced back at the list.

Persy sputtered and spat and tried to think of what she should say, but before she could speak Jake tossed the list back onto the counter and said, "No more of that fancy food. The men who come here don't want to eat trussed-up chickens with sauces that look suspicious."

His earlier outrageous and most improper comment was forgotten in the face of his insult toward her cooking. "Those were Cornish game hens, not trussed-up chickens, and I slaved over that sauce. The Queen of England should have it so good!"

"Let her. But at my table I want meat and potatoes, a good stew, fried chicken, pork chops. Surely you know the type. Food to fortify a man after a hard day's work."

"Fortify them so they can cavort with women!"

Jake laughed softly. "No, darlin'. To watch the women, nothing more, and spend their money drinking and gambling after a hard day's work."

"You lure these men to sin!"

"No, I simply provide them with the best of what they want. If I didn't someone else would."

"Is that what you tell yourself at night when you can't sleep?" She spat the words at him, hoping they would hit home and hurt.

Jake only stared at her for a moment, then laughed out loud. "I sleep like a babe in his mother's arms every night. Though perhaps not last night because I was too busy dreaming of you."

Her heart slammed against her ribs. She went weak in the knees. And that made her all the angrier. "Save your fancy talk for the ladies who want to hear it. I for one do not!" She backed away from him for fear that at any moment her knees would give out altogether and she would end up in his arms.

She grabbed up the nearest pan and banged it down on the stove. "Where's my help?" she demanded.

"Ah yes, Howie warned me."

"Warned you? What do you mean? You promised me that I'd have help in here today. I can't prepare meals for a hundred and fifty people every day all by myself."

"Two hundred for tonight."

"Two hundred!" She staggered back a step at the very idea.

"Miss Lola sings this evening. She's a big draw."

Her head craned forward and her eyes bored into him. "Miss Lola sings tonight," she said sarcastically, "and you expect me to prepare all those panting, mule-headed males supper—by myself? Get Miss Lola to cook for you, because I quit!"

And she meant it. Ruined dress or not. She had disregarded her conscience, disregarded her family, but she would not, could not, perform the impossible.

Jake hung his head for a moment before he rolled up the sleeves of his expensively tailored shirt. "No need to act so hastily. I'll help," he announced as if this were some sort of a prize.

She looked at him as if he had lost his mind. "You?"

Jake pulled his shoulders back and raised one slash of dark brow. "You doubt my abilities?"

"You bet I do."

With that he laughed. "When it comes to cooking, you probably should. But I'm a quick study. Always have been."

Persy groaned. What was she to do? She really did need the money. And how hard could it be to cook for two hundred people if she only had to prepare something like stew? Good heavens, she had been cooking stew since she was a child. She could probably make it in her sleep. "Oh, all right," she grumbled, picking up a new slip of paper. "I'll stay."

He was quiet for a moment before he said, "Good."

Persy glanced up from the list she had begun, and hated that she was pleased.

She finished a new list, and within a half hour the delivery boy had returned with her box of ingredients.

Persy had put on a starched bib apron, pulled out all the

pots and pans she would need, and began preliminary preparations. She looked back over her shoulder. "Scrub and chop the vegetables while I braise the meat."

Jake glanced between Persy and the vegetables, before he shrugged his shoulders and got to work. He talked all the while, unaware that she was hardly listening. In fact, she made a point to not listen, concentrating on her new dress and her debut to come. Not until she was ready for the vegetables did she finally turn back to him, only to find Jake leaning back against the counter, taking a bite of the carrot he held in his long strong fingers. The rest of the pile of vegetables sat on the counter, still unwashed.

At length the story about which he rambled on came to a halt when he finally noticed not only her furrowed brow but her angry gaze as well.

"What are you doing?" she snapped.

He glanced down and seemed surprised by the dirty vegetables. "Oh, yes. The vegetables. I'll do that now."

With a grumble, Persy set the meat aside, then started on the pie crust while she waited for the vegetables. Jake started in on a whole new set of tales. When she turned back again the vegetables were certainly washed and clearly pared, but washed and pared down to nothing!

Persy's growl brought a teasing grin to Jake's lips and he started to say something, no doubt something inappropriate, she thought, before she grabbed the knife away from him.

"Careful, darlin', you might hurt yourself."

"I'm going to hurt you," she muttered, pointing the knife in his direction. "You promised to get me help."

His smile broadened and he held out his arms as if presenting himself. "What more could you possibly want?"

Her eyes narrowed and with a boldness that was unheard of in the Persephone Daltry she had been for the last twenty years, two months, three weeks, four days, and fourteen hours, she looked the length of him, then said, "A lot."

Jake only laughed good-naturedly.

"You're about as worthless in the kitchen as a bull in a china shop!" she grumbled mulishly when her barb didn't hit home.

"Now, Persephone," he began, but was cut off before he could proceed.

"Find me some help, Mr. Devlin, or you and Howie and Mr. Bills are going to be cooking the rest of this meal, along with every one of them from here on out!" She glanced at the pile of what used to be vegetables. "You might boast of the finest liquors in town, but with your culinary skills that's all you'll be boasting about." She seemed to consider. "Though maybe Howie would surprise you and serve up a meal to rival the finest of chefs." She looked Jake in the eye. "What do you think?"

Jake grumbled in response. His good humor evaporated. At length, he stalked from the room, leaving Persy alone to wonder what exactly he was going to do. Her question was answered not five minutes later when he pushed back through the swinging door with two sleepy-eyed women in his wake.

"Oh, my goodness!" Persy exclaimed, both shocked and amazed at the same time.

"Miss Lola, Miss May, meet Mrs. Daltry, our cook who is in desperate need of your help."

"You didn't hire me to cook, Jake honey," the woman named Miss Lola protested.

Miss Lola had the whitest hair Persy had ever seen, with big brown eyes and a beauty mark just below her left cheekbone. And from the way she cuddled up to Jake, Persy thought with a strange flutter of her heart, the woman knew the man a great deal better than as simply an employee.

"That's right, Jake," the other said. "We dance, not cook."

Where Miss Lola had the whitest hair Persy had ever seen, Miss May had the reddest hair Persy could imagine. Neither one, it would seem, did anything halfway. Though on second thought, she amended, dress halfway might apply, for surely she had never seen more scantily clad human beings in all her days. Why when Miss Lola moved just so, Persy could make out the curve of what she was certain was, dear Lord, say it isn't so, a breast.

Persy noticed just then that Mr. Devlin had noticed the cleavage as well and when he lifted his eyes and met hers he had the gall to smile—no apologies or blushes of shame, just a shameless smile. Truly she was living and breathing in the world of eternal fires if ever there was one. And Jake Devlin was the fire master.

"Well, my lovelies, if we don't help our Mrs. Daltry, we will have no supper to serve."

"If last night's fare was any indication we might be better off without any," Miss May responded, brushing a lock of red hair from her eyes.

Persy sucked in her breath and May turned, instantly contrite.

"Oh, I'm sorry, ma'am. It's just that I was sound asleep when Jake barged in and I'm never very nice until I've had a cup of coffee." May shrugged her delicate shoulders. "The chickens really weren't all that bad."

"Cornish game hens," Persy said tightly. She didn't know if she should be outraged or insulted. "Mr. Devlin, I believe we need to talk."

She turned on her heels without waiting for his response. After a shrug and a smile to the two dancing girls, Jake followed Persy out the door. No sooner had he pushed through to the hallway and the door had swung shut than she started in on him.

"What is the meaning of that?" she demanded, pointing back toward the kitchen.

"Of what?" he asked.

"Those . . . those . . . women in my kitchen!"

All smiles and good humor fled from his face like storm clouds swept off on a winter wind. Persy had to force herself not to step back.

"Those women," he began, his voice tight, "are in *my* kitchen, and only because *you* demanded that I get you help."

"You expect me to work alongside . . . them?"

His chiseled jaw clenched. "Are you implying that they shouldn't be there?"

"Implying, nothing. That is exactly what I am saying!"

"Really," he said, leaning back against the wall, looking at her in a way that should have forewarned her. "So you think you're better than Lola and May, I take it?"

She opened her mouth to speak, then snapped it shut. She realized, belatedly, where this was heading. He was going to make her look callous and snobbish. But if she was truthful with herself, she had no one to blame but herself. "It's just that . . ." she began, looking for words to explain that it was indecent for her to socialize with such women. Why she shouldn't even be speaking to them much less working side by side with them. They were dancing girls! Women of lesser virtue. How could he possibly expect her to work alongside of them?

"It's just that what, Mrs. Daltry?" His countenance hardened and his green eyes blazed like slits of jade. "What were you going to say? That you, a widowed working woman trying to scrape together enough money to feed your child, think you're better than they are?"

Persy tried to speak, to explain, but the words died on her lips.

"Or maybe you're not a working girl after all and you're

some high-class society girl getting a few laughs working in a saloon."

Getting a few laughs was about as far from the truth as was her being a widow, but the society girl part shook her to the core. It was too close for comfort. But thankfully Jake didn't seem to notice her concern through his haze of anger.

"Did it ever occur to you that those women don't have a skill like cooking to get them a proper job?"

"Well, I—"

"Did it ever occur to you that those women could have made more money selling their bodies, but they dance for less instead."

He took a step closer, she took a step back.

"Not one of my girls sells her affections . . . Mrs. Daltry. The men can look, but they can't touch. I see to that."

Persephone forgot her concerns in the face of his absurd rationalization. "And that makes it better?" she stated heatedly.

Jake stared at her, hard, for one long, interminable second. "Yes, that makes it better. I pay them well, I provide a roof over their heads, give them clothes—"

"Clothes?" she scoffed, as she recalled the kind of clothes each of the women had walked into the kitchen wearing.

Frustration wound up in Jake's gut. "They don't wear that kind of thing all the time," he said as if reading her mind. "Not in front of an audience. And before you go casting stones, go look in the mirror. For reasons of your own, you, like them, are working in this den of iniquity as you so quaintly put it. I'm not forcing you to stay. But you do. Though I can't imagine why since apparently your sensibilities are so abused. But you stay. Just like those girls. I don't make them stay either. But like you, they need a job. Nothing more."

And with that shame washed over her. He was right.

She *was* working here. And while she wasn't kicking her legs up in the air for all to see, she was using those men's appetites to make money. And her need was simply for a dress! The others probably really had a child at home, or perhaps they had nowhere else to go.

Just remembering the thoughts that had run through her head made her cringe. Who was she to think she was better than anyone! Only yesterday she had told this man that in the West people didn't judge others. And here she was judging two women without so much as a single word of conversation, as if she could take their measure by simply looking them over.

Who knew why they had become dancing girls. Persy certainly didn't know. And if there was one thing her parents and grandmother had always taught her, it was that all people were equal and not to be judged unfairly. Every one of those values had vanished in the face of the prejudices she had learned from reading too many books on strict propriety.

"It's just that . . ." She started to explain, but what would she say? Nothing. There was nothing to say. Instead she said simply, "I'm sorry."

His eyes narrowed. "You're sorry?" His tone was cautious.

"Yes, I'm ashamed of myself for what I said, and for what I thought. I had no right." She smoothed her dress and then her hair. "And now I'd best get back to the kitchen to finish the meal."

Their eyes met and held. For a moment she thought he was going to say something, something meaningful, something filled with emotion. But then he smiled and he simply said, "Good," as if he was proud of her. And yet again, she was pleased.

She returned to the kitchen, but when the door swung closed, it closed on her alone. Jake had not followed. She felt a stab of disappointment, but brushed it off as disappointment that he wasn't going to be there to see that she was not as awful as she had seemed. But when she turned back around to find Miss Lola and Miss May lounging on high stools like they were in the queen's boudoir, still scantily clad, she couldn't help herself and she blushed.

Dropping her eyes, she moved forward toward the stove. "All right, Miss Lola, Miss May—"

"Just Lola . . ."

"Just May . . ."

Persephone looked up and found the two women smiling at her.

"Mrs. Daltry," they finished in unison.

"Please, call me Persephone."

"Ooh, such a fancy name," May cooed. She tossed her hair and tilted back her head. "I always wanted a fancy name."

Without thinking Persy snorted. "And I always wanted an ordinary name like Mary or Susan or . . ."

"May," May said.

They all laughed.

"Yes, like May," Persy added.

"Why don't you shorten it?" May asked. "Like Pers, or Pheeny."

"Pers or Pheeny?" Lola pashawed at this. "What kind of names are those. Something like Persy would be better."

"That's what my brothers and sisters and even my parents call me at home. Only my grandmother calls me Persephone."

"My word, it sounds crowded," May said.

Persy smiled. Talk of her family immediately put her at ease. "No, not really. Well, sometimes, maybe," she conceded.

"I always wanted brothers and sisters," Lola said, her voice suddenly overly soft and dreamy. "And a mother and a father. All of us living in a big sprawling house, with lots of space all around."

"But what about Jake?" Persy asked without thinking, remembering the way Lola had acted toward the saloon owner. Surely she didn't want to be anywhere but with Jake. The thought filled her with a poignant ache.

"Jake is wonderful, don't get me wrong, and I owe him, but . . ." Lola's words trailed off. She shrugged her shoulders beneath the flimsy material and feather boa. "I don't know. It would be nice to get away from here. Carriages everywhere you turn. Buildings everywhere you look."

An uncomfortable feeling began to seep into Persy's mind, and it had nothing to do with Jake Devlin.

May sighed. "I know what you mean. What with all kinds of crazy people everywhere you go, you have to be so careful who you get mixed up with. And Jake is great, he saved us both, but . . ." Like Lola, May's words trailed off and she looked toward the windows, her gaze unfocused.

The unease Persy had felt intensified. These women sounded strangely like she had when she was back in Paradise. Discontented. Unhappy. Unfulfilled.

But then Persy shook her head and began to push the braised meat around in the pot with a large spoon. Certainly it had to be that Lola and May were unhappy because of their profession. If they had a society life, like her cousin Betty had, and like she was going to have very soon, they wouldn't be so unhappy.

But as the women got to work, Persy couldn't quite forget the conversation.

"Well, what do you want us to do?" Lola asked, turning to study the vegetables on the counter. "Don't tell me you put Jake in charge of these."

They all laughed again when Persy nodded her head.

Within minutes, to Persy's great surprise, the women

were working side by side like cogs in a clock. With aprons covering their silky nightclothes, Lola and May pitched in and helped make everything from the beef stew to the mincemeat pie, from the sausage rolls for appetizers to the hard sauce to top the pie.

"Where do you and all those Greek gods and goddesses live, Persy honey?" Lola asked from the sink where she was cleaning the dishes.

Persy's hands stilled as she dried a plate. "What do you mean?"

Lola glanced over at her and chuckled. "Your family. Where do you all live?"

"Oh," she said, kicking herself for telling anyone anything about her private life. The less people knew the better. "All over."

"All over?"

Persy noted from the inflection in Lola's voice that Lola was suspicious. "Yes, all over the city." Frantically she tried to remember the details she had made up of the life she had told Mr. Bills and Mr. Devlin about. "Yes, we live all over. Different places. I'm widowed, you know . . . with a child." Yes, she had said she had a child, but she had hardly been thinking straight and she couldn't remember what kind of child she had told them she had.

"Albert!" she blurted suddenly. "Yes, Albert." She smiled at the women. "Yes, my sweet baby Albert." Not used to lying, foolishly she began to tell them all about this fictitious child, making it up as she went. She didn't know yet that if she was going to lie she should keep it simple.

"Well," Lola stated, studying Persy, "all that about your brothers and sisters seems true enough. You might even be widowed. But I'm not so certain about the kid."

Persy cringed. "What do you mean?"

"It doesn't sound like you know the first thing about having a kid."

"Oh, dear." Persy looked away.

"Don't worry too much, though," May said. "We won't say anything. Just don't tell anyone else that you're a mother."

Persy sighed. "It's too late."

"Don't tell me you already told someone."

Persy nodded her head.

"Who?"

"Mr. Bills . . . and Mr. Devlin."

Lola and May glanced at each other, then looked back at Persy.

"And Jake didn't question you?" Lola asked, clearly in disbelief.

"Well, not in so many words."

"Then he must have been desperate for a cook."

"Yeah, he detests people who lie."

Persy groaned.

"He's a real stickler about that kind of thing. You can be sick and poor, or have done . . . other things before you got here and he won't say a word, but lie to him . . ." Lola shrugged.

"And you're gone," May finished for her.

"Finee!"

"Caput!"

"Out the—"

"I get the point," Persy interjected.

Her smile was tight and Lola and May reached out and patted her hand.

"Try not to worry, love," Lola said. "If he hasn't said anything yet, he probably won't. Now it's getting late and we've got to get ready for tonight."

"It was nice meeting you," May added over her shoulder as she was pulled out of the room.

Persy was left alone, realizing that indeed it had been nice meeting Lola and May. And she hated that she had lied to them. As she stood there it pressed in on her that her string of lies was growing longer. But what was she going to do? Tell everyone, or even anyone, the truth? No, she couldn't do that. Her only answer lay in surviving the weeks it would take to earn enough money for her dress, then disappear from this kitchen never to be seen again.

With that she heard the bells toll, announcing the hour. Persy threw her apron aside and headed for the door. How was it that she kept forgetting the time? But before she could flee Jake returned.

"Ah, Mrs. Daltry. On your way home, are you?" he asked.

His smile seemed genuinely kind and she thought that maybe, just maybe, he didn't really suspect her of lying. "Yes," she said in a small voice.

"To see . . . what's your child's name?"

"Albert."

"Really? I thought you said it was Alberta?" He eyed her closely.

She cringed. Now that she thought about it she had said Alberta, a girl. Lord, how was she going to get out of this mess. "Albert, Alberta," she said, tilting her head from side to side and shrugging her shoulders. "Sometimes I even call her Albertie. I really am going to have to stop that. When she gets older I'm sure she won't like it at all."

He was silent then, not saying a word. He merely stared at her long and hard. Her heart began to pound. What was he going to say. Get out! Never come back, you lying hussy! Her imagination ran wild with all the things he might say to her. So when he reached out, took her arm, and pulled her close, she went without a fight.

"Who are you, Mrs. Daltry?" he asked softly.

His voice was so soft and low that she had to strain to hear. But she was hardly listening. He had taken her chin between his thumb and forefinger. She could feel the heat of his skin pressed against hers, and her heart fluttered in her chest. Good sense deserted her. The admonitions of earlier that she had simply experienced a moment of insanity the day before when she had longed for his kisses fled in the face of his heated touch.

He took her hand, running his fingers over her knuckles before turning it over and looking at her palm. "Who could you be that you have hands as soft as a dove's breast, but need to work in the kitchen of a saloon?"

He ran his hand up her arm to her shoulder. "You say you have a child, but you can't seem to remember its name."

"I told you," she said breathlessly, "nicknames."

"Ah, yes, nicknames." He ran the backs of his fingers up her throat to her chin. "You say you're a working-class woman, but you are offended by dancing girls."

"I've already said that I was ashamed of myself."

"So you did." He traced her jaw and cheek with one strong finger.

"Didn't you believe me?"

He smiled then, slightly. "That you were ashamed of how you acted? Yes." He ran his fingers across her lips. "But still I wonder who you are?"

Her body tensed.

"No doubt you're not who you say you are, but who exactly I can't quite figure out. From your smooth skin and haughty attitudes I'd say you were part of the upper crust of New York."

Her heart seemed to stop altogether.

"But you don't speak with the same inflections they use. And certainly if you were, all you'd have to do was ask your papa for money if you were in need."

Her mouth went dry.

"But since I suspect you aren't going to tell me who you really are, I'll just have to wait until you slip up enough so I can learn the real story."

He looked at her lips and her heart and stomach were in turmoil. Anticipation battled with concern. Her body was on fire from both, leaving her dizzy.

He lowered his head until he was only inches away. Her eyes fluttered closed.

"And rest assured," he said, his breath warm against her lips, "I'll find out who you really are . . . Mrs. Daltry."

He stepped away and minutes ticked by before it registered in her mind that he had. Her eyes snapped open to find him looking down at her, a devilish smile curved on his lips. "Were you waiting for something?"

Red surged through her cheeks. Mortification nearly overwhelmed her, but anger, intense burning anger, drowned it out. "Yes, I was waiting for something, Mr. Devlin. Your head on a platter, served up for two hundred guests."

And then she was gone, down the hallway and out the door, his resounding laughter echoing in her ears.

Seven

CHOPPED BEEF? NO.

Pigeon pie? Perhaps.

Skewered pork? That was it! Persy exclaimed to herself as she made her way home. If she could, she'd turn that slime ball, Jake Devlin, into skewered pork. She would make him weep. Make him get down on his hands and knees and beg for mercy.

She hated him! Hated every strand of nearly black hair on his perfectly shaped head. Hated every speck of color in his dashingly beautiful green eyes. Hated every muscle on his finely sculpted form.

Her breath caught in her throat at the vision that suddenly loomed in her head. Strong and handsome enough to take her breath away. What would it be like to feel those finely sculpted lips pressed to hers? she wondered.

But then she cursed herself. She would not turn into a simpering miss over that low-life saloonkeeper. He was scum. He was dirt. He wasn't worth the time of day it took to think about him. But why, she wondered, was she having such a difficult time making the appellations stick in her mind?

She shook her head with force. The labels *were* sticking, by George!

She had thought she had merely experienced a moment of insanity the day before when she had first encountered him. Now she knew differently. It hadn't been insanity that she felt, it was hatred—pure unadulterated hatred for a pure unadulterated cad! Yes, she hated Jake Devlin with a passion! And that idea was sticking quite nicely in her mind, thank you very much.

Persy didn't take the time to try to determine the cause for this intense hatred. In fact, the moment the thought popped into her head that she wasn't sure why she did, she discarded it as hogwash, chalking the traitorous notion up to the fact that he had addled her brain on top of everything else.

It took her forever to make her way home that evening after rushing from the saloon's kitchen. She couldn't find a hansom cab, every horse-pulled bus that had gone by was overflowing with passengers, and she didn't know how to ride the Third Avenue New York Elevated Train, the El as it was called. So she walked, block after block up Fifth Avenue in the frigid cold until she saw one of the arched roofed buses with some space on it. She dropped her five cents into the fare slot, then sat down on one of the two benches that ran the length of the bus. Leaning back, her head pressed against the window, she did not care in the least about the grime that covered the steamed glass that undoubtedly was rubbing off in her hair. She didn't even bother to study the many faces of her fellow passengers. She was exhausted, and by the time she dragged herself up the front steps of the Olsons' home she wanted nothing more than to drop facefirst onto her bed. Just the thought of having to sit through supper, much less an entire evening, and make small talk made her want to weep with weariness.

No sooner did she walk through the door than she met her aunt.

"Persy, dear, I was just wondering where you were."

Panic threatened. Yesterday when she had returned home no one was in sight and when the four of them had sat down at the dining table it appeared that no one even knew she had gone out. Today she wasn't so lucky. Was she found out? she wondered. But Persy quickly assured herself that panic was uncalled for. She was exhausted and simply overreacting. Or at least she hoped that was the case.

"I've been to St. Patrick's Cathedral," Persy stated.

Aunt Margaret glanced in a mirror and smoothed her hair. "Oh, that's nice, dear. It's so . . . huge."

Relief washed over her. She was safe. At least for now. "Yes, it is majestic. I walked all around. It was wonderful." She sighed. "But now I'm exhausted."

"Then you should go to bed right after supper."

Persy rubbed her temples, then glanced at her aunt through lowered lashes. "In fact, Aunt Margaret, I have a splitting headache and I thought I'd go lie down."

"Oh, dear, of course. You need to rest. Why don't I have Lucy bring a tray to your room. We certainly don't want you getting sick." Margaret clasped her hands together and her brow furrowed. "Do you think I should call the doctor?"

"Oh, no!" Persy said a little too hastily, causing her aunt to look at her oddly. "I don't want to be any trouble."

"It's no trouble, Persephone, if you're ill."

"All I need is a little rest and I'll be fine. Really."

"Well, if you're sure."

"I'm positive." Persy leaned over and kissed her aunt's cheek. "Tomorrow I'll feel as good as new."

Margaret turned and called out to the servant.

Success!

And before her aunt could change her mind, Persy gathered her skirts and took the stairs as quickly as she could. Not until she reached the relative safety of her room and the adrenaline wore off did she collapse on her bed and fall into a deep sleep.

But if her day had been plagued by a demon named Jake Devlin, her night was plagued by a devil who bore a suspicious resemblance to the very same man.

The next several days passed in a whirlwind of activity. The Olsons' daily schedule had changed. Suddenly Persy was expected to make calls and attend luncheons with her cousin and aunt. Only after these were through for the day did Aunt Margaret depart for her perennial meetings, and Betty snuck out of the house, allowing Persy to dash off to catch the bus that took her downtown where she cooked more food than she had ever dreamed possible. She wasn't certain which made her crazier: watching the clock and praying the call or meal would come to an end in time for her to make it to the saloon, or the deafening sound of iron-shod horses pulling buses with iron wheels over cobbled streets. Both left her mind and body taut with tension.

But oddly enough, after Persy had been certain she'd be a wallflower in this great huge city, due to her harried schedule that didn't allow her to make or receive as many calls as she was invited to make, she was in greater demand than ever, and she hadn't even made her debut yet.

The very proper and very sought after Lewis Abbot called regularly, as did the very wealthy and very handsome Nathan Winters. They had started out bringing flowers, filling the house to overflowing with myriad scents. A person couldn't walk into the house without sneezing. Though after Aunt Margaret had ever so subtly let it be known that they had received more than their share of flora, Persy's callers had taken to bearing baubles and trinkets instead. Her "season" was becoming a greater success than she ever dreamed possible. She should have been thrilled. But she wasn't.

The twenty-minute trek down to the saloon, followed by all afternoon of preparing vast quantities of food that never seemed to get any compliments, left her exhausted and desirous not of the sophisticated life she had come to New York to experience, but the soft comfort of her bed. Returning home after five and slinking upstairs to clean up and try to rest her rapidly tiring body before she had to smile and make small talk around the dinner table made her head spin from the effort. Even when she awoke, what energies she managed to restore were vanquished by yet another caller or another luncheon and certainly by another afternoon of cooking. She was visiting the grandest of parlors and garden rooms in town, all in preparation of her big night. She only hoped by then she wouldn't have succumbed to exhaustion and be confined to bed, forcing her to miss the very event she had come all this way to attend.

Day after day it was the same. The only difference in the rapidly growing monotonous routine was the absence of Jake for several days in a row. And she hated that she noticed.

But then one afternoon, having arrived a few minutes early at the tawdry saloon, with no one in sight in the cavernous kitchen, Persy had no idea how her life was about to experience yet another drastic change.

"I think you're lying!"

Jake stopped dead in his tracks as he made his way down the long wood-paneled hall that led away from the barroom. The small crowd that was following close behind him nearly cannoned into his back. His green eyes blazed as he turned a cold, hard stare on Velda. "Lying?" he asked, the word cold and implacable.

But Velda didn't seem to care. "Yes, lying."

Howie and Mr. Bills looked on with stunned disbelief. Never in Jake's life had he allowed anyone to call him a liar. He had been scrupulously honest in all his dealings, no mean feat when one starts in the gutter among thieves and cutthroats who gave no more thought to lying than breathing.

"Careful, Velda," Jake said quietly into the wide hallway that seemed oppressive by the weight of his sudden anger.

"Careful yourself, mister. You're lying. You simply don't want to marry me. You just keep making up excuses for my father because you . . . you . . . you're not man enough to tell him that you don't want to marry me. Admit it," she cried, her voice shrill. "Admit it or I'm going to tell Daddy myself. Then he'll finally know what an ungrateful . . . gutter rat you really are."

The muscles in Jake's jaw worked and his mind spun with thoughts, spun with all he'd like to say to her. Ungrateful! Gutter rat! Not man enough! He'd show her not man enough! But as always the thought of all her father had done for him halted his tongue. "You're lucky you are your father's daughter," he said, his voice tight.

Slowly he turned away, his teeth clenched, and continued down the hall. The situation had become worse than even he had imagined. Harold pressured him at every turn, reminding Jake of all he had done for him over the years. Financing his endeavors. Offering advice. Making important introductions. Quickly obtaining the permits he needed. Conveniently forgetting all Jake had done for him in return. God, how he hated the obligation he felt, though he hadn't felt that way until Velda became old enough to marry. Before that he and Harold had always worked so well together. And he missed that.

Deep down Jake didn't think Velda really wanted him or even liked him all that much. He had thought on more than one occasion that her pursuit seemed more like some perverse way of making him suffer, as if she were jealous that he was close to her father.

He shook his head, his footsteps resounding as he strode down the hardwood floor. He had told himself he needed to come up with some great way to get out of marriage once and for all. But nothing had come to him—no reason good enough that Harold would agree marriage between Jake and Velda was not possible.

With that thought circling in his head, his entourage on his heels, Mr. Bills berating Velda, Velda cursing him, Howie shaking his head, Jake pushed through the kitchen door.

"If you're not lying," Velda demanded, "then give me one good reason why you won't marry me, Jake Devlin!"

Persy's head popped up from where she stood concentrating on the cup of flour she was measuring out. Jake came to a halt, his eyes locking on Persy.

And inspiration struck.

A simple, nice girl who was interested in kitchens and cooking, homes and children. He disregarded the fact that he had already learned that Mrs. Persephone Daltry was anything but simple. And he had no idea what her feelings on homes and children might be. But she had said she had a child, didn't she? Though he hardly believed a word she said. But none of that mattered in the least right then. Whoever or whatever Persephone truly was, she looked the part of a simple maiden who would cause about as much trouble in a man's well-ordered life as a newborn kitten, he thought to himself. Jake Devlin had a lot to learn about newborn kittens.

"I'm engaged," he announced suddenly.

The silence that fell over the kitchen seemed unnatural for the sheer weight of it. No one was aware of the distant sounds of the bustling city, or the water that came to a boil on the stove. Persy, Velda, Mr. Bills, and Howie stood in the kitchen perfectly still, staring at Jake.

Jake only smiled. "Yes, Velda," he said, looking at Persy, "I didn't want to make any announcements yet, but since you're so determined to have the truth, I'll tell you. I'm engaged to be married."

"Married?" Mr. Bills blurted out before he could think better of it, bringing a suspicious look from Velda. But he recovered quickly and shrugged. "Yes, married. The secret is out."

Velda's mouth dropped open before she snapped it shut, then demanded, "To who?"

Jake sauntered over to Persy, turned back to the others with a flourish, and draped his arm around her shoulders. "To my little Persephone, here."

This time it was Persy's mouth that dropped open, but before she could utter a word, he turned her toward him, his eyes suddenly filled with silent pleading, then pulled her into a crushing embrace.

In the turmoil that ensued, Velda, Mr. Bills, and Howie all talking and carrying on at once, Persy managed to pull free far enough to look up at him. She tried to break free altogether but his grip was like bands of iron around her arms.

"Listen to me," he said, his voice quiet and insistent.

"No, you listen to me," she hissed in return. "I don't know what this is all about or what game you are trying to play, but I will have nothing, I repeat, nothing to do with it, do you hear me!"

"Yes, I hear you, and if you don't keep your voice down everyone else is going to hear you, too!"

"Good! I hope they do! Marriage! Marriage indeed, like I'd marry you if you were the last man on this earth."

Persy would have laughed at his reaction to her statement, somehow both amazed and hurt at the same time, if she hadn't been so furious.

"Like I'd really ask you to marry me if you were the last woman on earth!" he replied, strangely childish for such a dangerous man. But he was used to women falling all over him, using whatever tricks they knew to lure him into marriage. But this little imp stood there telling him she wouldn't have him!

Persy's eyes narrowed. "No, you didn't ask! You just announced!"

Her voice shimmered through the room and Jake hastily glanced over at Velda, who thankfully still wailed while Mr. Bills alternately tried to soothe her, then reprimand her for whatever it was she was saying. Such a sight, Jake thought before returning his attention to the matter at hand. His engagement. His supposed engagement.

As soon as he walked into the kitchen the idea had hit him. Persy needed the money. He needed a fiancée. It was perfect. Now if she'd only give him the opportunity to explain before she went and ruined his perfect plan. He refused to think about the strange feeling he had felt when he had wrapped his arm around her shoulders and announced their engagement—as if it should have been real. But that was absurd. If there were two people more totally unsuited to each other, he didn't know of them.

"Just hold on before you ruin everything," he grumbled.

"Ruin everything! Good Lord, you have nerve."

His grumble faded and he started to smile at this, rather pleased with himself for his quick thinking. "Just play along, for now, until I have a chance to explain."

She eyed him angrily.

"I know you need money. So, if you agree, I'll make it worth your while."

He could see the shift in her thoughts immediately. She certainly hadn't learned to hide her feelings, he thought, and was oddly pleased.

"How worth my while?"

Greedy little thing, came his next thought, and this didn't please him nearly so well. But what was a man to do? "Extremely worthwhile," he said simply, disgruntled enough that he didn't think about the fact that it was suddenly very important that she agree.

"All right," she said at length. "For now, at least, I won't deny anything. But I won't confirm anything either until I hear what this is all about."

He grabbed her close and kissed her forehead. "You won't regret it," he whispered in her ear.

"Well, well, well!"

Lola and May strolled into the kitchen, their attire only slightly more suited to cooking this day than previous days. "What's going on in here?"

No one answered right away. "Jake's engaged," Howie said happily into the silence.

Persy groaned.

"To who?" Lola asked.

Velda's lips pursed.

Jake pulled Persy close once again. "It was supposed to be a surprise. But since the secret is out, I know you'll be happy for us." He looked down at Persy. "I know we are. Isn't that so, darling?"

Persy smiled though Jake thought the effort had more in common with bared teeth than anything having to do with good cheer. But just then he wasn't in a position to complain.

Lola and May did nothing more than stare with wide-eyed amazement for a second until Lola stepped forward and hugged Persy. "Congratulations, honey."

"Let's celebrate," May announced.

Velda huffed, then stomped away, pushing so hard on the swinging door that it banged against the outer wall, only to find her father on the other side.

"What's this?" Harold asked. "My Velda, crying?"

The door swung back on its hinges, Harold following with Velda in his wake. Jake grimaced.

"He says he's engaged, Daddy!" Velda half cried, half accused.

"Who's engaged?"

"Jake!"

Harold turned a hard glare on the younger man. Everyone else in the room seemed to fade back. Jake met the older man's gaze and said, "I wanted to tell you myself."

The kitchen filled with tension as Harold and Jake stared at one another. Persy didn't understand what was going on around her. But she could sense, as if they were her own thoughts, that whatever was going on here was very important to Jake. The fact remained that she couldn't wait to get Jake Devlin alone to give him a piece of her mind. But right that second it was this Harold and his daughter who had her attention. Clearly there was more to this situation than met the eye. Jake was obviously going out of his way to put on an elaborate charade for him. But why? she wondered. Jake Devlin didn't strike her as the kind of man who put on shows for anyone.

With that, Persy decided Jake was in some sort of trouble and now he was wrapping her up in it, too. Or if it wasn't trouble, then it was some sort of con game. But who, she wondered, was getting conned? Regardless, she came to the conclusion that whatever reason Jake had for this charade it was one completely lacking in altruistic value.

"Harold," Jake said, "this is my fiancée. Persephone Daltry. Persephone, this is my dear friend, Harold Harvey."

Harold slowly took the few steps that separated them. "Congratulations, my dear."

His sharp eyes traveled the length of her and had he been even ten years younger she might have thought he was being lewd. At his age, however—sixty she deter-

mined, if he was a day—he seemed to be appraising her as
if she were no better than a piece of livestock. And she
didn't like that one bit. In turn, that part of Persy that was
becoming all too dominant pulled back her shoulders,
tilted her chin defiantly, and ran her eyes down the length
of him. "Thank you, Mr. Harvey," she responded inso-
lently.

One bushy gray eyebrow raised and he glanced at Jake.
"I thought you said you were looking for a docile female
who knew her place."

Red surged through Persy's cheeks but her embarrassment quickly turned to indignation when Jake pulled her
close and said, "She does, Harold, she was just noticing
your shoes. Weren't you, honey?" When Persy did nothing
more than stare at Jake, mouth agape, he added, "She
likes clothes and fashion. You know how women can be."

Persy's gray eyes darkened with outrage. "And how,
honey," she began, the endearment a sneer, "is that?"

Mr. Bills smirked but instantly washed his face clean of
emotion when Jake shot him an ominous scowl.

Harold smiled slightly as if considering. "Looks like
you're getting yourself in trouble before the vows are even
spoken, Jake. I think I'd like to get to know your little
fiancée better. We'll arrange something. For now, Velda
and I have an appointment on the Ladies Mile."

The door swung shut behind them. No one else moved,
they only stared at Jake.

"What are you all looking at?" he demanded, his smiles
and good cheer magically gone. "I would think there are
plenty of things to be done besides staring at me." He
glanced around the kitchen. "Like cooking, for one."

He turned to leave.

"Excuse me," Persy said, her tone tart and sharp in the
quiet.

He hesitated and she could just make out the grimace
that flitted across his face. He turned back and Howie and

Mr. Bills came to stand on either side of him like they were protecting him from a fearsome opponent.

"It's time we talk," she said. "Alone."

Reluctantly he nodded his head. He ushered her out of the kitchen and down the hall until they came to a staircase she had never noticed before. At first she was hesitant to venture forth into places unknown. But what were her choices? Besides, how much worse could this situation get? She had gotten herself in too deep to turn back now.

He showed her into what appeared to be his office. Lots of hardwood and leather, austere paintings and ornate clocks. With the exception of wearing purple vests and owning tawdry saloons, she thought how very similar Jake Devlin's trappings were to her uncle's. For a moment she felt disoriented, that feeling where she had to remember, with effort, that she was in the very heart of a den of iniquity, not in the seat of a respectable man's home.

"You wanted to talk to me?" he asked, breaking into her reverie.

Instantly she was firmly placed. She whirled around to face him, her simple dress swirling around her ankles, stray wisps of hair curling around her cheeks. "Don't give me that. You owe me an explanation about what's going on here. Now start explaining."

He leaned back against the edge of his desk and studied her. "You shouldn't be so bossy, Mrs. Daltry, or you'll never find yourself . . . another husband."

"I don't need instructions on deportment from the likes of you. What I need is for you to tell me why you told them we were engaged."

"Ah yes. The engagement." He crossed his arms and considered. "Let's just say it was necessary."

For ill doings, she stated silently, just as she suspected. "Why is it necessary?"

"That is none of your concern—"

"None of my concern!"

"Exactly. What *is* your concern, however, is that if you will pretend to be my fiancée for the next three weeks," he became engrossed in picking lint from his sleeve as if what he was about to say disgusted him, "I'll pay you—extremely well."

"I'm already getting paid for cooking!"

"True. But I'll pay you twenty-five dollars extra if you go along with my . . . little arrangement."

This caught her attention. "Twenty-five dollars?" she said quickly, too quickly.

Jake looked pleased and Persy knew he thought he had her. That, like everything else about this man, made her angry. Besides, she needed ninety-six dollars. If she could get the money in three weeks she could cut the amount of time she had to slip out of the house in half. If she went along with his "little arrangement," little innocuous arrangement, she added to make it more palatable, she could earn enough and more to pay for the dress and be done with it. "A hundred and fifty."

Jake's eyes widened slightly before he smiled. "Fifty."

"One twenty-five."

"Seventy-five."

"One hundred dollars on top of my regular wages and not a penny less."

"You've missed your calling, Mrs. Daltry," he said dryly. "I could have used you in my business dealings more efficiently than in my kitchen."

"Save your compliments for someone who's interested."

A smile spread on his full lips. "It wasn't a compliment."

Blood burned her cheeks, and it was all she could do not to flee. "Do we have a deal or not?" she asked through gritted teeth.

"Of course we do. One hundred dollars plus your wages for . . . services rendered."

Services rendered. Hearing it put that way made it sound

even worse than she had suspected. It no longer sounded so *innocuous*. And it made her furious that his shenanigans were making her look so bad. He was the one who was trying to deceive his friends. Not her. But of course, though it was about something altogether different, *she* was deceiving her friends as well.

Her bravado fled. Her heart clenched in her chest. What was happening to her? Every moral and value she had been taught was flying out the window. "You're saying that just to be mean," she said, her voice pained. "Services rendered. Like I'm no better than a common . . . soiled dove. Why is it that you don't like me?"

He was quiet for a long time as he stared at her, as if he could see deep into her soul. The clock ticked quietly on the credenza behind his desk. Teamsters hollered in the distant streets. And then he reached out and touched her cheek with infinite care. "That, I think, is part of the problem. I like you too much, it would seem."

The touch was like fire. Hot, liquid, molten fire that melted her reserve. His fingers were callused, rough against her skin. But the heat of the simple touch drew her as if she had come in from the cold. Her lips parted. And she felt her body come alive with sensations that she had never experienced before.

But then she locked her heart against the feelings. She didn't want his touch, she told herself. She didn't even like his touch. In fact she didn't like anything about him. She didn't!

She slapped his hand away. "Don't think you can use that fake charm on me, Mr. Devlin. I've been around. I've seen things." Hopefully he wouldn't ask where she had been or what she had seen. Such responses would be harder to come by.

"Hmmm," he said, studying her, his countenance growing dangerous. "You do look a little like you've been around." He ignored her gasp. "I couldn't put my finger on it at first, but now that you mention it, it all makes sense. Are you sure you're a *missus* with a child and not a *miss* with a child?"

If she had thought of it she would have slapped him again, this time across his face. But her mind was too filled with outrage and, as much as she hated to admit it, hurt to come up with such an idea. She hardly noticed that he was watching her, his brow deeply furrowed. But when he reached out to take her hand and he whispered that he was sorry, she jerked her hand away. "If I didn't need the money so badly I would walk right out of here and never come back. But I *do* need the money, more's the pity. So it's three weeks. Not a second longer. And then I'm gone."

His body stiffened. "Gone?"

"Yes, gone."

Then silence.

At length he asked, "What about the kitchen?"

The kitchen. Her anger trailed off and her heart fell. Absurdly. She hated that she was disappointed that his only concern obviously was for his stupid kitchen. His concern had nothing to do with her. Though why she should care she had no idea.

Her mind was a jumble, filled with conflicting emotions that she didn't understand. And through it all, no matter how angry she always seemed to be with him, she realized that for the next three weeks she actually looked forward to seeing where this adventure might take her. For the moment sophistication and propriety, museums and art galleries, were forgotten. All the things she had come to New York for faded into the background of her mind.

"I asked you about the kitchen. Are you planning to quit working here after you get your money?"

She looked at him and hated the absurd hope that flared in her breast. "Do you care?"

Jake shifted his weight, then turned away to look out

the window. She watched him, much as he had watched her earlier. The lines of emotion that suddenly etched his brow filled her with concern. He was a mystery to her, with his moods changing with lightning quickness. It was hard to keep up. One minute he was boyish and playful, the next he seemed to carry the weight of the world on his shoulders.

Knowing she shouldn't, but not caring at that moment, she reached out and touched his arm. "Do you care?" she asked again.

He glanced down at her fingers, so delicate against the stark white of his sleeve. After what seemed like forever he met her gaze. "Why should I care, Mrs. Daltry?"

Hope vanished, and she dropped her hand away. "You shouldn't, Mr. Devlin," she said, her chest tight. "Now if you'll excuse me, I have a good deal of work to do."

Eight

PERSY LEFT THE SALOON WITH THE FIRM COMMITMENT TO PUT fake engagements and shady characters from her mind. She had neither the time nor the inclination at this point to study how she felt. She had her first dinner party this evening and if she didn't hurry she would never be ready in time.

A dinner party. One of the many reasons she had wanted to come to the big city. Her dreams were coming true. If only she hadn't ruined her dress. If only she hadn't promised Mrs. McFee not to tell anyone. If only she hadn't gotten herself mixed up with that libertine Jake Devlin. He was quite handily turning her dream into a nightmare.

Her fists clenched in her lap as the bus rolled up Fifth Avenue. Anger started to build and her eyes narrowed. But then she realized what she was doing, thinking about the very man she said she wouldn't think about. So she took a deep breath and concentrated on polite conversation and sweeping lines of forks and spoons and knives around a single place setting that she most undoubtedly would find this evening.

In Paradise they never bothered with formalities. The one time she had set the table with both a salad fork and a dinner fork and, heaven forbid, a dessert fork on top, not only had her family not used the extra pieces of cutlery but they had teased her unmercifully for weeks afterward about being pretentious. She could still see Lee bowing to her for a full week after the meal, calling her madame, acting like a footman every time she walked into the room. When anyone came to the front door and knocked, Atlas had jumped up, told everyone to be still, then looked at her and said, "Let the butler get it."

Fortunately time wore on and eventually someone else in the family did something stupid enough to divert attention. In spite of herself, the memory made her smile. And suddenly she felt a surge of longing for her brothers' and sisters' outrageous antics. Beds short-sheeted. Bugs in drawers. Buckets of water splashing down from the barn loft. Then as suddenly as the longing came to her, the thought that Jake Devlin would fit in like a missing piece of the puzzle to her outrageous clan came as well. The thought startled her. And she didn't like it one bit. This man who was so clearly disreputable had no business being anywhere near her so very reputable and loving family any more than she wanted him near her. Persy wanted polish and sophistication, and the big city life—big city society life, she amended on the thought that Jake Devlin certainly led a form of big city life.

She wanted to go to this gathering tonight and sit down at a table where conversation was of important things and everyone expected to use each of the myriad utensils without question. And that was that. She had dreamed of it for ages. Her dreams were coming true. They were, she told herself firmly.

She had laid out her clothes before she left for the saloon. She wanted to bathe and redo her hair and dress perfectly for her first dinner party. Excitement tingled down her spine. Tonight it was all about to begin in earnest. A dinner. A formal dinner. With an invitation written in a fine cursive hand, addressed directly to Miss Persephone Daltry. As if she truly belonged.

She relaxed as best she could on the hard bench, leaning her head back against the plate-glass window with a contented sigh, Jake Devlin finally and firmly dismissed from her mind.

The night was bright with moonlight and clear of any clouds when Persy arrived with her aunt, uncle, and cousin at the home of Mr. and Mrs. Beaufort Weathersley. A silk-stockinged footman opened the door and took their wraps, before they were led into a grand receiving room that was nearly the size of the Daltrys' entire first floor.

Introductions were made, gentlemen bowing without taking Persy's hand, a right reserved for those who had already been introduced. The Weathersleys, according to Betty who had taken Persy aside when she arrived home that evening to fill her in on a great many things she had been unaware of before, were at the upper echelons of New York society with both a great deal of money and an old, good name. The long line of Olsons, Persy had learned in that same conversation, the family into which Aunt Margaret had married, descended directly from one of George Washington's generals, but had only a decent amount of money. So it was their very old and very good name that, barring social disgrace, would keep the family on the social register for generations to come.

Betty's detailed account had filled Persy's head. In all the books she had collected on cooking and social graces, not one of them had prepared her for the intricate array of unwritten and very seldom spoken rules of this society. Suddenly the sheen on her excitement grew hazy. Up until this night she had been blissfully unaware of her lack of true status. She was scared to death that being nothing more than the niece of the wife of a man with a very old and very good name left her in the very gray areas of acceptance.

But her worries proved unfounded when she found not only Lewis Abbot in attendance, who, of course, had shown his undying support, but Nathan Winters at the party as well. In fact, the only male at the intimate dinner party of twenty who wasn't vying for her attention was Thomas Weathersley, the host and hostess's son, who very politely bowed but then was commandeered and cornered reluctantly, Persy was inclined to think, by her cousin Betty.

"So you're from Texas," said a man named Marcus who sat on her right at dinner.

"Yes, from Paradise Plains."

"Paradise," Nathan snorted, his stark white formal collar and shirtfront looking too stiff and too tight beneath his cutaway jacket. "From what I hear, Texas is a long way from paradise."

The sentiment startled her, but so did the fact that the image of Jake Devlin loomed unexpectedly in her mind. Jake had longed for a place like Texas, had thought it *was* paradise, whereas this man clearly looked down his nose at her home state. She started to say something, to defend the vast land where she was born, and would have regardless of the fact that Betty had warned her not to speak her mind on any issue—it was just not done. But it was the fact that yet again she remembered that she herself had thought her home somehow lacking just as this man did that stopped her. How could she fault him for what she had felt? In the end she simply smiled and asked very politely about the weather, feeling strangely like a traitor as she did.

After a short discourse on the elements, the conversation turned once again to Persy and Texas. The questions came, this time from both sides, Marcus on her right, Na-

than on her left, even from Lewis who sat across the table.
They asked her absurd questions—did Texans travel in
carriages, what food did they prefer, what, if any, newspapers did they read—as if she were from another country, a
backward one at that. Her anger rose. She longed to tell
them that Texas was only a mere fifty-eight years younger
than New York, that Texas was old and established, with
folklore and traditions of its own. But then she tamped it
down. She had no interest in starting an argument or being combative. She was where she wanted to be, and she
was enjoying herself! She was!

"From what I've heard, Texans hardly speak the same
language as we do."

"And they pledge allegiance to a different flag!"

Well, that did it! Her good intentions flew right out the
mullioned window.

"Just because Texans have lived under five other flags
besides the United States *in the past* over a long, very long
history, I might add, is no reason to cast aspersions on our
loyalty now."

Marcus, Lewis, and Nathan looked at her with something akin to shock stretched across their handsome faces.
But Persy only felt elated that she had spoken her mind.

Taking a deep breath she cast them a smile as sweet as
cherry pie, then took a sip of the soup that sat before her.
But with that one sip, history, ancestors, and dos and
don'ts of society life fled from her mind with a vengeance.
It was all she could do not to spew the contents across the
table. Good Lord, the soup was awful. And unfortunately
the meal didn't get any better from there. The lettuce was
limp, the vegetables soggy, the fish burned, the sauce . . .
ugh. Her mother, blindfolded, could have done better.
And the meal went on for hours, course after course of
food that was bland, wine that was not worth drinking,
and conversation that would have put an insomniac to
sleep.

But she wrote her displeasure off to needing to educate her palate. The finest of wines, her father had once told her, tasted horrible to a person who had never had a sip before. Yes, she concluded, a New York society dinner party was like a fine wine. She needed to develop a taste for it. Next time, she was certain, she would like it better. She disregarded the thought that luncheons and social calls had been equally distasteful and she had been attending those for a week now.

Betty, on the other hand, seemed to be having the time of her life, that is if lowered lashes and subtle glances could be considered great fun. Nothing, Persy concluded, was overt at this gathering; everything was as subtle as the glances Betty cast at Thomas Weathersley. The conversation was muted, almost coded. It was as if a dangerous current ran beneath the surface of all conversation that could pull a novice under if she weren't careful. It seemed to be a language spoken with raised eyebrows and meaningful nods, a sort of sign language that New York society had developed all on their own. Nothing outrageous or intimate was ever expressed in words. Nothing of any seeming importance was voiced out loud. In fact, she couldn't remember the last time she had engaged in such seemingly banal conversation.

After dinner the women took their hand-worked shawls and plumed fans and ascended the stairs to an upper drawing room. The men remained below to drink port and smoke cigars. The women's conversation, while still restrained and circumspect, was a good deal livelier than at dinner. Persy became fascinated by the subtle references to who was doing what, and she was engrossed in trying to interpret the women's many gestures to understand the meaning between the spoken words. It wasn't until the women began a long and tedious discussion on one woman's dress that Persy noticed Betty was nowhere in sight. When several minutes had passed, still with no sign of her cousin, Persy left the room without drawing attention to herself.

She walked down the hall, her footsteps muffled by the plush carpet. She passed the gilded chairs and brocade benches and the rich tapestries hanging on the walls. When she came to the grand curving staircase that led to the foyer she heard voices. Peering over the railing, she found Betty standing much too closely to Thomas Weathersley, his arms encircling her waist.

Anyone who came to the top of the stairs would see them. And though Persy hadn't been in New York society long, she knew without having to ask that such a scene could very well cause the scandal that could bump the Olsons right off the social registry. But when she started to clear her throat to announce her entrance, Thomas leaned even closer and pressed his lips not to Betty's mouth, which would have been bad enough, but very low on the slender column of her neck. Persy's eyes opened wide and she waited for Betty to put the forward man in his place. But after only a feeble attempt to say no, Betty succumbed to the pressure and pressed her body to his.

Dumbstruck, Persy stood at the top of the stairs and stared. What was she to do? Turn and flee was what she wanted to do, but the sound of voices approaching made her act without thinking.

"Uh-hum," she announced.

Thomas pulled away with a haste that nearly tumbled Betty to the floor in her massively bejeweled gown. But when he saw that it was only Persy who had interrupted his illicit pursuit, a slow smile curled on his lips. "Betty, love, your cousin is here."

Betty giggled in response.

"If I were you," Persy said tightly, "I'd fix my hair before my hostess was upon me."

Suddenly Betty became aware of the voices and muffled footsteps approaching from above. In an instant Thomas disappeared without so much as a good-bye. Betty smoothed her hair. "How do I look?"

Persy took the steps and said, "Fine."

"You're not going to say anything to Mother or Father, are you?"

Persy studied her cousin, then shook her head. Who was she to cast stones or tell tales. "I will say nothing to anybody, Betty, but I'd be careful if I were you."

But Betty only laughed, then linked arms with her and hurried to join the other women.

Nine

"I *LOVED* MY FIRST DINNER PARTY, I DID," PERSY WHISPERED TO herself over and over again as she lay in bed for hours, still wide awake.

She didn't care that Lewis had the intelligence of a gnat, and that was being unkind to the gnat. She didn't care that Nathan had about as much goodwill toward his fellow man as a bear come springtime. She didn't care that something not altogether on the up and up was going on with her cousin. None of these things bothered her, she tried to tell herself. None of them! But throughout her nighttime declarations she was unable to fall asleep.

She had the niggling little thought that the sophisticated life wasn't all she had dreamed it would be. But that was absurd, she quickly interjected before the traitorous thought could take hold and run amuck in her brain. She was simply too tired and too worn out from her misadventures at the saloon to fully appreciate the very life she had come all this way to experience. In a matter of weeks she would have her money, her new dress, then she would never have to set foot in the Dusty Rose, or lay eyes on its menagerie of inhabitants, ever again. And that was exactly what she wanted. She did, she muttered aloud as she rolled over, punched her pillow, and flopped back down onto the bed, trying to get some sleep.

After what seemed like ages she finally drifted off, her mind filled with discordant images, only to wake a short time later. The room was dark and the moon was high in the nighttime sky. She was disoriented and all she could think about was that she had to get the devil out of hell and take him home to Paradise. The need was persistent and troublesome. But she was still half asleep and had yet to make sense of her feelings.

But before she had a chance to clear her mind she became aware of a noise at her window. At first, when every few minutes a soft clink sounded against the glass, she was merely surprised. But when the noise continued, waking her completely, bringing sanity to the forefront, a shiver of fear raced down her spine.

She had grown up hearing gruesome tales of murder and mayhem in large bustling cities. Most anyone in the small, safe town of Paradise had either heard or told such a story. Persy had never paid much attention to them. She had always been too enamored of those places to allow such petty little details spoil her opinion. Now, however, with someone or something clearly tapping against her second-floor window in the middle of the night, she wished she had paid more attention.

With the utmost care, she slipped out of bed and crept toward the window. The moon was full, and silver light slipped through a crack in the heavy velvet draperies. Taking a deep breath she moved the curtain ever so slightly and peeked outside. She sucked in her breath at the sight that met her eyes. Sure enough she hadn't been imagining things. There was a man standing among the bushes, his face cast in shadows by his hat and the moonlight, tossing pebbles at her window.

She jerked back, pressing against the wall. She knew she

should call out. Raise the alarm. Send out the dogs. Then
she laughed. They had no dogs. Besides, she thought, her
breathing having slowed, it wasn't like the man was wearing sinister clothes, nor did he look as though he was trying to break in. He wore a high-crowned silk top hat and a
ruffled shirt as white as freshly fallen snow, for goodness'
sake. It looked more like he was on his way to a ball than
a burglary. And as far as him being a possible thief, unless
things were different in New York, she couldn't imagine a
robber first gaining his prey's attention, then divesting
them of their goods. No, this had all the earmarks of an
illicit liaison.

She parted the curtain once again just as he reached
down to pick up another stone. And when he straightened
and apparently saw her, first a smile parted his lips before
he stiffened with apparent shock. If only he would remove
his hat so she could see the rest of his face. But that was
not to be, and when finally he seemed to gather his wits,
he hastily disappeared through the bushes. Clearly she
was not who he expected to find.

Could he have been searching out Marie, the upstairs
maid? she wondered. Or Lucy, the downstairs maid? Or
dear old Mrs. McFee? This thought made her laugh out
loud once again, before she discounted all three possibili-
ties. Even in the moonlight Persy had made out the shim-
mery gold chain of his watch fob—an expensive gold
watch fob. She doubted the man was there for an illicit
rendezvous with someone from the staff. Nor did she
think he was there for an illicit rendezvous with her, unless the hapless Lewis or the self-absorbed Nathan had
more gumption than she realized. The very idea made her
laugh even louder. If it had been either of them the mere
sight of her in nightwear obviously had filled them with
grave reservations.

No, the man hadn't been there to pilfer either household goods or the maid's or her virtue, which left only one

other explanation. He was there to see Aunt Margaret or Cousin Betty. Persy thought about Betty's long walks in the park, without escort, dressed and acting like a young woman in love. The man lurking in the bushes had more than likely been seeking out Betty, whose room was right next to hers. And then suddenly she wondered if it was possible that the lurking figure had been that of Thomas Weathersley.

Good Lord, surely not. Men of manners didn't skulk around in the bushes—did they? Perhaps she should tell Betty of his arrival? Or maybe it was best if she told Uncle John. But what if she was wrong? What if the man was simply lost and had thrown pebbles at not only the wrong window but the wrong house altogether?

No, she'd best tread carefully. Wait and see what happened in the morning. Besides, she was still in no position to point out anyone else's secret doings. For now, she should simply go back to sleep before the sun was up and she was once again forced to make her way back down to the Dusty Rose—and Jake Devlin.

Jake. To whom she unexpectedly found herself engaged. Mrs. Jake Devlin. Persephone Devlin. She suddenly remembered her dream. Taking the devil out of hell and home to Paradise. The memory made her feel warm all over—for a second. In the next second she felt the fool. Mrs. Jake Devlin! Ha! There wasn't a chance in hell that she would ever become that man's wife. She disregarded the fact that he seemed about as inclined to make it really happen as was the Czar of Russia.

Jake Devlin was a cad and a lout, a debaucher of women. He was at home in his devil's lair. He had no interest in the sedate, boring in contrast, place of her birth. And she'd do well to remember that fact.

The next morning it was late when Persy finally awoke. Sounds of the day wafted up to her room. She nearly forgot everything else and simply lay there until she felt like getting up. But then she remembered work and the nocturnal visitor, bringing her up out of the bedsheets in a flash.

She was dressed and downstairs in record time. Apparently she wasn't the only one off to a late start, as all three Olsons still sat around the dining table breaking their fast.

"Good morning," Persy chimed.

Only Uncle John looked at her with a smile when he lowered his paper. "Good morning, Persephone. Trust you slept well."

"Yes, thank you."

Aunt Margaret looked worriedly at her daughter before turning her attention to Persy. "We didn't have a chance to talk about the party last night. Did you enjoy yourself?"

Persy hesitated. "It was an evening I'll never forget." And that was true enough, she conceded, not wanting to lie any more than she already had.

"Yes, yes, I'm sure you won't," Margaret said, her tone distracted as she turned back to her daughter. "Can I get you some more tea, love?" she asked Betty.

Betty sat with her eyes cast down, without responding, endlessly stirring a full cup of tea.

"Perhaps some coffee," her mother asked. "Or milk, or juice."

"I'm fine, Mother," Betty said finally, exasperated.

Lucy brought a plate and set it down at Persy's place. Fluffy eggs with melted cheese. Slices of ham grilled to perfection. Freshly baked bread dripping with butter. Even Persy herself couldn't have done better. But for all her grumbling stomach, she was tied in knots over her cousin's mood. She wanted to inquire after the cause. Was it possible it had something to do with the nocturnal visitor? Certainly she couldn't ask with her aunt and uncle present, and she wasn't sure when she'd get a chance to talk to Betty alone later.

"Well," Uncle John began, folding the newspaper and setting it aside, "got to go." He stood and walked down the length of the table and pressed a quick kiss on his wife's forehead. "I'll be home late, dear. Don't hold supper."

He left before Margaret could assimilate his news, and when she turned around to question him, the front door had already slammed shut. With a sigh, she turned back and reached out and placed her hand over Betty's. "Tell me what's bothering you, love."

"Nothing, Mother," she responded, her tone impatient. "I'm fine, really."

"Well, I can tell when my only child is fine and when she is not. And since you won't tell me, I'll just have to cancel my meeting with the Women's Guild at the Museum of Natural History and stay home with you."

This, Persy noticed, drew an invigorated response from Betty.

"Now, Mother, I'm not a child. I'm fine. Just as I said. I didn't sleep well last night, that's all. And in fact, there is no need for you to stay home because I won't be here."

"Where are you going?" Margaret asked, her tone firm.

Betty appeared not to have expected her mother to question her further. For one long surprised moment she sat perfectly still with her eyes slightly widened. Persephone could practically hear the wheels churning in her brain as she tried to come up with an answer. Like Margaret, Persy was interested in hearing where Betty planned to spend her day.

"The milliner's!" Betty blurted out. "Yes, I'm going to the milliner's down on the Ladies Mile."

"Then I'll go with you. It will be fun," her mother said, removing the napkin from her lap and setting it on the table. "We'll start with a ride around Madison Square, then work our way through all the shops, not just the milliner's. We've both been so busy that I've barely seen you. And the Women's Guild can do without me for a day."

"Come with me? Oh, Mother! I'm so sorry." She turned to Persy. "But I promised Persy that we'd go together."

Persy's eyes opened wide and a bite of ham halted halfway to her mouth.

"You know, Mother," Betty continued, "some time for some . . . cousinly talk . . . girl to girl. That kind of thing. You understand, don't you?"

"Well—"

"And," Betty continued, "she's been anxious to look at the latest in hats. One with feathers and bows, or lace and flowers."

Persy's eyes widened still farther. Feathers and bows? Ugh!

"Isn't that right, cousin?"

Both Margaret and Betty stared at her with expectation. Good heavens, she was being forced to align herself with either her aunt who so graciously allowed her to stay in her house, or with her cousin whom she had come to love like a sister. "Feathers and bows! I just can't imagine what something like that will look like," she stated obliquely, hoping that would do.

And apparently it did.

"Well, all right," Margaret said reluctantly. "If you say so."

"In fact, we'd best hurry," Betty said, jumping up from her seat with surprising energy for someone who had sat staring at her cup lethargically only moments before.

Persy didn't move and when Betty got to the diningroom doors she turned back, laughed, then skipped back, grasped her cousin's wrist, and pulled her from the room, Persy following along trying to swallow her last bite of breakfast without choking.

When they reached the relative safety of the second floor, Betty finally set her cousin free.

"That was close," Betty mumbled more to herself than any other.

"What was close?"

Betty glanced over at Persy as if noticing her for the first time. "Oh, nothing," she scoffed. "It's just . . ." Her face began to fall. "It's just that . . ."

The words trailed off and Persy watched, dumbfounded, as her cousin began to cry. Persy was having a difficult time keeping up with Betty's moods. Instinctively she reached out to comfort her and Betty fell gratefully into her arms.

"Why does my life have to be so difficult?" Betty wailed. "Why can't my life be simple and fun?"

Persy tensed. "Don't you love your life?"

Betty gave a very unladylike snort to this and pulled away.

"Betty! How can you not love your life? You have everything a person could dream of. Museums and teas, and sophisticated conversation."

Striding to the window, Betty gazed out over the barren garden dusted with winter snow. "That's what my mother keeps telling me. But . . ." Her words trailed off into a sigh.

Once again, Persy had that disconcerting feeling she had when Lola and May had expressed their discontent. But this time Persy could think of nothing to explain away her cousin's unhappiness.

"It's so unfair," Betty said, pushing away from the window, anger mixing with anguish. She began to pace, one minute throwing her head back and bemoaning her state, the next balling her hands and cursing her circumstances. But when the upstairs maid climbed the stairs, Betty wiped her face clean of all emotion, grabbed Persy's hand, and pulled her back downstairs. "Come on," she said. "Let's go to the milliner's. A hat will make me feel better, I'm sure."

Persy resisted the pull. "I can't go." Her sudden resistance gained her freedom.

Betty stopped abruptly and turned back and surveyed her cousin's plain wool dress with raised brows, her distress magically gone. "Whyever not, Persy dear?"

With her mind racing, much as Betty's had earlier, Persy tried to come up with an explanation as to why. By now it was eleven-thirty and she only had two hours before she had to be at work. With the way Betty shopped, it could be well into the afternoon before she was done. On the other hand, the milliner's shop was not more than a handful of blocks away from the saloon. It might prove easier to go to the shop, then once her cousin was well ensconced with salespeople and frippery, she could make her excuses and be gone before Betty could drag her attention away long enough to notice.

"No reason," she said finally. "No reason at all. In fact, I'd love to go."

Betty eyed her with great speculation in her huge blue eyes before she smiled, then led the way to the waiting landau. They circled Madison Square slowly, in a long line of beautiful carriages. Betty waved and nodded her greetings before the circling finally ceased and the carriages started down the Ladies Mile.

The milliner's shop was a quaint little store that made the finest and most desired hats in town. Mrs. Werner, who owned the shop, made a point of knowing her better customers by name.

"Miss Olson," she chimed, "how good it is to see you."

Persy could have sworn that for all the woman's haughty facade, she was rubbing her hands together at the vision of dollar signs that Betty apparently brought to mind.

"Thank you, Mrs. Werner. And you remember my dear cousin, Persephone, don't you?"

"Of course, of course," she said, barely offering her a glance.

Persy had made the huge mistake of telling her aunt and cousin, the first and only time they had been in the store together, that she refused to wear a hat that was three times the size of her head. Mrs. Werner, apparently, hadn't appreciated her candor. So Persy merely offered her a polite smile, then began to wander about the store while Betty discussed the latest fashions with the proprietress.

Time passed and after Persy had studied just about every swatch of lace and length of ribbon, and had tried on every hat to be found, she glanced at a clock ticking discreetly on a table and noted that it was nearly one o'clock. Her heart began to pound. She had to make her escape, and soon. But no sooner had she determined she was going to make a run for it than the door pushed open, ringing the tiny bell suspended above. And when she turned away from the row of hats she had been studying, her heart seemed to leap out of her chest at the sight that met her eyes.

Jake Devlin! With the most beautiful woman she had ever seen!

Quick enough to billow her skirts, she turned back and grabbed the first hat at hand. She didn't care that the headpiece was a frilly concoction of feathers and bows and lace and who knew what all, not three times the size of her head, but four! Looks were the least of her concerns just then—anonymity was.

"Mr. Devlin!" Mrs. Werner exclaimed. "And Miss Norman. How good it is to see you."

With her stomach firmly lodged in her throat, Persy glanced surreptitiously over her shoulder from beneath the wide brim. Mr. Devlin, as well as everyone else in the store, seemed entirely unaware of her presence. Her heartbeat steadied, but when she noticed Jake Devlin's strong hand pressed intimately to the small of this Miss Norman's back, another sensation, one she had never experienced before, raced from her heart to her stomach, then back to her heart, making her teeth clench.

She looked at the woman. Her dress was finely made of what Persy deduced in her unknowledgeable way was some sort of silk—and red silk at that. Her hair was the deepest brown, done up in an elaborate design of twists and curls. Her eyes were so blue they appeared to be purple—violet she was sure they were called. Another shiver of feeling that she didn't like one bit raced down Persy's spine when Jake reached out and with very gentlemanly care removed the woman's finely woven shawl. But the shiver evaporated when she caught sight of the low-cut dress. Never in her life had she seen such cleavage, in fact she didn't realize so much cleavage was possible. Good Lord, Persy thought, how did the woman see her toes!

Suddenly she forgot all about the saloon. Suddenly she forgot that she had no interest in being there. Her interest was growing by the second.

"Miss Norman," Mrs. Werner enthused. "I have just the thing for you."

The proprietress's smile hardened as she glanced around the store. "Miss Daily!" she called sharply.

Persy glanced around the shop as well, wondering who in the world the woman could be calling. Clearly no one was in sight. Then, as if by magic, curtains parted and a frazzled-looking older woman hurried forward.

"Yes, Mrs. Werner."

"Show Mr. Devlin and Miss Norman to the private showing room," she instructed. "She is so slow, Mr. Devlin, and I apologize."

Jake scowled, making him look just like the dark and dangerous man he was. "I'm sure Miss Daily will do fine."

Mrs. Werner had the good sense to look uncomfortable. "Yes, of course. She'll bring you coffee and get Miss Norman started with some samples, and as soon as I finish up here I'll be right with you."

Persy watched as Miss Daily did as she was told and escorted the couple through the curtained opening. Persy felt a tingle of pride that Mrs. Werner was put in her place. But the tingle of pride turned to a tingle of fear when just as Jake reached the doorway he unexpectedly turned back. She barely managed to drop her head and pretended to study the hem of her dress before he glanced in her direction.

No one spoke. The clatter of carriages rolling through the streets filled the shop. Dogs barked and people shouted to be heard. But still no one in the tiny, feather- and ribbon-laden shop said a word.

At length, when Jake didn't speak or move, Persy carefully, without moving an inch, peeked through the fringe of feathers that hung down in her eyes. Her breath caught in her throat when she realized that he was staring right at her, his brow furrowed as if he was trying to place her.

"Jake!"

Miss Norman's voice shot out to them from the back room.

"Jake, darling, what are you doing?"

Jake seemed to snap out of his reverie. He ran his hand through his thick dark hair, leaving ridges where his fingers had passed. After one more penetrating look, he turned back, then disappeared through the doorway, the heavy curtain rippling in his wake.

Persy's breath came out in a rush. Seconds later Betty flew to her side and hissed in her ear. "Can you believe it! It's him!"

Persy did her best to pretend indifference. "Whoever do you mean?"

Stepping back just a bit, Betty eyed her cousin. "You know good and well who I mean." She leaned close again. "Jake Devlin!"

"I don't recall the name."

"Of course you do. You saw him on Fifth Avenue. Remember, you asked who he was."

"Oh, him," she said with feigned nonchalance. "Is he the same man?"

"You know he is, Persephone Daltry. Quit acting as if you don't." She clutched her hands to her chest. "And to think he's with Lilly Norman, the opera singer! Oh, how delicious! In this very room. If I had reached out I could have touched either one of them."

"Really, Betty. He's nothing but a scamp! You told me so yourself."

Betty laughed at this. "No, Mother told you that. And as I recall, not but a few weeks ago you were practically hanging out the carriage window gawking at that very scamp!"

"I was not!" Persy exclaimed, pulling herself together. "I was simply . . . observing."

Betty laughed even harder at this. "Observing, cousin? Drooling, maybe. Gawking, more than likely. But simply . . . observing, I think not." She peered toward the back. "I wonder if she's his new paramour."

"Paramour?" Persy followed her gaze.

"You know, lover, mistress, fancy woman, inamorata—"

"I get the idea." She scowled. "Surely not."

"Surely yes. Why else would he bring her in to a milliner."

"To purchase a hat." She didn't like the idea that Jake had a . . . a . . . woman friend who perhaps he was . . . intimate with. Especially when he was supposed to be engaged to her! Real or not, he could at least have shown her some consideration.

"Yes, he's here to buy her a hat," Betty answered, heedless of Persy's churning mind. "But only a lover buys his mistress such personal things." She nodded her head with superiority. "A gentleman with proper intentions buys a woman who holds his affections flowers or some little trin-

ket as a proper gift." Her tone grew heavy and troubled.
Her eyes filled with pain. "If he loved her and cared for
her, that is." Betty turned away, her face crestfallen once
again, Jake and his supposed fancy woman seemingly forgotten.

"Have you decided on a hat, Miss Olson?" Mrs. Werner
asked, bustling over to them.

"No, Mrs. Werner," Betty said softly. She glanced over
at the clock that Persy had noticed earlier, and her eyes
widened. "Oh, heavens. I must be off." She turned to
Persy. "You take the carriage. I'll find a cab. I've got to
go." She stepped closer and whispered in her ear, "And
don't tell Mother." She hesitated. "Please."

Persy was surprised yet again by her cousin's rapid
change of mood. But she was too relieved that she wasn't
going to have to come up with some excuse to leave Betty
to care. "I won't tell. Don't worry. And you take the carriage."

"How will you get home?"

"I'll take a cab later, or I'll catch the bus. I thought I'd
look around a bit more."

"You're a dear," she said, leaning over and pecking
Persy on the cheek. "I'll see you this evening then."

And it wasn't until Betty was out the door, the bell
jingling to a halt overhead, that she thought to ask where
the devil she was off to. She suddenly remembered the
man in the garden the night before and Betty's upset over
some man who supposedly didn't love her. Was it possible,
she wondered, that the two events were related? Could
that man skulking through the darkened night like a common criminal be the man for whom Betty pined?

Persy wondered about that and a great many other
things suddenly. But it was too late for questions now.
Only a whiff of Betty's perfume lingered. She'd have to
inquire later. And then she heard the deep baritone laugh
floating out from the back room, reminding her that she

had her own appointment to keep—at the saloon owned by the very man whose laugh she now heard.

But she hadn't gotten much past heading for the door when it was pushed open again, the bell jingling in response, bringing the woman who had followed Jake into the kitchen the day disaster had struck. Velda. Velda Harvey, she remembered the woman was called.

Persy twirled on her heels and shoved her head into another hat. Oh, dear heavens, how was she going to get out of this one?

"Mrs. Werner!" Velda announced. "I'm here!"

Mrs. Werner looked slightly disconcerted. "Yes, you are, and how glad I am."

Just then, to make matters worse, Jake stepped back into the front room. Persy would have laughed out loud at the look on his face had she not been so concerned about detection. He tried to retrace his steps but was halted in midstride when Velda cried, "Jake!"

Jake's body visibly stiffened, though his face remained unruffled. "Velda," he said simply, his voice rumbling through the feminine domain like thunder.

Mrs. Werner clasped her hands together in obvious relief. "Yes, Velda! Miss Velda Harvey."

Velda scowled at her.

"Such a beautiful name, I was thinking," Mrs. Werner quickly added.

Persy watched as Velda only humphed, then returned her attention to Jake. "Jake darling, what are you doing here?" Her voice was nearly a purr as she moved her considerable form seductively closer.

Clearly, Jake wasn't pleased to see the woman. Ha! Persy laughed with satisfaction to herself. Juggling too many women at once. He was bound to drop a ball at some point and get caught. The thought pleased her immensely.

Jake opened his mouth to speak.

"Jake, love." Lilly Norman's voice floated out from the back room.

Jake closed his mouth and grimaced.

"Jake?" Lilly called again.

"I'll be right there," he called, only to have Lilly poke her head out between the curtains.

Velda and Lilly stared at each other.

"My, my, my," Velda said, her tone acidic.

At this point Persy could have whipped off the hat and no one would have noticed. All eyes were locked on the drama that unfolded before her. Velda looked furious. Lilly looked upset. And Jake Devlin looked as if he'd like to be just about anywhere else in the world except here in Mrs. Werner's millinery shop.

"Who might this be?" Velda probed.

Jake grimaced, seeming to debate, then finally said, "Miss Harvey, please meet Miss Norman; Miss Norman, Miss Harvey." He took hold of Lilly's arm. "We'd love to stay and chat but it's late."

Lilly looked surprised by this announcement and Miss Daily looked panicked. "Why we only just started with the hats," Miss Daily said, her tone pleading, casting a surreptitious glance at Mrs. Werner.

No one, however, paid a bit of attention to Miss Daily. Velda took a step forward, a smile that didn't reach her eyes tight on her lips. "Is this a . . . sister we've never heard of before, Jake darling?"

Jake groaned.

"In all the years Daddy has known you," she continued, "he's never mentioned a sister."

Miss Norman tilted her head in question. "A sister? What are you talking about? Jake, what is she talking about?"

"Nothing, Lilly," Jake interjected, yet again making an attempt to steer her toward the door. Lilly, however, wasn't going anywhere.

Velda smiled. "So you're not his sister? Well, well. I just assumed you were since now that he's engaged I wouldn't have thought he would . . . or at least so quickly . . . be seen with other women."

"Engaged!" Lilly turned on Jake. "You're engaged?"

Jake cursed audibly. Velda laughed. Lilly looked to be on the verge of tears. Persy stared blatantly, nearly smiling at this melodrama that played itself out.

Jake glanced back and forth between Lilly and Velda. "Well, you see—"

Velda stepped forward and pressed her gloved hand to Lilly's forearm in a caring, sisterly fashion. "So he's engaged. Mark my words, it won't last. The woman is a mousy little thing."

Persy's smile vanished, and she gasped. Jake, Velda, Lilly, Miss Winters, and Mrs. Werner turned to her. She ducked her head back into all the feathers, her heart pounding. She wasn't sure if she was outraged or insulted. After a moment she decided she was both.

Silence reigned, until finally, thankfully, Lilly said, "Engaged," once again as if she couldn't believe it.

"Yes, engaged," Velda continued. "To a hired hand in his saloon, no less. In fact, a person has to wonder how a man like Jake Devlin could end up with a woman like that." She eyed Jake. "Yes, it makes a person wonder."

"Velda," Jake said, his tone warning.

"Velda what?" she asked. "Are you offended? Aren't you going to defend your little betrothed?"

Persy wondered the same thing as she peered back at him. But he didn't look as if he was on the verge of coming to her defense. He just looked mad, mad as hell!

"Or perhaps," Velda continued, "the little mouse isn't your betrothed after all. Is that it, Jake? Have you been lying to Daddy?"

"Jake," Lilly said, her voice shaky, pleading. "What is she talking about?"

Jake groaned.

"Is it true, Jake?" Lilly asked, pulling her shoulders back.

"Yes, Jake," Velda added, "is it true?"

Jake cast Velda a look that would have slayed a lesser woman. Velda only laughed. And Persy didn't wait to find out what his response would be. She saw she had a clear shot for the door and that everyone there was engrossed in their own little tragedy. So without a word she hurried for the door, slipping out unnoticed, then headed for the Dusty Rose.

Ten

"YOU'RE LATE!"

Persy stopped in her tracks, after having just pushed through the swinging door to the kitchen, only to have the door swing back and smack her from behind. Her normally impeccable chignon was slightly askew, tendrils of silky brown hair escaping to curl about her face.

Lola and May covered their mouths to stifle their laughter. Persy sent them a scathing glare before she marched over to the pantry to start the day's work without ever saying a word.

"Aren't you surprised to see us?" May asked from her place on a stool at the end of the counter where she had been studying her nails, trying to determine if she would have enough time to redo them before the night's performance.

"Of course she's surprised," Lola said, who sat next to May on another stool, the collar of her satin robe lined with flimsy feathers, her high-heeled mules swinging provocatively from her toes. "She surely couldn't have expected to find us here," she added, loud enough for Persy to hear. "At least not before *she* arrived."

"Imagine that," May teased just as Persy reappeared from the pantry, a load of cooking supplies in her arms, "you and me arriving before our Perky Persy."

"Though from the looks of that scowl on her face our Persy doesn't appear too perky today."

"Could it be that she can't think of a thing to cook?" May asked with a smile.

"Or that the delivery boy is late with her order?" Lola countered, mischief glimmering in her coal-lined eyes.

"Or maybe, just maybe, she's worked up into a lather because she's desperate to see her *fiancé.*"

May and Lola laughed cheerfully.

Persy merely shot them another scorching glance, then dumped the pans and utensils onto the counter. The metal and wood clattered onto the hard surface. "If you have nothing useful to say or do, why don't you get to work and leave me in peace. You know good and well that he isn't really my fiancé. And it would be a cold day in hell before he was!"

Taking up a heavy skillet, she slammed it down on the stove, the sound reverberating through the high-ceilinged kitchen. "I hate him," she muttered to herself.

Lola and May slid off their stools with a questioning glance at each other.

"We were only funning you, honey," Lola said with a look of concern. "Do you want to talk about it?"

Persy's hand stilled in its task. *Do you want to talk about it?* Something her father would have asked. Suddenly she longed for home. Longed for the wide-open spaces and simpler ways of life. A place where dresses didn't cost ninety-six dollars. A place where she wasn't trying to juggle two vastly different lives in order to pay for that blasted dress, and not get caught.

She sighed and glanced at the other women. "No," she

said with a tired smile, "I don't want to talk about it. There's nothing to talk about, really, but thank you. And I'm sorry I've been so . . . ornery."

"Maybe there *is* something to talk about," May suggested. "Has anyone . . . hurt you? If it was anyone other than Jake I'd say he had made improper advances. What else could make you hate a man like you apparently do?"

"But we're talking about Jake Devlin, here," Lola added with a meaningful look that said as clearly as words that it was impossible.

Persy whirled around. "Why is it that everyone around this place thinks that devil man is a saint?" she demanded.

May and Lola exchanged another look, before they turned back and said, "Because he is."

With a snort of disbelief, Persy rolled her eyes. "A sinner, I'd believe; a saint, never."

Lola reached out and took Persy's hand in a surprisingly firm grip. "Whether you believe it or not doesn't matter. What does matter, however, is that you don't talk that way about him in front of us or anyone else around here. We like you a lot, Persy, really we do, but we love Jake Devlin."

The seriousness of the woman's voice filled Persy with the perverse need to prove her wrong, but when she pulled her hand away and would have made another snide reply, Lola seemed to sense it and headed her off.

"I mean it, Persy. Jake Devlin is the finest man I've ever met. He may not be considered a gentleman by many, but he's more of a gentleman than any one of those dandies up on Fifth Avenue." Lola furrowed her brow and stared at Persy hard.

Persy grew uncomfortable, and not just because of the look on Lola's face. Somehow, after weeks of socializing with the very men about whom Lola spoke, her words had the ring of truth. But that couldn't be, Persy told herself quickly. It wasn't possible for the fine men of New York society to appear wanting in comparison to a man like Jake Devlin! Surely.

Abruptly she turned away. Confusion twirled around in her head like a top gone out of control. Her thoughts had gone crazy. But then she sighed. This scheme to have her dress remade was crazy. The fact that she was in New York City at all seemed crazy. And suddenly she remembered the question that had circled in her mind during the long journey east. Why had her grandmother sent her here in the first place? What was she supposed to learn?

She nearly groaned out loud in dismay but held it down with effort. She felt inadequate and totally incapable of doing anything right. At the rate she was going, spending so much time and energy in a saloon instead of a ballroom, she'd never figure out what she was supposed to learn. Why hadn't she simply told her aunt and uncle about the dress instead of tangling herself up in a complicated web of deceit and lies that she was already having difficulty keeping straight.

But regrets did her no good at this late date, she realized with further regret. She had already determined it was too late to tell her relatives what she had done. So she was stuck. At least for the next two weeks, five days, nine hours, and fifteen minutes. Yes, for that period of time she could endure anything, including that two-timing, no-good reprobate, Jake Devlin.

The women worked side by side, each lost in their own thoughts. Though minutes ticked by, the passing time did nothing to soften the sharp edges of Persy's anger. Without realizing what she was doing, every time Persy heard a voice from other regions of the house she glanced at the door. She scowled the entire time and would have ruined the meal altogether had Lola and May not been watching.

"Careful!" Lola cried, her high-heeled shoes clicking

against the hard tile just in time to catch a loaf of bread from tumbling to the floor.

Persy stopped for a moment, seemingly startled. But then her scowl returned and she turned back to her task with a huff.

It was only a little after four o'clock when Lola and May untied their aprons from around their waists with a sigh of relief and headed for the door. The meal had been accomplished in all due haste, and Lola and May were in a hurry to be gone.

Just as Lola and May got to the door, Jake walked in.

"Hello, all," he called, his spirits high.

Persy stilled at the sound, a meat cleaver held in her fist.

Lola glanced at Persy before she leaned over to Jake and whispered, "You'd best steer clear of Persy today. She's in a mood."

"A bad mood," May clarified as if there was a need.

Jake considered, then smiled. "A bad mood you say?" He glanced across the room to where Persy had turned narrowed eyes on him before she whirled back, and lowered the cleaver with a resounding chop where it stuck in the cutting board, quivering angrily. Jake eyed the cleaver. "And what, pray tell, has caused this bad mood?" he asked the girls.

"Who knows?" Lola said, shrugging her shoulders. "She wouldn't say. She just came in late, then started muttering and banging things around, and sending looks around that would have sent a wharf rat scurrying away."

"She may have only muttered and banged," May conceded, "but she muttered enough to make it clear she's not too pleased with you, Jake."

"What have you done?" Lola asked.

Jake laughed. "Nothing that I know of. But we'll have to probe to find out."

"Probe all you like—by yourself," May replied. "We've got to get ready for tonight."

Lola and May left Jake alone with Persy.

Jake stood quietly at the door watching her. Her back was ramrod straight and her shoulders were stiff. And he didn't understand the strange tightness in his chest that he felt whenever she was near.

His smile disappeared. For some time now he had longed for wide-open spaces. That he understood. But since Persy's unexpected arrival into his life the longing had turned into a nameless hunger that gnawed at him.

"What's wrong?" he asked quietly.

His words washed over her like a caress. His voice never ceased to amaze her. So deep and melodious, not proper or practiced, but still a voice that made her think every word he spoke was a work of art. Just like his person, she thought. So handsome that he might have been chiseled from stone by the greatest of sculptors, but wrapped in clothes as extravagant as a minstrel in a parade.

She turned toward him, forgetting the scene at the milliner's shop momentarily. "You have a beautiful voice," she said without thinking.

His normally iron-clad composure slipped, and she was absurdly pleased with herself for having caught him by surprise.

He shifted his weight, then eyed her more closely. "I asked you what's wrong and you respond by telling me I have a beautiful voice? I think the kitchen heat is making you mad, love."

Love. He had called her "love." The simple word washed away any pleasure she had felt. In that second, she suddenly felt like a madwoman. He didn't love her. And he never would. A strange feeling of emptiness wrapped around her. But that was impossible. She didn't care about this man, and she certainly didn't want his love.

"I'm not your love!" she snapped, disconcerted. "And you'd do well not to forget it."

He chuckled into the room, his composure slipping back into place. "Why is that?"

She practically growled at him. His humor, at her expense, made her seethe. She hated him, she reminded herself. She hated that she had no control over him and she hated that he knew it. And that made her even angrier. But then a thought occurred to her and slowly, very slowly as the idea began to grow and take shape, a smile softened the harsh line of her lips. "You'd do well not to forget because the next time you do, I'll just have to let it slip that I'm not really your fiancée." She fluttered her lashes at him. "I can just imagine what *Harold* would have to say about that. From all I've heard, he's quite serious about seeing you married, if not to me, then to his charming"—she said the word like it was poison—"daughter Velda."

Jake's eyes narrowed in turn. "Don't play with me, Persy, love."

"I'm not your Persy—"

He cut her off. "You forget, I might end up without a fiancée, but you'll end up without your money."

She snapped her mouth shut. The truth of his words infuriated her. Well, he might have bested her for now, but one of these days she was going to have the last word. She would!

They stared at each other across the room, their eyes locked, teasing green with violent gray. Not until the door pushed open and in its wake came Lilly Norman, did they finally look away.

"There you are, Jake," Lilly said, her tone impatient.

"I told you to wait for me in my office, Lilly."

"I've been waiting a full half hour for you to come back and explain what that Velda woman was talking about. I'm tired of waiting!" Lilly said, stamping her dainty foot.

"Lilly," he began, his voice tight. "This is neither the time nor the place to discuss personal matters. Let's go back upstairs to my office."

He started to usher her out of the kitchen but she jerked her arm free. "No, Jake! I will not be put off any longer. I want an answer, here and now. Are you or are you not engaged?"

Persy raised an eyebrow, then leaned up against the counter, her arms crossed on her chest. "Yes, Jake . . . love . . . are you or are you not engaged?"

For the first time since her arrival, Lilly looked at Persy. Confusion etched her brow.

"Persephone." He spoke her name as a warning, his voice dark and dangerous.

Lilly glanced between the two, her porcelain-white skin stained with red, her gloved hands clasped tightly at her waist. "Who are you?" she finally asked.

Another day Persy would have listened to reason, or at least thought things through before she acted. Wasn't she supposed to be nice, sweet, kind, and caring if nothing else? But this wasn't another day, and nice, sweet, kind, and caring seemed as far away as Texas, and had been since the day Jake Devlin stepped out of the kitchen shadows and into the light on her first day of work.

Yes, nice, sweet, kind, and caring were a long way off. This was a day when she had been callously called mousy in front of, and shamefully not defended by, the very man who stood before her now, trying to warn her off from gaining her vengeance. But vengeance she would have.

Persy ignored Jake and her smile broadened. "Why, I'm Persephone Daltry." She took the few steps that separated her from Jake and took his arm. "And last I had heard, I was this . . . dear man's betrothed."

Jake groaned. Lilly paled. And Persy suddenly felt horrible. The world seemed to come to a careening halt. No sooner were the words out than Persy willed them back. In her desire to get even with Jake she had forgotten about an innocent woman's feelings.

What was happening to her? she wondered. Where was the Persy she had always been? She dropped his arm as her throat grew tight, and a frown settled between her delicate brows.

An uncomfortable silence filled the kitchen as Persy tried to come up with something to say to undo the damage. She could laugh and say it was all a joke—a bad joke. She could slap Jake and say the engagement was off, that Lilly was the woman he really loved. But that she knew was entirely too dramatic and just might make a bad situation worse.

But she was saved from doing anything at all when a distant scream interrupted the silence. The simple scowl that had played on Jake's face evaporated like a tiny spill of water on a blistering hot day. His countenance hardened and she was reminded yet again that in spite of his constant teasing and outrageous ways, Jake Devlin was a dangerous man—a man she had no business toying with as she had just done. He was a man at home in a notorious saloon. A man not to take lightly. She remembered the people parting for him on the walkway when she had first seen him. She had thought him dangerous then. How, in the intervening days, could she possibly have forgotten that?

Another scream sounded, followed quickly by the crash of furniture. Jake leapt into action. He raced through the swinging door, Persy and Lilly close on his heels. Persy had never been in the actual barroom, so when her eyes took in the opulent room with its shiny brass, red velvet draperies, and the largest painting of a woman without a stitch of clothing on right before her very eyes, Persy nearly forgot that they had raced in there because of trouble. But then she saw May clutching the lapels of her gown together and a strange man stalking her, a broken chair in their midst.

"You're not going to leave me, woman," the man hissed. "You're mine, you hear me, you're—"

The words were cut off when Jake leapt forward, grabbed the collar of the other man's coat, and dragged him backward with Herculean strength. No sooner had Jake thrown the man up against the opposite wall than Howie, Mr. Bills, and an assortment of women piled into the room.

Jake had the man pinned against the velvet curtains, his strong forearm pressed against the other man's throat. Persy watched, stunned, as the man's face began to redden and his eyes bulged in his head.

"She is not yours," Jake said in a murderous tone. "Do you understand me?"

Despite the deadly hold, the man started to protest but stopped when Jake's grip tightened.

"Do you understand me?" Jake repeated.

The man began to panic as veins began to bulge on his forehead and temples. Persy thought he would die right there in front of them. But finally, when Jake didn't let up the pressure no matter how hard the man struggled, agreement was finally gained.

"Yeah, I understand," the man choked out.

Abruptly Jake let him go and stood back, the man dropping into a heap on the floor, gasping for breath, his fingers coming to his throat.

"Stay away from her, do you hear me. If I ever catch you around her or my saloon again, you won't be as lucky as you were today. Now get out of here before I change my mind."

The man sat on the floor, his back against the smooth, wood-lined wall. For a second it looked as if he wouldn't leave. He glanced up and found May. But when Jake took a menacing step forward he pushed himself up and said, "I'm going, I'm going."

But just after the man reached the door and Jake turned to check on May, the man whirled around and charged.

It happened so quickly that Persy had no time to think. She simply reacted. Just when the man raced past her, she stuck her booted foot out into his path, sending him on a headlong flight until he landed at Jake's feet.

Jake glanced between the man and Persy, before Howie was there, gathering the man up, then tossing him out the door.

After a moment of silence Jake turned away. Persy wanted to go to him or say something to him, but it was Lilly who finally spoke.

"Jake," Lilly whispered.

But Jake didn't go to her. He stood perfectly still, staring at the closed door. "You'd best be getting home, Lilly," he said quietly. "Howie will take you."

Without having to be told, Howie jumped to attention and held the door for Miss Norman. Lilly looked at Jake one last time before she allowed Howie to lead her away.

Persy looked on as all the women and even Mr. Bills circled around May, making sure she was all right. Persy wanted to go to May, help her in some way. But she was an outsider here, had intended it that way. And she should have been happy. But she wasn't.

The crew from the Dusty Rose circled around May like a family around a wronged sibling. Persy knew the feeling well, she realized, without ever having appreciated it before. The longing she had felt for her family earlier intensified. A shared word or hug. A smile or a joke.

And she realized as well that this man named Jake Devlin was a great many things, and no sooner did she peg him as one than he showed her he was many others. But how to make the pieces fit? She didn't know—wouldn't know, she realized. She would never know any more about this notorious saloon owner other than that he was a great protector of those he cared about. No wonder Lola and May so vehemently defended and loved the man. Persy realized now that their love was not romantic, but the kind of love she felt for her own family.

At length Jake turned back and went to May, the others stepping back to make room. "Are you all right, sweetheart?" he asked in a tone so soft and gentle.

May offered him a watery smile. "Yes, Jake, thank you."

His lips spread in what Persy thought was supposed to be a smile of reassurance, but looked more like a grimace of pain. Her heart clenched when he reached out and touched May's hair, like a father to a child. "Why don't you go on upstairs. Take the night off."

"Oh, no, I couldn't."

His smile was genuine this time. "Of course you can. I insist."

The crowd began to disperse, Lola and another woman guiding the teary-eyed May up the wide carpeted stairs.

Jake had stepped off to the side, staring out at the street through the huge mullioned window, as if to ensure that indeed the man was gone and not coming back. The anger in his expression remained, but the tightness began to ease like a panther with its hackles finally settling after an intruder had left its domain.

"You were wonderful," Persy whispered.

He sighed. "No," he said, looking through the windows at things only he could see. "That wasn't wonderful. Just necessary."

From the way he said the words she had the distinct impression that he hated that it was necessary, and from the look in his eyes she had the feeling, yet again, that he would rather be someplace else. But where, she wondered. Unbidden, Paradise came to mind, and her dreams of taking the devil home to Paradise seemed so very real.

She walked up next to him and looked out the window much as he did. "What do you see, Jake Devlin?" she asked in a voice so soft that she hardly realized she had spoken.

With infinite slowness, he turned until he faced her. "I see a woman whom I don't understand, who continually surprises me, and has more backbone than I ever imagined a woman could have."

Persephone blushed. She was oddly pleased by his words even though she knew she shouldn't be. "If you're referring to my sticking my foot out, it was just a reaction."

A shadow of a smile flitted across his lips. "A timely reaction, I must say. But that's only part of the reason. You certainly aren't afraid of danger or dangerous people. Nor are you afraid to fight back when you're angry."

She looked at him in confusion.

"I was referring to your telling Lilly about our engagement."

Persy grimaced. "Oh, that. I'm sorry. I had no right."

"True. You had no right at all."

Her heart clenched. "Will she ever forgive you? I could talk to her, you know. I could tell her it was all a farce, that I was mad at you and was trying to get even."

He stared at her for an eternity. At length, he asked, "Is that true?"

Her blush of embarrassment intensified. "Is what true?"

"That you were angry with me?"

She tried to turn away but he staid her by taking her hand.

"Answer me, Persephone." Though the words were a demand, his voice was gentle, almost pleading.

"Yes," she whispered, trying to resist the unfamiliar longings he made her feel.

"Why?" he persisted. "Tell me why you were angry. Please."

How could she answer his question? She hardly understood the reasons herself. And she wondered, suddenly, why he cared. She was nothing more than a pawn in his game, and only a convenient pawn at that. What would have happened had Lola or May been standing in the kitchen when he had needed a fiancée? Or Miss Lilly? Or anyone else wearing a skirt?

"Were you jealous?" he asked.

Her shoulders stiffened and she started to speak.

He only laughed softly and pressed his finger to her lips. "You have no need to be jealous of the Lilly Normans of the world. You are a beautiful woman." He reached out and very gently touched her hair. "With silky brown hair, and stormy gray eyes that very nearly sweep me away every time I look at you."

Feeling shimmered down her spine, intense feelings that she only experienced in his company—feelings she was certain she had no business feeling.

With infinite slowness, he leaned down and pressed his lips to hers. Her mind swam. And when she should have pulled away, slapped his face, called him a cad, she damned better judgment and lost herself to the feel—lost herself to the soft, intimate touch of this hard, beautiful man whom she neither understood nor liked, she tried to tell herself as his lips whispered across her skin.

He pulled back, barely, and when he spoke again she could feel his warm breath against her cheek. "Who are you, Persephone Daltry?"

His voice was like sandpaper, but Persy hardly noticed.

He watched, mesmerized, as Persy ran her tongue over her lips. He groaned at the sight, his loins aching for this woman as if he were no more than an adolescent.

Carefully, almost reverently, he pulled her to him, no longer caring if she answered, and claimed her lips with his own. "Persy," he groaned, before kissing her again, gently, as not to scare her, until he could feel the tension melt from her body and her eyelids flutter closed. His tongue caressed her lips, parting them, to taste the sweetness within.

His mouth was searingly hot, his tongue making her quiver with astonishment. Never in all the times she had longed for this man's kiss had she imagined the intensity she would feel. A sweet ache filled her, centering at her very core. She tried to pull back because she knew she should, but he only pulled her closer. Then, succumbing to the warmth that beckoned, she forgot all reason and molded her body to his.

Hesitantly she flicked his tongue with her own, relishing the feel, reveling in the new and wondrous emotions that exploded in her body.

Jake moaned deeply at her clearly inexperienced attempt, surprised that such a gesture could fill his body with unbridled passion. Never had he desired a woman more. Not even the experienced touch of a woman who knew how to please a man had made him feel so alive. His hand froze at the thought. He realized then that unlike a woman who knew how to pleasure a man, Persy did not. Persy clearly wasn't experienced. This widowed woman who supposedly had a child was not experienced at lovemaking, didn't seem to know the first thing about kissing and holding. He had never completely believed her story from the start, but he had never suspected that this woman he held in his arms could be an innocent miss.

Better judgment bade that he pull away, pursue this thought. But then she moved just so, accidentally brushing against his desire, and the feel of her warm curves banished all thought from his mind.

A soft, barely audible moan sounded from her as his strong hands gently caressed her back, moving slowly downward. His tongue became more insistent, moving with a rhythm as old as time. His arm circled her shoulders, pulling her close, guiding her until her back was against the wall. He couldn't get enough. He wanted to rip her clothes free, feel her bare skin beneath the palms of his hands. He looked down at her, her eyes closed, her breath heavy with desire, and he knew she wanted him, too. But when he whispered, "My sweet, mysterious Persephone Daltry. How long will it be before I find out who you really are?" but as his hand traveled from her lower back to her midriff, then slowly ascended to claim her breast, he felt her body stiffen and he cursed his stupidity.

His words as well as his intimate touch were a harsh dose of reality. Panic made her angry and she wrenched back and reached out with a force that surprised her and slapped him hard across the face. "How dare you take such liberties!"

He stared at her for a long while as if trying to comprehend what had just transpired. Very slowly he brought his hand up to his cheek.

She stepped back, her fingers touching her face, her mouth opened in silent surprise as she stared at the vivid red handprint that swelled angrily on his cheek.

"Well, that settles that," he said, testing his jaw with a grimace.

Her eyes narrowed suspiciously. "What are you talking about?"

"I haven't been able to determine who you are. But one thing is for certain. You're not a"—he seemed to look for the right word—"fallen woman." His green eyes darkened. He reached out and ran one strong finger down her cheek. "Or if you are, you didn't fall easily. I find I like that in a fiancée."

Her mind reeled. She couldn't imagine how to respond. Too many emotions warred within her to allow coherent thought. The only thing that stood out in her mind was the feel of his finger brushing against her chin.

"Now, my pretty lady, you'd best hurry home. It's already a few minutes past five." He smiled. "And you wouldn't want to be late for wherever it is you go off to in such a hurry every day."

She seemed incapable of comprehension much less movement, and when she did nothing more than stare at him, he turned her around by the shoulders and pointed her toward the door. "Good-bye, Mrs. Daltry. We'll see you tomorrow."

Eleven

"COME AWAY WITH ME."

Betty gazed up into Thomas Weathersley's dark brown eyes and wondered if she dared believe him. She wanted to believe, needed to believe, because she loved him. Desperately. Had for years. "Where would we go?"

His deep, rumbling laughter filled her frilly white-laced bedroom, wrapping around her. He ran his knuckles down her cheek, stopping at her lips. "Anywhere you like. London, Paris, Philadelphia. I'll take you there."

She pulled away and walked around her room, slowly, running her fingers along the items she had been surrounded by for a lifetime. Madame Suzanne, her favorite doll, sat with her old smiling face looking up at her expectantly. It was all Betty could do not to pick her up and hold the doll tight to her breast. But she was a woman now, full grown, though her parents didn't seem to realize it.

The skirt of Betty's light blue chiffon dress rustled as she walked from one item to the next. She touched each toy and ribbon, each necklace and painting, as if something she came across would hold the answer. Should she go with Thomas? Should she stay? Did he really love her? Or not? The very idea that he didn't was painful, unthinkable. She loved Thomas Weathersley with all her heart, and had since she was no more than a little girl of five and he an older man of thirteen. Of course he hadn't noticed her, not then or even later. Only in the past month or so had she gained his notice. Now she was prepared to do whatever it took to keep that attention. Yes, whatever it took. The thought made her sigh with frustration and sadness. She wished it didn't have to be that way.

Her parents didn't like him even though he was the son of close family friends—wealthy friends. He was the type of man Betty thought her parents would have wanted her to marry. She couldn't understand her parents' vehement reaction to Thomas's attentions. They should have been thrilled. Instead, they had forbidden her to see him, offering some mumbled excuse that he was not right for her.

But even as angry as she had been with her parents over their declarations, and no matter how strongly she denied their words, she hadn't been able to close her ears to the rumors that floated around town that Thomas's parents had cut him off. Without a cent. He was only allowed to live at home because they were trying to avoid a scandal. But she simply wouldn't believe it, couldn't believe it. Thomas himself had denied the reports as jealous rumors, and had gone out and bought a brand-new pair of Hessian boots on his father's account to prove his point. "If I had been cut off, Betty, I wouldn't be able to make purchases such as these," he had said, displaying his new footwear with a flourish, before taking her arm and leading her to the secluded part of the park where he always took her.

And of course people were jealous of him, she told herself. His looks, his money. His easy charm. Everyone thought he had everything. But she knew better. They didn't know him like she did. He was hurting deep inside.

He was wounded by callous parents who didn't understand him. She understood him, however. He needed her. And she knew she could heal him with her love.

"Betty," he whispered as he took the steps that separated them.

When he pulled her into his embrace, her back against his chest, she let him. He cared about her, she told herself. He did! Scaling the ivy trellis that led to her bedroom to see her proved it.

The feel of his hard muscled chest against her back sent shivers of longing down her spine. He had never kissed her before, or at least the kind of mouth-to-mouth kiss, a sharing of passion that she so desired. At first she had thought it odd. Never in all the afternoons they had met had he pressed his lips to hers. He only touched her, in places where he shouldn't, leaving her breathless and wanting more.

Her mind filled with memories of his smooth palm slipping beneath her bodice, and covering her naked breast. Cupping, holding. His fingers pulling, first gently, then with pressure, on her nipples. Just the memory made her body burn.

"Betty," he said again, leaning down, his breath a warm whisper against her skin, "don't you want to come away with me? Don't you want me?"

The words stung her heart. Of course she wanted him. But she wanted to be Mrs. Thomas Weathersley as much or more. And she knew that she had to proceed carefully if that was to happen.

She stepped away and looked back at him. "Thomas," she said, her voice low and deep, seductive, "you have never stated your intentions."

She would have sworn his brown-eyed gaze flickered with impatience, but when she looked closer it was gone, and most assuredly, she told herself, it had never been there. She was simply imagining her fears coming true.

"My intentions, love? I didn't realize that what we shared needed to be expressed. Cheapened by words that could never adequately convey all I feel for you." He sighed and started to turn away. "I thought we had more than that, Betty. I guess I misjudged our bond. I guess I should go."

"Oh, no! Please don't go." His tone as much as his words made her heart race with panic. Instantly she blamed herself. She was wrong. She was ruining everything. And it was easy to come to that conclusion in a society that teaches women to believe in the wisdom and knowledge of men, and to fear their own. "Forgive me, Thomas. I love you," she cried, grasping his arm.

He turned back, though only slightly, and looked down at her dainty hand clutching the sleeve of his coat. She followed his gaze. Milky white against starling black, stark in its contrast. So different. So harsh. So incompatible. Like the two of them, she suddenly thought. She realized with a start that their meetings were always like this. She asking questions. He growing angry that she asked. She putting the questions out of her mind until they surfaced once again when she forgot that she had to keep them suppressed. The same scene played itself over and over again like a bad dream that refused to go away.

But she loved him. And he loved her, too. Surely. Why else would he have spent so much time with her. Showing her off around town. Taking her to his special place in the park.

She glanced up and she found him looking at her. All she saw was the face that had plagued her dreams since childhood, and she knew then that even if he didn't love her, she would make him love her one day. She could. They were meant to be together. And weren't all things that were worth having worth fighting for? Well, she would fight for Thomas Weathersley. And she would win.

"I'm sorry, Thomas. I'm talking nonsense. It's been a

long day. And I was so upset when you didn't come last night as you said you would."

"But I did come." He smiled slyly.

"You did? When?"

He chuckled. "Just when I told you I would, only I came to the wrong window."

Betty's eyes opened wide. "Oh, no! Whose window did you go to? Did anyone see you?"

"Your cousin's window."

Betty thought about this. Persy had said nothing to her. "How did you know it was her room?"

"She came to the window. Scared the devil out of me, I'll tell you."

"But she didn't say anything to me about it!"

"I don't think she could see me clearly. I wore a hat. Besides, she was probably titillated by the idea of a man sneaking into her room and didn't want to share her secret." He smiled. "It wasn't until this afternoon when I came back that I realized I had gotten lost in the dark." He stepped closer. "Now I have come to right my grievous wrong."

Her mind was awash with worry. What if Persy told her parents? But she wouldn't, she reassured herself. Persy hadn't told on her so far. And she doubted Persy would have put the afternoon walks together with the man in the garden anyway, especially if Thomas was correct and she hadn't been able to see his face.

She smiled her relief. "I'm glad you came. I've missed you. I thought about you all night and all day."

He leaned down again and pressed a fleeting kiss on her neck. And then, finally, after all these weeks of waiting, he kissed her on the lips. A tiny gasp of sound escaped her lips and she closed her eyes. It was heaven.

"When will your parents be home?" he murmured against her skin.

"Later. Much later."

"What about your cousin?"

"Later, as well."

For a second she wondered where it was that Persy went every day, dressed so plain, and gone for so many hours. But then he kissed her again, and she wondered no more. There was no room for anything in her thoughts other than Thomas Weathersley and the glorious way he made her feel.

His breathing grew heavy. Labored. He kissed her again. Full on the mouth. Hard, startling her. She had never imagined kissing to be like this. She had dreamed that his kisses would be like all the caresses he had plied her with, sweet and gentle, making her want more.

His breathing became harsh. She stiffened. His kiss was cold and hard with no emotion, no feeling. Like a command, like he was wielding power over her. And she didn't like it.

At length, she forced herself to relax. She was imagining things again. It was the fact that she had never kissed a man before that made her uncertain now. It would get better once she got used to it. Just like his caresses.

She gave in and let his kiss continue. At this he groaned. Her heart began to pound. He brought his hand up to the back of her head, holding her close—captive. His mouth slanted over hers, and he forced his tongue between her lips. When his tongue touched hers she was so unprepared that she forgot her intentions to relax and she panicked. Pressing her hands against his shoulders, she tried to free herself.

"Thomas!" she cried, tearing her face away.

"Baby," he panted against her neck, his hands groping.

Her resistance only seemed to spur him on. His hands traveled down her hips and he pressed her body to his. She felt his hard arousal, again and again, as he pressed her rhythmically against him.

"Thomas! Stop this. You're scaring me."

But still he continued, seemingly oblivious to her concerns.

Her fear mounted and she began to twist and turn in his embrace, until finally she caught him off-balance and she wrenched herself free. "Thomas!"

When he found his hands empty he seemed surprised by the sight of Betty, as if he didn't know who it was who had so ravaged her. His eyes were wild, even desperate, before they settled into cajoling brown pools of good humor.

"Thomas, you frightened me."

"I'm sorry, sweetness." He was still slightly breathless. "So terribly sorry."

"You scared me," she repeated, her voice small and childish.

"I know, baby, and I'm sorry. I didn't mean to scare you." He smoothed his jacket and glanced at the window. "It's just that I want you so badly." He quickly glanced at her before he turned away again. "You're so beautiful and desirable that you make me crazy. And I do crazy things like crawling in your window in the middle of the afternoon and getting carried away with my desire. Forgive me."

She felt crazy, too. She had allowed him to sneak in her room—proof enough that she must be insane. So she believed his words, wanted to believe his words. "Do you really think I'm beautiful?"

She watched as a smile slowly curved on his lips before he turned back to her.

"The most beautiful of women." He came to stand before her, then reached out and very gently caressed her cheek. When she flinched, he said, "Don't be afraid. I won't hurt you. I could never hurt you because you are the other half to my whole."

Just as she had believed. They were meant to be together. Elation filled her. So when he leaned down and very carefully kissed her, this time slowly, gently, across her cheek to her lips, she let him. He didn't linger there but pressed her forehead with his lips all the while whispering sweet endearments until her body began to relax still further, gently molding to his.

"Hmmm," he murmured. "Nice. So nice."

And it was nice, Betty thought. Just like it had been before, in the park or garden or carriage. The way it was supposed to be. "You do love me, don't you, Thomas?"

She thought for a second that he stiffened, but then he cupped her cheeks and tilted her head until she met his eyes. "Do you think I would kiss you this way if I did not?"

But when she started to question further, realizing that he hadn't truly answered her question, he bent his head and kissed her, long and deep, though ever so gently until her body melted entirely and she forgot everything else but the feel of his arms around her.

"Oh, Thomas, I do love you."

His murmured response was nothing more than a buzz of sensation against her skin that traveled down her spine to the core of her being. And when his hand came up and cupped her breast, she stiffened only a moment, then relaxed and relished the feel. When his finger slipped beneath her chemise, her head fell back and she groaned. The feeling was exquisite and she thought no more, heard no more, simply lost herself in sensation.

The tiny buttons slipped open with an ease that any other time would have made her question his apparent adeptness with such things. But this time she was only aware of his tongue gliding across her nipple and the wisp of breath that made her shiver with wanting. "Thomas," she breathed, arching her back, crying for more.

"Betty!"

She nearly fell to the floor when Thomas suddenly released her. She staggered back and caught herself on the bedpost. And only then did she become aware of the person who stood in the doorway.

"Persy!"

Betty's cousin stood perfectly still, her eyes wide with surprise, staring. Betty followed Persy's gaze and noticed for the first time her bare breasts. "Oh, my word!" She covered herself with suddenly clumsy hands. The tiny buttons did not button up nearly as quickly as they had been unbuttoned only minutes before. When she looked up Persy hadn't moved but now stared at Thomas. Thomas stared back and Betty felt ill.

"Have you gone mad?" Persy finally asked, turning back to Betty, her voice filled with incredulity. "What if it had been your parents who came home early instead of me?"

"Well," Thomas said, taking a slow step forward, a lazy smile lifting one side of his lips, "it wasn't her parents who arrived so unexpectedly, and uninvited I might add, it was you. No sense in bemoaning something that didn't happen, now is there, Miss Daltry?"

Her eyes narrowed. "I would think that something did happen that is well worth bemoaning, Mr. Weathersley," she said, her voice as severe as his was indolent.

Thomas only laughed, straightened his cravat that had come slightly askew. "Nothing happened worth discussing. And unless you go and shout it out to the world no one will be the wiser." He gathered his hat that he tipped, then placed on his head. "Ladies," he said before he walked not to the window through which he had entered but to the door, and exited as if he owned the place.

Betty and Persy watched him go, both too amazed at his audacity to speak. They heard his steps trod down the carpeted stairway, then hit the marble entryway floor. The front door opened, then shut with finality, bringing Betty around in a flash of concern.

"You're not going to tell, are you?" Betty finally asked, her blue eyes wide with pleading.

Persy shook her head slowly. This had become an all too frequently recurring theme in her relationship with her cousin. But yet again, she had to concede, she was in no position to point fingers regardless of the fact that she sensed a great deal of trouble was brewing. She had to sneak out of this very house that evening for a rendezvous of her own. If fingers were going to be pointed, then they should be pointed at her as well.

But that didn't make it any easier to keep quiet, she found. Thomas Weathersley was no good. That was as clear as a bright summer day. But somehow Betty had either overlooked that fact or had simply missed it altogether.

"He's no good, Betty."

Her cousin's quiet voice evaporated in a flash. "No good! What do you mean?"

"He's nothing but trouble as my grandmother would say." She tried to sound sweet and caring, soothing.

"You're just jealous!"

The venomous tone scathed Persy. And she didn't understand it. "Betty—"

"You want him for yourself!"

"Betty!"

"I saw the way you looked at him!"

"If I looked at him in any way at all it was in disgust!" Persy's tone was no longer so sweet. "Any man who would sneak up into a woman's room is no gentleman!"

"He loves me, he does!"

Persy sighed. "Oh, Betty, can't you see—"

"We're to be married!"

Persy glanced down and noticed the buttons on Betty's dress, done but slightly askew, a blatant reminder of what had gone on before she arrived. "Has he asked your father for your hand in marriage?"

Betty grew uncomfortable. "Well, no. But he will. He's just waiting for the right moment."

A fragrant breeze blew in the window through which Thomas had entered. White eyelet curtains fluttered, then fell, then fluttered again. Persy stood silently, not knowing what else to say. She felt as if she were caught up in a bad dream, someone else's bad dream. She couldn't believe the way her cousin was acting. Anyone with a lick of sense could see that Thomas Weathersley was one, no good, and two, using Betty terribly. But what could she do? Just then she longed for her grandmother's no-nonsense advice. Minerva always had a way of putting things in perspective. Today, standing in the extravagantly decorated room of her high-society cousin that was so different from her own bedroom at home, levelheadedness seemed a long way off.

"Don't just stand there. Say something, Persy!" Betty's voice was shrill.

Persy looked at her. "What do you want me to say? That I believe that he plans to marry you?" A scowl crossed her face. "I'm afraid I can't do that. I think it would be best if you stopped seeing Mr. Weathersley. I'm worried about you. I'm worried that you're going to get hurt."

Betty's mood change was so swift and unexpected that Persy felt a moment of unbalance.

"Persy dear," she said, her voice sickeningly sweet. "Why is it that you are gone every afternoon?"

"What do you mean?"

Betty stepped closer and actually sniffed. "And why is it that you always return smelling like food?"

Persy couldn't breathe. She was about to be found out. And for a second she felt pure unadulterated relief. She was so tired of sneaking around, of leading a double life. She would get the truth out in the open and deal with the results afterward.

But Betty only laughed, a sound that wasn't nice, making it clear she didn't care for confessions, only in making

Persy uneasy. So much for Betty being like another sister, Persy thought.

"Cousin, cousin. At a loss for words?" Betty asked. "My guess is that I don't have to worry about you telling on me. You'll be too worried that I might tell on you." She glanced at herself in the mirror and noticed the buttons done incorrectly. She laughed even louder, then began to redo her dress. "Yes, cousin, we're a pair, you and I. Each with our secrets to hide. So run along now and get cleaned up before Mother and Daddy come home and become suspicious of you all on their own."

Twelve

SEVERAL HOURS HAD PASSED SINCE PERSY'S ENCOUNTER WITH Betty and Thomas. Hopefully it would be her last. She had little interest in witnessing Betty in the throes of passion ever again. Heavens above, the way that man had been touching her! On top of which, the venomous words Betty had uttered left Persy shocked, but more importantly saddened.

She leaned back against the closed door of her bedroom, her eyes pressed shut. She had made it, had safely escaped dinner with her relatives once again. No one seemed suspicious. Or so she hoped. Even Betty had been so preoccupied with her own thoughts that she had hardly afforded Persy a glance. Now all Persy had to do was sneak out of the house without anyone knowing.

Good Lord, what had she gotten herself into! Needing to sneak out of the house under the cloak of darkness, as if she were no better than a common criminal! What would her family say if they ever knew? But they would never know. That was the point of this whole masquerade.

Persy's dress and shoes were carefully packed in a satchel. She'd have to change at the saloon. Did they have places to change, she wondered, or would she have to go *up to the rooms* to dress? It didn't matter. She had to take a change of clothes. She surely couldn't climb out of her window in a full skirt, corset, and pantaloons, much less in shoes with any kind of heels, be it an inch or two or none.

She gritted her teeth. She wished she didn't have to climb out the window at all. She wished she didn't have to go to this stupid dinner either. But there was no use in wishing for things that couldn't be. She had to be at the saloon in thirty minutes, and if she didn't hurry she would never get there in time—in time for her "official betrothal dinner" to Jake Devlin.

Her head swam. Her stomach quivered. Her heart pounded. But Harold Harvey and his daughter had insisted on having the party, and at the time the cogs in Persy's brain hadn't turned quickly enough to come up with an excuse not to attend. Though what she would have been able to come up with to get out of her own betrothal party she couldn't imagine.

She muttered a curse that, thank you very much, she had never heard let alone uttered until she stepped into the depraved confines of the Dusty Rose saloon. Good Lord, how had she gotten herself into a position to be socializing with the likes of Harold and Velda Harvey, not to mention learning profanity from the likes of Jake Devlin? To think she had envisioned a life at the pinnacle of New York society, only to end up with the dregs instead. How had things gone so wrong? she wondered in dismay. But of course she knew. The dress. That blasted dress.

She arrived at the saloon at five minutes after eight, her attire dusty and ripped due to her fall from a good ten feet above the ground. The trellis hadn't been as easy to descend as the one at her home in Paradise Plains.

Paradise Plains. Paradise. How she longed for home at just that moment. But that was absurd. She didn't want to be there. She wanted to be here, or at least she wanted to be in New York. She did.

When she pushed through the swinging door, she found Jake in the kitchen pacing. He didn't notice her at first and she stood for a moment and simply stared, struck by his striking good looks as she had been that first day she saw him from the carriage. Oh, Jake, if only things were different, she thought before she could think better of it.

But "if onlys" didn't amount to a hill of beans, she quickly admonished herself before her errant mind could take the thought any further.

She let the kitchen door swing shut and he turned. "You came!"

He sounded a bit like a schoolboy, even looked the part with his dark hair falling forward on his forehead. With a smile he swept the hair back and came forward. "I was afraid you wouldn't come."

Persy hated the way her heart skipped a beat, hated the way she wanted to reach out, smooth his hair, and say, "Of course I came." Instead she scowled and said, "A deal is a deal."

Jake threw back his head and laughed. "Of course. How foolish of me. The money. I never should have doubted that you would come." But his laughter vanished when he finally noticed her attire. "Despite the fact that you are quite appealing in britches—rips, streaks of dirt, mud and all . . ."

Persy glanced down at herself and blushed.

"I had hoped you'd have worn something a bit more appropriate for a dinner party. You're supposed to be *my* fiancée, after all."

One delicate brow arched. "Are you implying that *someone else's* fiancée could arrive in such attire? Perhaps you think better of yourself than circumstances warrant, Mr. Devlin."

She watched the good cheer vanish from his beautifully

chiseled face as quickly and as thoroughly as a rabbit in a magician's hat. He looked dangerous, the man of the underworld, and she was relieved. The dangerous man was the only man she felt comfortable thinking of him as. Because if he wasn't dark and dangerous, if he wasn't bad, then all her preconceived ideas would be mistaken. *She* would be mistaken, wrong, and that just couldn't be. She was Persephone Daltry. Everyone knew she was nice, sweet, kind, and caring. She had lived her whole life with people telling her just that. And nice, sweet, kind, and caring people didn't wrongly accuse others of things they were not. So he had to be bad—so that she could still be good. She couldn't be anything else, or she wouldn't be anyone at all.

She realized then, however, that not only had she not acted like the person she had always been, but the people in this great huge city of New York didn't know her from Adam, didn't know if she was good or bad, and frankly didn't seem to care. Certainly, if she was thought to be bad, the invitations she had been receiving would be yanked away so quickly her head would spin. But they would be withdrawn because she was perceived as not good enough. One more or less debutante hardly mattered in the scheme of things. But at home, in Paradise, people would have noticed that she had changed, would have cared about and inquired after the cause. She would have people around her who cared and listened.

Suddenly she was struck with the thought that the very people from whom she had fled were really the only people who truly cared about her. They might not have any interest in multiple forks or social hierarchies, but they loved her and cared about her. They were the very people and things that defined who she was. All that had happened in her life, and all those she had met and spent time with, were who and what had shaped and molded her— made her who she was. She had the sudden unsettling thought that here in New York she seemed to have lost her identity. She had become someone she neither liked nor respected.

She scowled, feeling uncertain and confused. That very fact that no one knew her in New York had been such a pleasure to realize when she had first arrived. Now it simply made her feel alone and lonely.

With more force than was necessary, she thrust out the bag she held in her hand. "Of course I brought something else to wear. What do you think I am? A social mooncalf? I wore this because I couldn't very well climb down the trellis in—"

She nearly choked on the words. Her brain, she was convinced, had ceased to function, or at the very least, she was a mooncalf. Good heavens, what had she almost said?

"Climbing down the trellis, my sweet widowed mother of one?" His eyebrow quirked and the darkness evaporated from his features, leaving only the rays of good cheer that he so frequently exhibited. In fact, he looked quite pleased with himself. "Won't your baby daughter . . . or is it a son . . . let you out of the house tonight?"

Her scowl was meant to sear him, but Jake only laughed. "Such an example you're setting."

This time she made a low gurgling sound that sounded suspiciously like a growl, but Jake only chuckled and said, "Soon he or she will be following in Mother's footsteps, sneaking out to meet someone or something, and engaging in who knows what illicit activities."

"After what I've been through today, Mr. Devlin," she said through clenched teeth, "I'm in no mood to listen to your sarcasm."

His smile only broadened. "Then what kind of a mood are you in? One to listen to romantic prose, perhaps? Or sweet soliloquies?"

"One to see your sweet ass on a platter, more like it!"

His eyes opened wide for half a second, and she would

have been pleased with herself for catching him off guard had she not been so embarrassed. Good heavens, what had she just said!?

"Persephone, Persephone, Persephone," he said, shaking his head. "Such a surprise you are. What am I to do with you?"

"You, sir, are to do nothing," she replied, her face crimson. "Now are you going to find me a place to change so we can get on with this farce, or am I going to turn around and return home?"

"You could change right here."

His expression was as angelic as a cherub's, but she knew better. Beneath that handsome exterior lurked a mischievous scoundrel. And he proved it in the next second.

"You could show me *your* 'sweet ass,' with or without a platter."

This time she did growl her outrage, after which he held up his hands, his smile intact, and led her to his office where he left her in peace to change.

The dinner party was being held at the Dusty Rose, in a private room so far removed from the bar area that not a single catcall or holler could be heard. Persephone had craned her neck to peer inside the barroom when they passed, fascinated despite herself. She had never seen it when it was being used. The room with all its wood and brass was transformed by the hordes of men who had arrived, and by the girls, including Lola and May, who moved among them with welcoming smiles.

Part of Persephone was incensed. The other part, the part that she was fearful was taking over, longed to enter, toss back a drink, and kick her heels up. A heated blush seared her cheeks. Good Lord, what would her family think of her now. But then she smiled at the thought that her father and grandmother would probably join her. She suspected even C.J. and her sister-in-law Meredith might join her. Venus, too. How different her family was from the rigid New York society that didn't allow straightforward conversation much less straightforward actions such as drinking and dancing in a saloon.

"Miss Daltry," Harold stated in a tone that was half gentleman, half scoundrel, from where he stood in the corner talking to Velda. "Good to see you again, doll."

For some reason, Persy nearly laughed out loud. Doll. He had called her doll. He was all scoundrel. Someone straight out of the darker side of life. Perfect company for the likes of Jake Devlin.

She glanced around. Certainly the dining room was expensively decorated, but it couldn't compare to the opulence of the last dining room in which she had attended a dinner party. They both had crystal chandeliers, with imported oriental rugs, and even fine china. But in this dining room, in the farthestmost recesses of the Dusty Rose, the chandelier was gaudier, the wallpaper more heavily laden with brighter colors and bigger designs, and the china was new, not handed down from generation to generation. And certainly there had been no one who called her doll at the Weathersleys' gathering. But crazily enough she liked it. She felt free and alive. People weren't watching her every move, nor were they listening to every word she uttered, as if waiting, hoping, she thought suddenly, for one false move. Her cherished New York society somehow seemed more tarnished in comparison to this gathering in Jake Devlin's tawdry saloon. And that was odd indeed.

"Hello, Mr. Harvey," she replied.

"Call me Harold. Everybody does."

"All right then. Harold."

"Besides, we're going to be as good as family soon. What with you marrying Jake."

Persy blushed.

"Ahhhh," Velda said, her tone much too sweet, no smile in sight. "A blushing bride."

"Miss Harvey," Persy responded with a nod of recognition.

"Why don't we all have a seat," Jake said quickly, stepping forward.

Mr. Bills was in attendance as was Howie, both looking dapper in cutaway coats with silk lapels, wing collars, and ascot ties. It was a peculiar, but somehow endearing sight to see these two dissimilar men dressed so similarly. Howie looked extremely uncomfortable. Persy had the sudden urge to reach out and tell him he looked just fine. But of course she didn't.

But thoughts of decor and concerns for Howie fled when Jake casually draped his arm around Persy's shoulder. The casualness was belied, however, by the tension she could actually feel shimmering through his body. Yet again she wondered what game he was playing with this man and his daughter. Was it some intricate con? she wondered. A scandal? What?

But those thoughts were rapidly replaced by the feel of his strong arm around her. His taut muscles. His massive shoulders. And the smell of wild prairies and clear skies, though she was surprised she even remembered what a wild prairie or clear sky smelled like for as long as she had been away from home. Though it hadn't truly been all that long, she realized. It was just that when faced with nothing more than buildings taller than she could ever imagine, and roads filled with more carriages and pedestrians than she knew existed, and the need to travel beyond Fifty-ninth Street to find any significant open space, the memory had dimmed all the faster.

As the evening progressed, Mr. Bills was either talking to or watching Velda, she noticed. Persy got the distinct impression that he was interested in the woman. Even though Persy had no idea how the behemoth woman and wiry little man could ever come together, she thought it would do them both good if they did. Hmmm, she thought silently. Perhaps there was some matchmaking to be done here. Despite the fact that Velda had been less than cordial to her and had gone so far as to disparage her in public—mousy indeed—Persy's only thoughts were of the possibility of making two people happy. Some would have called her a fool; others, however, would have called her nice, sweet, kind, and caring. And she felt a tiny bit of relief that maybe she wasn't beyond redemption.

Soon servants were circling the table with dishes of food that everyone exclaimed over, and which Persy had slaved over earlier. For their special dinner, Jake hadn't wanted the plain fare that he served the regular customers. He wanted Cornish game hens, he had told her. Persy had smiled at him and said, "So you liked them after all."

"Not on your life," he had replied, "but it's just the kind of silly nonsense Harold Harvey would like." After that he had cast her one of his most devilish smiles and left her to cook.

Talk was lively, and nothing, it would seem, was off-limits, no topic too outrageous, no laughter too loud. For the first time since she had arrived in the big city, she experienced an evening that was reminiscent of home. Joking, laughing, storytelling. So unlike her meals at her aunt and uncle's home. She hadn't realized how much she had missed it.

Conversation flowed freely, turning something she had dreaded into an enjoyable event. Even Velda, whose attention was monopolized by Mr. Bills, rarely turned her acerbic tongue in Persy's direction. Persy began to relax for the first time in weeks, and when Harold poured her more wine, filling the crystal goblet much too full, she hardly noticed. She was animated and she simply drank.

She talked to Howie and Harold. Even Jake regaled the group with lively anecdotes of saloon life. But then Velda glanced over at Jake and with a sly smile that should have warned them said, "You've certainly come a long way from the gutters, Jake darling."

The laughter and stories trailed off as silence fell over the table. Jake visibly tensed. But then he forced a smile. "Yes, Velda, I certainly have."

"You know, I haven't heard you thank my father recently."

"Velda!"

"What, Daddy?" she snapped.

"No, she's right, Harold." Jake stood up and raised his glass of wine. "This is a perfect evening to toast the man whom I owe a world of debt."

"Though not enough to marry his daughter!"

"Velda!" her father said again.

Persy looked on, stunned. Suddenly it all began to make sense. She remembered thinking on that first day they met, that deep down Jake was vulnerable. Now she knew she had been correct, and she also knew why. Jake had pulled himself up from the gutter by the bootstraps with the help of Harold Harvey. No wonder Jake had such a difficult time avoiding Velda's clutches. No wonder he had mixed Persy up in his ruse. He wasn't trying to pull anything over, or take advantage of anyone as she had first suspected. He was indebted to this man and felt an obligation to marry his daughter on the one hand, and couldn't stand the woman on the other. He was simply trying to get out of a bad situation and hurting as few people in the process as possible.

Amazingly, for the first time, she wondered where he had come from, what had brought him to this point. Where was this gutter Velda referred to? She realized she didn't even know how old he was! Suddenly she wanted to know his middle name, his mother's name, his father's name, and if he had any siblings. She wanted to know everything about him.

She took another sip of wine. She felt so good, so at ease, so happy. She didn't care about shoulds or should nots. Suddenly she wanted Jake to kiss her, as he had before. She wanted him to wrap her in his arms, hold her tight, press her to his heart.

She glanced at him, conversation swirling all around, encapsulating her in her private dreams. She became all too aware of him—his profile so perfect, so handsome, and now seemingly so engrossed in the laughter that had thankfully returned. His fingers were long and strong, ever so lightly clutching the stem of his wineglass. His hands looked hard with muscles and bones, not plump and fleshy like so many men's hands.

It wasn't until her eyes traveled up from his hands to his shoulders, then to his face, that she realized he was watching her. But instead of blushing red or cursing herself, she found she could only smile, bringing that devilish smile that normally made her scowl in answer.

He leaned over and touched her fingers. "Are you enjoying yourself?"

The deep melody of his voice washed over her and she nearly closed her eyes and moaned her pleasure. Instead, she took another long, slow sip of wine.

"Careful, love, you'd best go slow with that."

Persephone giggled. "No need to worry, monsieur," she said with a slow French accent. "A little wine never hurt anyone."

Jake raised an eyebrow. "A little, no; a lot, yes."

And then she giggled again, louder, and everyone around the table stopped to listen. Jake quickly said, "You see, she even laughs at my jokes. The perfect wife, don't you think?"

The men laughed. Velda glared. But Persy didn't care.

It was nearly ten-thirty when the Harveys finally left. Howie and Mr. Bills disappeared. And Persy felt like she could sit in her chair and float forever. Her mind wandered. Her heart pounded slowly. Her legs tingled. She didn't give much thought to anything but how nice she felt. The worries that had plagued her since ruining her debut dress had magically disappeared. For the first time since that dreadful day, she was actually enjoying herself. And she had Jake to thank for that.

"What are you looking at?" he asked from the doorway where he had said good-bye to his guests.

Persy smiled. "Kiss me, Jake."

She never would have known that her words surprised him had she not learned to recognize that sudden darkening of his eyes. But then it was gone and he merely shook his head. "You're drunk, Persephone."

She tried to look abashed but she laughed out loud instead. "I'm not drunk! And even if I were, which I'm not, I would still want you to kiss me."

He walked over next to her and pulled out a chair. He sighed as he sat down. "Persy, Persy, Persy."

She sucked in her breath. "That's what my family calls me." She exhaled sharply and closed her eyes in pleasure. "It sounds nice the way you say it, though."

"Your family?"

Without realizing it, Persephone leaned toward him. "Yes, my family. Minerva, Odysseus, Hercules, Atalanta, Venus, Cupid, Atlas . . ."

"You're making this up."

"No, it's all true."

"Next, you'll be telling me you live on Mount Olympus."

This brought about another round of giggles. "We do. And Mount Olympus is in Paradise."

"Hell! You're drunker than I thought." He looked at her closely. "And you, the mother of an infant."

"Ah yes, an infant." She giggled. "Albert."

"I thought you said it was Alberta," he said, his eyebrow raised.

Persy thought for a moment, then giggled again. "I thought we'd already been through this before. Albert, Alberta, I still want you to kiss me."

And when he didn't make any attempt to comply, she simply leaned forward and pressed her lips to his.

At first he resisted. Through the cloud of wine and desire she felt his body stiffen. But just when her mind began to clear and she thought he would push her away, his body seemed to melt, and he molded her slight form to his.

She felt as much as heard the groan that rumbled deep in his chest. He wanted to kiss her as much as she wanted him to, she realized. Relief and satisfaction swept through her, and she pressed closer still.

He brought his hands up and gently held her face. He looked deep into her eyes, captivating her with his very intensity. Slowly, having no will or desire to resist, she touched his hand. His fingers, under hers, lingered on her skin. Persy swallowed, her pulse beating wildly in her throat, making it hard to breathe. With infinite care his fingers trailed back into her hair, freeing the tresses to tumble down her back.

"Persy," he groaned as his lips traveled over the smooth contours of her face, from her eyelids to her cheeks, ending once again at her mouth. His tongue caressed her lips, gently parting them to taste the sweetness within.

She reeled with unimagined sensations at the touch of tongue on tongue, so intimate. Hesitantly she flicked his tongue with her own, relishing the feel, reveling in the wondrous emotions that flooded her body. Her moan seemed to please him, and his kiss became a demand, heated, unyielding. His tongue became insistent, pulsating with rhythm. His hands traversed her back, and then down to her hips, cupping, molding.

Her hands traveled a path of their own. And she whispered his name against his neck. "Jake."

But with the utterance of his name, everything came to a careening halt. She felt it. It was as if she had screamed stop. The reaction was the same, for Jake did just that. He froze, their bodies still pressed together, his breathing ragged, mixing with hers, but he did not move a muscle.

"Jake?" she repeated, this time confused, wondering what had brought their heady flight to an end.

He didn't respond, but she could feel him start to ease away from her.

"Don't," she whispered, clasping his face between her palms. "Please don't stop."

But then she realized what she was saying, what she was doing—how she was acting. Reality rushed in to the empty void where desire had fled. She jerked as if she had been slapped. Her brow furrowed. Breathlessly they pulled back as reason set in. They gazed into each other's eyes, each a bit startled, uncomfortably aware that what had just happened should never have taken place.

"Don't look at me like that," he said.

"Like what?"

"Like I've wounded a small defenseless animal."

She tried to turn away. "I'm so ashamed. What you must think of me?"

He reached out and gently turned her back. "I think that a beautiful, wonderful woman wants me as much as I want her. But that woman has had too much to drink. I won't do this while you're drunk." He smiled into her eyes. "But that doesn't mean I didn't want to."

His admission wiped away her mortification, making her spirits soar. She hadn't been wrong. "So honorable, Mr. Devlin?"

"Have you ever doubted?" His dark brow raised in question.

"More than doubted." Her good humor made her

tongue bold and careless. "I was quite certain you were not."

But her humor was not well received and she desperately wished she could take back her thoughtless words. She grew quiet at the look that surfaced in his eyes, wishful and full of pain, eyes that had seen too much and only longed for simple things.

"That's not entirely true," she added hastily. Her words were breathless, impassioned. "In fact, if I am to be honest, I must say that I've wondered quite often if you aren't more than you appear."

His gaze intensified and she had the feeling that he looked at her with his deep green eyes as if he could penetrate to some truth. But he obviously had no interest in pursuing the issue of *his* honor. Instead, he asked, "Honest, *Mrs.* Daltry?"

It took a moment for her to comprehend what he was implying, but when it finally sank in she blushed. And then she got angry—with him, with herself, with the whole situation. How foolish she was to care who this man was, as if any of it would make a difference. She had come here to lead the sophisticated life. That is what she wanted! She did! And why wasn't it working as she had planned? And then she got even angrier—angry with the situation, angry that the people whom she had come to New York to see seemed shallow and undesirable compared to this man. "How is it possible that you, a dissolute saloon owner, exhibits more honor and interest than . . ." Her words trailed off. She felt angry and sad all at once, and confused as well.

"More honor than who, Persy?" He stared at her hard, his voice deep and unrelenting, as if she had no choice but to answer.

She jerked away but he caught her arm and held her in a grip of iron.

"Who, Persy?"

"None of your business, Mr. Devlin."

He pulled her so close that she felt his brandy-laced breath against her face. "You made it my business when you came into my kitchen and lied to me."

She tried to escape again, her face red, not with embarrassment but with anger. "Don't talk to me about lying, Mr. Devlin. You're in no position to cast stones."

Clearly this surprised him, for his grip loosened and she stepped free.

"When did I lie?"

"To Harold Harvey."

"What I said to Harold about our engagement was . . . necessary," he said like an incensed preacher.

"Did it ever occur to you that what I have done, I also did because it was necessary?" She hated the fact that a silly dress was what had made her plight necessary.

But her statement had gained its effect. He ran his hand through his hair as he leaned back against the table, looking as confused as she felt. "No, I hadn't considered that." He shook his head, then looked her in the eye. "And I won't ask you what your problem is. But maybe, just maybe, with time, you'll let me know. Perhaps I could help."

Just like her family would. Just like her friends in Paradise would. Just like people who cared about her would.

Shame washed over her. "I can't tell you," she whispered, turning away.

He turned her around until she faced him. "I can appreciate that, Persy. But just remember," he said as he looked at her for a moment before a gentle smile curved on his lips, "I'm here if you need me. All right?"

How kind he was. Caring. Thinking only of her. Yet again, she saw a glimpse of what it was about this man that made May and Lola so loyal to him. "All right."

And then he leaned down and pressed her forehead with a kiss. "Come on, I'll take you home."

Well, whether she was chastised, full of shame, or simply devastated before, every emotion fled in the face of his last words. *I'll take you home.* Good Lord, that was impossible!

Persy realized belatedly that she hadn't thought much past getting to the saloon. The thought that she had to get herself home, without the help of Jake, went far in sobering her up. She nearly snorted out loud at the look she knew would freeze on his face if she directed him to her aunt and uncle's luxurious home. Shock. Disbelief. And finally, inevitably, anger.

"No need to take me anywhere." She forced a smile. "I'm perfectly capable of getting myself home."

He was halfway to the door. He stopped and turned back. "Not at this hour, you don't."

"Jake, really—"

"Forget it, Persy. I'm taking you home." He started toward the door. "Wait here. I'll get the carriage."

Not until she heard his footsteps fade away down the hall did she move, and when she did, she moved so quickly that she didn't have time to think about possible dangers of the night. The dangers of allowing Jake Devlin to take her home far outweighed the dangers outside.

She slipped out into the darkness on Prince Street, and it wasn't until she was safely home, having thankfully hailed a hansom right off the street, snuck into her bed with no one seemingly the wiser, that she realized that when she had sought Jake Devlin's kiss, she had acted no better than her cousin had with Thomas Weathersley.

Good Lord, what was happening to her? Who was she, she wondered.

The Persephone Daltry of Paradise Plains, Texas, seemed to have disappeared altogether, replaced with someone who not only she didn't recognize, but who she didn't particularly like, either.

She buried her face in her pillow and groaned her distress.

Thirteen

"WHAT THE HELL DO YOU THINK YOU WERE DOING LAST night?!"

Persy's heart leapt into her throat as she came through the swinging door to the Dusty Rose kitchen. Jake stood waiting for her, and based on the time, two forty-five in the afternoon, he probably had been waiting for some time.

She completely forgot, for the moment, that she was trying to think of something she could cook for one hundred and fifty men that could be prepared quickly. She doubted the hotel could have had another cancellation at the last minute, providing her with another nearly prepared meal. Hungarian goulash had been all she had come up with just before pushing through the door.

"I don't know what you're talking about," she said, starting past him as she pulled her bonnet from her head.

"Like hell you don't!"

Persephone stilled and gave him a look that was meant to admonish. "Really, Mr. Devlin, I'll thank you once again not to use profanity in my presence."

He made a noise that sounded suspiciously like a growl as he crossed his arms and leaned back against the counter. And she could tell from the look in *his* eyes that she was in trouble.

"*Mr. Devlin,* is it?" he said, his voice laced with sarcasm. She cringed.

"Last night as I recall it was—"

"Don't, Jake, this is beneath you."

He stood very still for a moment before he pressed his eyes closed. And he sighed. "Not necessarily, Persy, not necessarily."

Her heart broke and she wasn't even sure why. She forgot about cooking, or that she had just been to a luncheon that was boring at best, downright catatonic at worst. The grandfather clock that had stood against a wall in the hallway off the dining room where the small gathering had taken place had announced each half hour that passed. Eleven-thirty, twelve o'clock, twelve-thirty. At one o'clock the group had barely started their soup. Persephone's stomach had begun to twist into knots, and not merely because the soup was about as edible as sea water. And when the clock tolled two-thirty and dessert had yet to be served, she had feigned illness and fled the opulent confines of the palatial dining room of the president of the Women's League. But she didn't care about possible consequences of fleeing such an influential home. She had to get to the Dusty Rose—and Jake Devlin, a tiny voice added in her head.

Jake Devlin. She focused on his countenance as he stood before her. She was reminded yet again of the first day she saw him, his gaze filled with longing. Without thinking, she reached up and carefully touched his cheek. "Why do I think you're much too hard on yourself?"

His body visibly tensed. "Because you're much too nice and sweet for your own good."

She dropped her hand away and laughed. His words were like water to a thirsty woman.

His brow creased. "And don't think I've forgotten that you ran out of here last night without letting me take you home." His tone grew fierce. "It was stupid. Pure stupidity. You could have been killed or worse."

Her smile widened. "I didn't realize there were fates worse than death," she said with a laugh.

"You obviously haven't lived in New York long," he responded.

Persephone had to stop herself from sucking in her breath. Did he suspect? She could only pray he didn't, and surge ahead, changing the subject. "So, what do you want for dinner tonight? I was thinking of Hungarian goulash."

She nearly sighed her relief when he merely grimaced and said, "What the hell is Hungarian goulash?"

"It's really very good," she offered hopefully. She bit her tongue to keep from telling him it was one of a handful of entrees that could be whipped up in less than an hour. And despite the fact that she had arrived late, she had to leave early to attend the opera that evening. How exactly she was going to explain her sudden return to good health to the president of the Women's League she was not altogether certain. But explain she would for Persy was not about to miss her first opera.

Jake pushed away from the counter and took a step toward her, startling Persy from her thoughts. Her delicate brows furrowed when a smile curled on his lips and he took yet another step forward. She had thought she was in trouble before. The look on his face told her that her troubles had only just begun.

"What are you doing, Jake?"

"I've decided on something else that would be good for dinner." His eyes ran the length of her. "Better than that Hungarian goop you were talking about."

Alarm swept over her, but she forced a smile. "Hungarian goulash. And if that doesn't sound so good, well fine. How about—"

He took a step forward, cutting off her words. She took a step back.

"I've just decided to have it early," he said.

There was laughter and teasing in his voice, but when he took yet another step forward, she took yet another step back, only to run into the counter on the opposite side of the kitchen. She knew he was serious. "Mr. Devlin, really. What are you doing?" she asked, trying to keep her voice from quavering.

"I'm going to kiss you."

"I thought you were going to tell me what you wanted for dinner?"

"I just have," he said, his voice as deep as a well in Texas.

"Mr. Devlin, really!"

"It's Jake, remember. Or at least it was last night. And last night you asked me to kiss you."

"And you did! It was plenty, thank you very much."

"That little peck wasn't anything, Mrs. Daltry. Like I said, I had no intention of kissing you when there was a possibility you . . . wouldn't remember."

Jake's laughter filled the room, warm and fun, wrapping around her, making her feel funny inside. Making her want his kiss. "Not to worry yourself, truly. I remember your kiss quite well enough, thank you." Too well, she added silently to herself. "No need to bother yourself on my account." The hardwood counter pressed into the small of her back.

"Well, *I* don't remember well enough."

She tried to dart away, but his arms came down on either side of her and gripped the counter, effectively cutting off all escape. She smiled a nervous smile, but despite herself her eyes drifted to his lips—the lips that had kissed her last night in a way that not only did she remember but that she doubted she would ever forget. "Oh, dear. It's getting rather late. We really should be thinking about dinner." She tried to concentrate. "You know, food."

"I would like to concentrate—on the feel of my lips on your forehead." He leaned forward and kissed her just there.

"Mr. Devlin," she tried to warn, though it was more like a sigh. "What about all those men who will be here in a matter of hours, expecting to eat their fill?"

"What men?" he teased softly.

"The men who need all their energies, remember?"

"I'd rather feel your cheeks . . ." His lips traveled lower.

"Dinner!" she announced. "Would you like pork chops?" she asked, unable to think straight.

"Or your chin."

Persephone closed her eyes and leaned back harder against the counter. "Maybe roast beef."

"Or your ear."

"Ahhh."

He chuckled.

"I mean . . . I mean . . . Ah ha! You want fish."

"Inventive, my love."

"Inspired, actually."

And they both laughed.

"But this," he said, kissing the sensitive skin behind her ear, "is more inspiring. And I know you like it."

"I do not!"

His tongue traced the shell of her ear and she gasped. "I don't like it one bit!" She told herself she needed to jerk free and run as fast and far away as she possibly could.

He only chuckled, then pressed his lips to hers.

The minute she felt his touch, not only did she lose the will to flee, but she lost the thought that she should do it at all. No thoughts of pork chops or roasted beef filled her mind. Hungarian goulash was long forgotten. Only thoughts of the sweet feeling that coursed down her spine and pulsed in her body were left to be considered. "Oh, Jake," she murmured as her hands came up of their own volition, her fingertips just barely touching his arms.

"Yes, love, touch me."

"Yes, love, touch me! Damnation, what's going on in here?"

The words sounded in Persy's head like an explosion. She heard Jake growl but he didn't let her go. She squirmed frantically to escape. And when finally she managed to duck beneath his arms and slip free, she found Lola standing in the door.

"Lola! Oh, dear," she cried, her hand coming self-consciously to her hair. "It's not what you think."

Lola laughed. "Now, Persy honey, I wasn't thinking a thing. You're engaged, after all." She laughed even harder.

Persy blushed. She was both relieved and disappointed that their encounter against the counter had ended. No, she quickly admonished herself, she was only relieved!

Jake turned an ominous stare on Lola whose laughter died in a cough.

"I hope you have a good reason for interrupting, Lola."

"She wasn't interrupting anything, really. There was nothing to interrupt," Persy said, turning around, trying to look busy. But of course, the counter was bare. She hadn't even taken off her coat, let alone made it to the pantry. Not even a pad of paper or leaded pencil was there to make out her list.

Lola looked back and forth between Jake and Persy. "We're practicing a new dance and wanted you to come and watch, Jake."

Persy twirled around without thinking. "A new dance?"

"Yeah, the cancan. At least it's new for us."

"No!" Persy cried excitedly.

"Yes!" Lola responded as if she were talking to an excited schoolchild. "Come on. You can watch, too."

Persy started to follow, but then stopped. "Oh, no, I can't. I haven't even started the meal. And what are you doing practicing when you should be in here with me? And where's May, anyway?"

"I told them practicing was more important," Jake supplied. "I was going to help you today. That's why I was here in the first place."

Persy snorted. "You were here to irritate and harass me."

"Me?" he asked with feigned innocence. "Never."

When she started to protest, he reached out and took her hand. "We're wasting time. Come on. We'll cook later," Jake offered.

The barroom was lively with dancers, though there wasn't a patron in sight. Herbie, the piano player, whom Persy had never met, played the brand-new upright in the corner. Lola ran up onto the small stage that was just to the right side of the bar and joined the line of women. May was the tallest and stood in the middle. Lola squeezed in beside her.

The music was lively and the dancing gay. Persy had a nearly irrepressible urge to join the women and kick up her heels. Short of doing something clearly so inappropriate, she tapped her black-booted foot in time to the melody. The music filled her mind, the dancing her senses, and she thought of nothing more than the freedom this improper dance made her feel. They certainly wouldn't be dancing like this at her debut. She laughed her delight at the very idea.

But her delight was quickly dashed when Velda entered through the front door. Persy's attention was diverted, however, by the sound of somebody stumbling down the stairs. She turned, as did everyone else, the music stopping in mid-stanza, the dance halting in mid-kick, to find

Mr. Bills catching himself on the banister, righting himself, straightening his attire, then casting a glowing smile on Velda. Velda snorted but preened just the same.

Next, Lilly Norman entered. This time it was Jake's good cheer that was vanquished. And not long after that, Harold Harvey pushed through the door. It was then that Persy remembered her conclusion earlier about performing a little matchmaking between Velda and Mr. Bills.

"Mr. Bills," she said, before she could think better of it, "why don't you help Miss Velda with her coat."

Mr. Bills looked first shocked, then inspired. "Of course. Here, let me help you."

Velda slapped at his hands. "I don't need your help, you little jolt."

Mr. Bills's smile hardened. "You have the manners of a pig come to trough! Now give me your coat!"

Persy groaned. So much for matchmaking, she thought. Thankfully Harold was busy talking to Lilly Norman and either didn't hear what Mr. Bills said to Velda or pretended not to. And then to Persy's surprise and, from the looks of it, Mr. Bills's surprise as well, Velda turned so he could assist her with her wrap.

Herbie burst into a new round of music. Then suddenly everyone was dancing. The girls on the stage. Mr. Bills and Velda. Harvey and Lilly. Jake and Persy.

Everything was forgotten. Persy simply lost herself to the feel of dancing and being held in this man's arms.

But then the dancing and music were interrupted yet again when the door banged open, a burst of cold winter air rushing into the room.

"Devlin! Where are you?"

Everyone turned and stared. At the sight that met her eyes, Persy thought her heart had up and stopped on her. Caput! Finee. She was done for.

"Over here." Jake's voice cut through the sudden unexpected silence. "What do you want?"

Just before Persy twirled around and stuck her head in the nearest potted palm, she saw the look on Jake's face that told of the dangerous man, the man who had dragged himself up from the gutter to make something of himself. A man she would never want to tangle with. Just then, however, she wasn't worried about tangling with Jake, her only concern was how to get out of the barroom and into the kitchen without being noticed.

When she had thought that her aunt and uncle's friends would not patronize such a place she had been wrong. For not only was one of their friends here, but it was Thomas Weathersley—a man with a direct connection to a member of her family who was already suspicious and would love to hear of such goings-on.

"Your giant here," Thomas sneered, pointing to Howie who had materialized behind him, "is harassing me. Call him off!"

Thankfully Thomas hadn't recognized her, or hadn't seen her more than likely. She was safe. At least for the moment. Part of her would have liked to stay around and find out what was going on. But the other part, the part that she so rarely listened to these days, demanded she flee with all due haste.

Without warning, she thought about the freedom she had felt earlier. It had been nothing more than perceived freedom—a false freedom. It was only an illusion. Thomas Weathersley standing in the middle of the Dusty Rose was proof enough of that.

Persy was no freer in New York City than she was in Paradise Plains, Texas. Only, in Paradise, she was surrounded by people who loved and cherished her. With a start, as she glanced surreptitiously around her, she realized that here, in the Dusty Rose, she was surrounded by people who loved her. She glanced at Jake. At least, she amended, in some strange way cared for her.

"He's not harassing you, Weathersley," Jake said. "He's simply collecting on a loan past due—well past due."

Thomas's face suffused with red, his eyes bulged, and one telltale vein bulged on his forehead. "Damn you, Devlin! I told you I'd pay."

Jake moved slowly forward, his outward demeanor calm and in control. But even from a distance Persy could make out the tightening in his jaw. She knew instinctively that Jake Devlin didn't like Thomas Weathersley one bit. At least there was something they agreed upon.

"Yes, you did tell me you'd pay. But that was last week. Time's up."

"You, bas—"

Jake took another step forward, this one clearly menacing, and Thomas's words cut off. "Damn you, Devlin. You aren't anyone. You're a nobody! I'm Thomas Weathersley. That should count for something."

"That only gives you more reason to pay your debts on time so no one else has to hear that you owe money to a . . . lowly person like me. Gambling debts at the Dusty Rose, I doubt, are the kind of expenditures dear Mama and Papa want to hear about."

This time she thought Thomas would strike out. She had turned completely around to stare, forgetting about needing to flee or possible recognition. The muscles in Thomas's face worked, his features strained. But he seemed to take notice of Howie on one side of him, Mr. Bills on the other, not to mention the dark towering form of Jake directly before him.

"I'll get the money," he spat.

"That's what you said last time."

Jake's voice was so cold and hard that a chill ran down Persy's spine. But she realized suddenly that everyone was preoccupied with the scene that was playing itself out. It was time to make her escape when no one would notice.

As quietly as she could she turned to slip out of the bar-room.

Jake stilled. His thoughts shifted. It was more that he sensed something than he had heard anything. He cast a quick glance to his right. And there he caught sight of Persy casting a quick, surreptitious glance at Thomas Weathersley before she slipped out the door. Something in him tightened. His jaw clenched. His hand fisted.

"Are you listening to me?" Thomas demanded.

Slowly Jake met his glance. "I'm listening. But are you? I'm not a patient man."

"Tonight, damn it. I'll have it tonight."

"You'd be wise to follow through. As I said, I'm not a patient man when it comes to money owed me."

"You'll get your money. Then I'm going to take my business elsewhere. Over to Mel's, in fact. He has rooms upstairs where a man can take a woman without question."

"I'm sure Mel will be more than happy to acquire your business, Mr. Weathersley. Now if you'll excuse me, I have things to attend to."

Grumbling, Thomas slammed back out the door. A quiet murmur of voices drifted through the room. Jake didn't move, only stared at the door. Thomas Weathersley and Persephone Daltry, he wondered. Is that what she has been hiding all this time? He knew that the man was particularly fond of ruining virgins. The thought made his insides churn with fury. He knew that Thomas Weathersley promised to marry them, then take them away. To the good life. He had bragged about it in the saloon often enough. That was one of the many reasons Jake could barely stomach the man. He would be more than happy if Weathersley stayed away. But he wouldn't. Jake's liquor was too fine, and his dancing girls too beautiful. It was only after men left the Dusty Rose that they could stomach a place like Mel's, when fine liquor had dulled their senses, making the filth of Mel's not so noticeable and the girls not so difficult to look at. He turned away from his thoughts in disgust.

The strange tightness intensified.

"Jake."

He turned around with a start and snapped, "What?"

Lola straightened at his harsh tone and he cursed himself for letting a man like Weathersley get to him. "I'm sorry, Lola. What do you need?"

"Are you all right?" she asked softly.

He noticed for the first time that everyone stood quietly with looks of concern on their faces. He forced a smile. "Of course, I'm fine. You know how much I hate scum like Weathersley. That's all. Now if you'll excuse me, I have things to do."

He strode stiffly from the room and went to his office. Leaning back against the carved colonnade, he pulled a cheroot from his pocket. With a minimum of ceremony Jake lit the cigar and pulled slowly at the smoke. He couldn't think clearly as feelings he didn't understand filled him.

He had determined that if Persy had given herself to a man, which he doubted, she hadn't given herself freely. And now, with Thomas Weathersley here, and Persy seeming to know him and trying to avoid him, Jake felt a sickening dread wash over him.

Was it possible that Persy had fallen for Thomas Weathersley, and now was forced to work to support a child of his making? Had Weathersley lured this working girl in with his empty promises of love and devotion, only to toss her aside once he had attained what he desired?

The thought filled him with sadness and fury. Sadness for Persy, and fury for Weathersley. But then he remembered her inability to even remember the child's name, and her innocent attempts at kissing. A second sense that had guided him through the streets reaffirmed that Persy had never been ruined by Thomas Weathersley or anyone else.

Relief washed over him. Not because he would have felt anything less for Persy if tragedy had struck, but because he would have hated for something like that to have happened to her. But why, he suddenly wondered, did he care so much?

He knew he wanted her—physically. He had known that practically from the start. But that was all he wanted, he had told himself over and over again. There was no place in his life for someone like Persephone Daltry, with or without a child. And she had made it perfectly clear how she felt about the saloon. It was only a matter of days before their bargain was done and she was out of his life forever. And he had no other life than that which he had established in a saloon to offer her. There was no way they could be together even if he wanted it. Which he didn't, he told himself firmly. He didn't even particularly like the kind of woman she was. Prudish. Opinionated. Bossy, even. He wouldn't have hired her had he been in charge of the interview even if they had been desperate for a cook.

But somehow she had managed to worm her way into his consciousness, filling his senses with the sound of her laughter, filling his mind with the look in her eyes taking in sights that he was certain she had never seen before, as if she had never been to New York.

As if she had never been to New York.

The thought resonated in his mind. He remembered her reaction earlier after he had said a fate worse than death and then added that she obviously hadn't been in New York very long. At the time he had said it more in jest than anything else. But suddenly it all came clear to him. She wasn't from New York City as she had said, or even New York State. For reasons he didn't understand, he felt certain that Persephone Daltry found herself in

New York and unexpectedly in need of money. And he knew as well as anyone how hard respectable employment was to come by. If only she would confide in him he could help her.

And of course that was all he wanted to do. Help her. Nothing more. Just like he would help a stray pup. Just like he would give a starving man a meal or a beggar a coin. Yes, he reassured himself to lessen the sudden unease that overcame him, he wanted nothing more than to help his fellow man.

But Persephone Daltry was no man, his mind inserted, no man at all. In fact, she was a beautiful woman with curves that would make a lesser man weep with joy. But he was not a lesser man, he quickly added to his mental conversation. In this world he couldn't afford to be.

Fourteen

PERSY BEGAN IN EARNEST TO COUNT THE DAYS UNTIL HER DEBUT, not because she was so excited about the party any longer, but because, as of that night, she would finally have washed her hands of Jake Devlin and his tawdry saloon once and for all. And that, she told herself firmly, was what she wanted. She would have her money, her dress, and she'd never have to set foot in the Dusty Rose again.

She held down the disappointment that tried to surge forth and overwhelm her at the thought, just as she had been doing for the last three weeks since the fraudulent betrothal party. She couldn't do it much longer. She couldn't hold back the strange feelings much longer, and she knew it.

Truly, Jake Devlin made her feel things he had no business making her feel, and it had to stop. Her defenses were weakening, as had already been seen when she had asked him—goodness gracious tell her it wasn't so—to kiss her. So she had begun avoiding him whenever possible, though tangled up in a fake engagement as they were, it wasn't so easy to do. It was clear to anyone with half a brain that Velda Harvey was just waiting for them to slip up.

And oddly enough, Jake seemed inclined to help Persy avoid him, at least most of the time. Generally he wasn't around more than the few minutes it took to bestow a chaste kiss on her forehead, but only whenever Velda or Harold was near. She had rarely laid eyes on the man except for a few heart-stopping times when she had turned from the stove to find him watching her.

"What are you doing?" she remembered snapping one of those times, disconcerted by the intensity she saw in his eyes.

"Just looking," he said softly, his brow creased.

"Well, look at someone else!"

With that he had sighed. "I wish I could," he said before pushing out through the swinging door.

Needless to say, it had been a difficult three weeks. Very difficult in Persy's mind. So when her last day of work finally arrived, with her debut the following night, she stood in the cavernous kitchen, her stomach churning with emotion.

She had finished the meal for the day, her last meal, she realized with those strange hollow feelings washing over her, and had given the new cook all the instructions the woman could need. She'd not leave the Dusty Rose in the chaotic fashion in which she had found it.

After one last look around, she wiped her hands on a linen towel, then pushed through the swinging door. Lola was waiting for her on the other side with a huge smile.

Persy stopped in her tracks, her heart feeling as if it were about to break. "You've come to say good-bye?" she said, trying to sound cheerful.

Lola laughed. "Yes, love, good-bye in a big way."

"What are you talking about?"

In answer, Lola took Persy's hand and pulled her down the hallway toward the barroom.

"I can't go in there! It's after five o'clock. Men . . . should be in there by now."

"Not a single one. Jake put off opening for an hour."

"He did?" she breathed, though why she was surprised she didn't know for she shouldn't have been. It was just like Jake to be so kind.

She allowed Lola to pull her into the high-ceilinged den of iniquity, but instead of thinking about sin and vice, she thought only of Jake Devlin and all the people around him whom she knew suddenly she would miss a great deal.

When Jake saw her, he smiled and started toward her. "I would have liked to throw you a huge going-away party—"

"Good thing you didn't," she interjected. "If I understand correctly, Velda and Harold don't leave until tomorrow. You're taking a chance as it is having any kind of a party. I'd hate to see all our hard work at being engaged fly right out the window if they walked in."

"Was it such hard work?" he asked her softly.

Persy grew uncomfortable, but she forced a laugh. "Very hard work, Mr. Devlin. Hard work, indeed."

"I'm sorry to hear that."

But he was given no opportunity to say more when the tiny gathering of people circled around and began talking all at once.

It was nearly an hour later when Jake motioned for Persy to follow him. When she looked at him, her countenance leery, he laughed and said, "You want your money, don't you?"

Her eyes widened with excitement, then she grimaced. "I'm not always . . . or let me say, I *haven't always* been so shallow."

Without warning he took her hands in his. "Who were you, Persy?" he asked, his tone intense. "Who were you before you came here, before you had to come here?"

Her gray eyes darkened with panic, and something else.

"I'm sorry," he said, dropping her hands. "It was foolish to ask. It's too late for an explanation now anyway."

And that, she realized, was the something else. It was too late, it was at an end, and she had never rectified her wrongs. She had come here as a liar and she would leave as one. The realization filled her with grave regret.

After he turned and continued on, she followed him to his study, then stood quite still as he went to his desk and pulled open the top drawer. Carefully, almost reluctantly, Persy thought, Jake held out a small velvet bag that jingled with coins.

"Here it is," he said without ceremony.

Persy stared at the pouch. A little over one hundred and fifty dollars. Enough to pay for the dress and then some. And her family, neither here nor back in Paradise, was any wiser. She should be ecstatic. Then why wasn't she, she wondered as her gaze drifted from the string-tied bag to the strong, surprisingly elegant fingers that held it.

The sun was fading, descending in the sky, casting the wood-and-leather-filled office in muted tones. Softer edges. Long rays of sun drifted through the mullioned windows, caressing Jake's cheeks like a lover. It was all she could do to keep her hands at her sides and not follow the sun's lead.

Pearl-white teeth tugged at her lower lip. She didn't move, couldn't move. Jake chuckled, though she had the fleeting suspicion that it was forced.

"After all your hard work, don't tell me you no longer want the money."

She hesitated. But then she took the few steps that separated them and she took the heavy bag. "It's not that I *want* the money, it's that I *need* it."

His lips settled into a hard line. "Why, Persy? Why can't you tell me? Or is it simply that you won't?"

"Oh, Jake," she said, the sound a sigh. "You wouldn't understand."

"Try me," he snapped impatiently.

The anger only shimmered in his eyes for a moment before he shifted irritably and the fathomless depths returned. His tone and sudden anger surprised her—bothered her. "Don't be angry, Jake. Please."

And then, unable to help herself, like the sunlight, she reached out and caressed his cheek. Her eyes closed and she felt as much as heard his groan. She wanted to sink against his massive chest, feel the heat of him, have it sear into her soul so she would never forget. She nearly wept out loud. As if she needed anything else to make her remember. No. As it was she knew it would take dying to ever forget him. And even then he would probably plague her in the afterlife.

The thought sobered her and she started to drop her hand away. But he caught it against his cheek, startling her. With infinite slowness, he turned his head until his lips brushed her palm. The touch was like fire and she sucked in her breath. He smelled of fine tobacco, brandy, and clean linen shirts. And she thought she could simply stand there forever, damning New York society, and be happy.

His hand left hers and went to her face. He tilted her chin until his deep green eyes met hers. He stared at her for an eternity and just when she thought he would do nothing more than look at her he spoke.

"Why is it that you couldn't have made my life easier by just making me desire you?"

His words confused her and made her heart hammer. "What do you mean?"

Jake chuckled, a deep sound that resonated with sadness. "Don't you know? Haven't you guessed?"

She knew she had no business pursuing this line of conversation, but she couldn't any more stop the words from tumbling from her lips than she could keep the ocean tide from the beach. "Guessed what?"

His smile fled and his gaze grew intense. "That I love you." He shook his head as if even he didn't understand. "Whoever you are, Persephone Daltry, wherever you came from, despite better judgment, I love you."

At first she didn't understand, or didn't want to understand. But unable to hold comprehension at bay for long, the words strung together in her mind, bringing meaning to the surface. She hated that his countenance flashed with pain when she gave no response. And she hated that she cared. She also hated that her life had gone so unexpectedly awry. He couldn't have her, just as she couldn't have him. In reality, the Persephone Daltrys of the world didn't damn New York society or any other.

She had the sudden urge to say no, scream no. No, I don't love you and you shouldn't love me. She felt she was losing everything. Jake, Lola and May, Mr. Bills and Howie. Even the life she had come here to lead, as it had certainly lost a good deal of its appeal. And she was no closer to learning what the purpose of her labor was now than when she had left Paradise Plains. The thought seeped into her mind that she did know, or at least that she should know. But it fled before she could put a name to it, bringing her frustration to a peak. And it was all Jake's fault, she blamed him unreasonably. She wanted to hurt him, felt the need to make his pain as intense as her own. But something stopped her just short of uttering the words—something that seemed suspiciously like panic at the thought of the consequences of such an utterance— consequences to him, but to her as well. And when the words were suppressed, pushed far back, very different feelings surged forth.

The sounds from the barroom and the calls from the street below faded in her mind. Thunder clapped in the distance with the force of an avenging God.

He loved her, he had said. Her. Persephone Daltry.

Loved by this devil man who alternately made her laugh, then shake her head in dismay.

Jake dropped his hand away. She knew she should run as fast as she could. But she didn't. She was finally free of this absurd entanglement. She had the money in her hand. She would pick up the dress tomorrow, attend the ball tomorrow night. She would officially enter New York society. She would be finished with the Dusty Rose once and for all, and be in a position to move forward in her life—finally she could start living. And then everything would be all right.

Then why did she feel like she were dying. Her heart ached and her mind swam with visions of emptiness. Did she love him? she suddenly wondered. The very idea hit her with the impact of a sledgehammer. She nearly staggered back from the force. Confusion wrapped around her like a spider's web until with determination she shook free.

Of course she didn't love him, she quickly reasoned. She couldn't! But still his admission of his love washed over her like a warm pool of water on a cold winter day.

She knew then what she would do. She could very easily live to regret the act, but she feared regretting not having done it more. Common sense told her to flee, that she was in need of finding safety in an unsafe world. Propriety bade that she do just that, but something else that she had no interest in putting a name to, stronger than propriety, made her stay. And before she could think better of it, or of the myriad possible repercussions, she spoke his name.

Their eyes met and held. They stood quietly. Staring. Until Persephone took his hand in hers.

"Love me, Jake Devlin."

She watched the emotions play across his face. Confusion. Amazement. Uncertainty.

And desire. She was sure.

She remembered their kisses. And if ever there was a

time when she could have turned back from this reckless and surely insane path, it was gone. She wanted him as much as he wanted her. For now, that was all that mattered.

"Don't play with me, Persephone."

She raised his hand to her lips. "I'm not. I want you to make love to me. Here. Now."

His voice was laced with anger. "You don't know what you're talking about."

His tone jolted her free of insanity like nothing else could. How presumptuous of her to think he wanted her, like she was some sort of expert. She blushed to the roots of her hair. Heat suffused her body. As suddenly as it had come over her that she wanted to be there, she wanted desperately to be gone. "I'm . . . I'm sorry to have . . . been so forward." She started to gather herself together to leave. "I'll be going now."

"Ah, Persy," he groaned. "Don't look at me like that."

"I don't know what you mean," she said stiffly before she turned away and headed for the door. But before she could escape the suddenly overwhelming confines of his office, he took the few steps that separated them and pulled her to him, her back to his chest.

"Don't leave like this. You surprised me is all. I'm sorry."

Her spine was stiff, unyielding.

"And I guess my pride was hurt," he added quietly. "I've never told a woman that I loved her before."

She squeezed her eyes shut.

He ran his hands up her arms to her shoulders with infinite care. "When I was a boy I used to dream about finding someone to love. As a man I had just about given up the dream . . . until I walked into the kitchen and found you."

"Jake—"

"Let me finish. Please."

She took a deep breath but remained silent.

"When I finally said the words . . . and received no response . . . like that little boy"—he shrugged his shoulders—"I was hurt, and I lashed out . . . foolishly. Just because I love you doesn't mean that you love me in return."

Slowly she turned in his arms to face him. "Dear God, I don't know what I feel," she whispered honestly. "But what I do know is that for reasons unknown, I love that you love me." Ever so gently, reverently, she took his hands and lightly kissed each strong finger.

"I'm afraid to say anything," he admitted, "and afraid to let go for fear that this is all a dream and words will wake me up."

She kissed the palm of his hand, much as she had earlier. "But you did speak and I'm still here."

She could feel a shiver run the length of his body before the tension lessened. And then words were no longer necessary, no longer desired.

He kissed her, long and slow, and this time the tension in her body melted away. The bag of money slipped from her grasp to lay forgotten on the thick oriental rug. She was acutely aware of him, the hard, sinewy muscles of his chest beneath her fingers. She gave in to the luxury of letting go. She forgot possible consequences altogether. She thought only of this man, who loved her, dear God. But she wouldn't think about that complication. At least not yet.

His strong arms circled her shoulders, and he leaned down to bury his face in her hair. Lightning flashed through the sky and thunder rolled through the heavens. The early evening light cast by the gas street lamps was darkened by the thick clouds and downpour of rain. Jake and Persy held on to each other, each a little afraid to speak, and despite Persy's words to the contrary, each a little afraid to let go for fear the moment would be washed away like winter-dried leaves in the rain.

At length, Jake pulled back. He clasped her chin and carefully forced her to look into his eyes. "I love you, Persy. And despite the fact that I don't know who you really are or where you came from, I want to spend the rest of my life with you. I want you to be my wife."

His words took her breath away. She didn't trust herself to speak, for the sudden fear that she would damn all else and say yes. Instead she reached up, her hand shaking, and pressed her palm to his cheek. "Oh, Jake, love me. Please love me."

His eyes darkened with what she suspected was pain, and he started to push away.

"Love me, please," she repeated, clasping his arms.

"Persy," he groaned, his voice tight and strangled, as if part demanding, part pleading.

Her hands skimmed up his arms to his shoulders. "Love me," she said one last time before with a desperate groan he gave in.

Gaslight washed the room golden as Jake swept Persy up into his arms and carried her up a set of stairs leading away from the office.

When they reached the room above, his bedroom, she thought fleetingly, he released his hold on her legs and slowly lowered her, though his other arm still held tight, held her close. Her body ran the length of him, pressed together, intimate.

He didn't kiss her as she expected, he only looked deep into her eyes, as if giving her one last chance to turn back. When she didn't, if possible, his brow furrowed still farther. "You give me a precious gift, Persephone."

Wanting badly to erase the pain from his face, she reached up on tiptoes and pulled him down to her. But he turned his cheek to her lips, then set her at arm's length.

Their eyes met and held. Mortification surged through her. She was wrong. He didn't want her. But when she started to pull away, he held her captive. Very gently, reverently, be began to work the fastening of her gown. She all but stopped breathing as her clothes fell in a puddle around her ankles.

"Beautiful," he whispered as he ran his hand down her arm, turning her slowly until she faced the mirror beside the bed.

This time their eyes met in the silvered frame.

"Beautiful," he repeated.

He ran his palm down her body, barely touching, hesitating at the sweet curve of her hips when she sucked in her breath, but only for a moment before his hand continued its path, downward, slowly, over her buttock, lower still until his fingertips grazed the tightly curling hairs between her legs.

"Jake!"

"Hush, love." He leaned down and pressed a kiss at the nape of her neck as he brushed her hair away. "Let me love you, just as you asked."

"But I didn't ask for—"

"Hush," he repeated. "Let me show you how wonderful love can be."

She caught her lower lip between her teeth. "I'm not sure. I thought . . . Well, you see . . ."

He chuckled. "If you don't let me ready you, I doubt you will enjoy lovemaking. The first time is always difficult for a woman."

The first time. The words registered in her mind. "It's not the—"

His body stilled. She could feel his tension return.

"Don't say it. Don't lie to me, Persephone. At least not tonight."

She pressed her eyes closed. "I'm sorry," she whispered.

And she was, sorry for so many things. But then she realized that there, in the muted light, held close by this devil man, with those seemingly simple words spoken, the truth was laid out before them at last. In some small measure she had made amends.

In essence she had told him she had no child. She was not a widow. Not even married. She held her breath, afraid that he would curse her and leave. Not until she opened her eyes and saw his shirt fall to the ground did she start to breathe again. If he was leaving, she thought crazily, he was leaving without his shirt.

Stepping away he cast his clothing aside until he stood behind her once again in nothing more than his trousers. The soft wool brushed her skin when he moved close. The sensations made her mind reel.

This time when his hand traveled over her body, his lips followed. Nip and suck, his teeth gently biting, his fingers lingering at her hips before they slipped lower once again. But unlike the first time when they only grazed her most intimate spot, this time they teased, around and around, maddeningly slow, again and again, until finally he made one long velvet stroke over the swollen bud of her desire. Her hips thrust forward of their own volition.

"Yes, love, yes," he murmured against her skin. "That feels good, doesn't it?"

She couldn't speak, could only nod her head. But when he started to withdraw his hand, shamelessly she whispered, "No. Please don't stop."

Persy lay in Jake's large feather bed, a contentment she had never known before washing over her. He was asleep, looking like a tousled, dark-haired angel, all traces of the devil gone.

She glanced at her surroundings for the first time. Like his office, his bedroom was filled with leather and wood. But unlike the room just below them, this room had proof of the many facets of Jake Devlin. The supple leather and smooth-polished wood was interspersed with not paintings depicting hunt scenes and hounds, but wide-open spaces with prairies, high plains, and jagged mountain peaks that she had only seen out West.

The paintings reminded her of home. And lying there wrapped in this multifaceted sleeping man's arms she longed not for the sophisticated life but for the prairies and plains of Texas—of home. Home. Family. Children. A two-story, clapboard house. A white picket fence all around. And best of all, Jake Devlin.

The vision was so clear in her mind that for a moment it seemed real. But for the hundredth time she had to remind herself it was not. And never would be. Ever.

Jake Devlin didn't fit into her plans for the kind of future she wanted—had dreamed of for years. A voice she wasn't familiar with tried to assert itself, tried to tell her he was everything she could want and more. But she didn't want to listen to the voice. She was making her debut tomorrow night. She had not come this far and worked this hard to throw it all away. This was what she had been longing for, dreaming of, and she couldn't let go of it so easily.

Easily?

She bit her lip against the disparaging laughter that threatened. She had just made love for the first time to a man, practically demanded that he make love to her. How could she have done it? she wondered. How could she have been so shameless? But looking down at his dark curly hair and, in sleep, almost boyish face, she knew. If she couldn't have him forever, then she wanted the memory of him etched in her mind. After she walked out the door she would never see him again. But she would always remember the feel of his hard, muscled chest, the touch of his lips, the smell of his skin, the curve of his smile, and most of all she would always remember the sound of his words when he had told her he loved her.

Her throat tightened. How could she leave? Very carefully she ran her fingers down the sides of his face to his lips. How could she stay?

Knowing she couldn't, she leaned close and whispered, "I'll never forget you, my love." Then she extracted herself from his embrace, gathered her clothes, and fled through the door without looking back for fear that if she did her resolve would shatter into a million tiny pieces.

The night was still young in the bustling city when Persy slipped out of the Dusty Rose. She felt empty and alone when she hailed a hansom. But she was not alone, though she didn't know it. She didn't notice the sleek carriage that pulled up just as she was stepping into the cab. She didn't notice Velda Harvey peer out the carriage window at her. And she didn't notice when Velda instructed her own driver to follow Persy's hired coach.

The carriages covered the distance up Sixth Avenue, then over to Fifth with little trouble. After Persy paid the man she walked the last two blocks to her aunt and uncle's home, then slipped around the back to climb the trellis. Only minutes later, when Velda was just about to leave, none other than Thomas Weathersley strolled up, glanced around, then slipped around the back of the house just as Persephone had done moments before.

For the first time since her arrival in New York, Velda felt a surge of hope. This was what she had needed all along. A way to ruin the perfect Persy in Jake's eyes. She couldn't wait to see the look on his face when she told him just who his little fiancée was meeting in the darkness of night. Everyone knew how Jake felt about Thomas Weathersley.

Velda didn't return to the Dusty Rose as she had planned. Earlier she had thought to try to reason with

Jake one last time before she and her father left the following day. She no longer needed to reason with him. She needed time to think. She needed time to plan how to make her dreams come true.

Fifteen

JAKE WOKE WITH A START. HE WAS FILLED WITH A STRANGE, unsettling heaviness he couldn't name. But then he remembered his dream. Loneliness stretching before him. Love elusive. Persy whispering that she will never forget him. And then she is gone.

A dream, he said silently, though firmly to himself. Nothing more than a dream.

Taking a deep breath, he rolled over, the soft, rumpled sheet falling away, revealing smooth bronzed skin and dark curling hair across his chest. He reached out to pull Persy into his arms, to reaffirm that all his concerns were truly groundless, indeed only a dream.

But the space next to him was cold and empty. Persy was gone.

His heart started to pound, hard and steady. Glancing about the room Jake told himself he would find her curled up in a chair, or leaning against the sill watching the early morning sky. But the chair sat empty and the sky stood unwatched, causing Jake's heart to lurch in his chest when he remembered how Persy had never said she loved him.

He took another deep, calming breath and forced himself to relax. After what had transpired in this very bed he felt certain she was his—no, he corrected himself forcefully, he knew she was his, and he tried to believe. She *hadn't* left him. It was impossible that the only person he had ever loved deeply as an adult would desert him.

Throwing his hard-muscled legs over the edge of the bed, he dressed, trying to still his pounding heart. He tried to concentrate on what Persy's reaction would be when first she saw him. A touch of embarrassment, more than likely, but not entirely. He could just imagine the look of startled excitement, as if an adventure loomed just around the corner. And for them it did. He would ask her to marry him, once again, but this time he would demand that she agree. And she would, he had to believe, how else could she possibly have given of herself as she had if not.

Telling himself he felt certain and confident, he headed downstairs, hating the doubt and insecurity he felt more readily, so much like the feelings he had carried constantly with him as a child. His study was empty, but that didn't surprise him. She had never taken much interest in his books or papers. She had always preferred the heat and warmth of the kitchen. Yes, she was in the kitchen, surely, keeping herself busy while she waited for him to awaken and come downstairs.

She was probably this second talking and laughing with Lola and May, or even Howie since the likelihood of either Lola or May being up at this hour was highly unlikely. But when he pushed through the swinging door, the kitchen stood empty and unwelcoming, as dark as the dungeons of hell. The hearth was cold and the gaslights hadn't been lighted.

The barroom was the same. Cold and deserted. The card room. The dining room. All empty. Only after searching the entire building did he finally allow the undeniable truth to sink in.

She was gone.

His tightly fisted hand smashed into the hardwood casing that surrounded a huge plate-glass window. Pain shimmered up his arm into his shoulder, but he didn't care. In fact, he welcomed the pain. Anything was better than the mind-numbing feeling in his heart.

She had left him.

She had let his hands move over and caress her body, touch her most intimate places. She had let him impale her so deeply he had felt her womb—that sacred place where this very moment his child could be growing. Yet after he had drifted off to sleep, nearly overwhelmed with what they had shared, she had snuck from his bed like a common harlot.

Anger seared him. Fury riddled his mind. And he welcomed it, was happy for it. For where pain had filled his heart before, a sense of betrayal rushed in to fill the void. Leaning forward, he pressed his forehead against the window frame, relishing the bite of hard wood on his skin.

He had given his heart—for the first time ever—only to have it thrown back in his face.

The day progressed with no sign of Persy. Every time the door opened or someone called out, his heart leapt in his chest as he wondered if it was her. He cursed himself as an idiot every time it wasn't. She wasn't coming back, and he'd do well to remember that fact.

His blood boiled. And his anger mounted with each hour that passed. Once the girls woke and began to venture out from their rooms, they quickly learned to steer clear of him. Mr. Bills stopped trying to ask questions about supplies that needed to be ordered, or lines of credit that were overdue. Howie, soft-hearted as he was, asked what was wrong, only to have his head bit off in response.

But Jake hardly noticed that the only family he had ever

known moved quietly about the Dusty Rose on silent feet, trying to determine what could be wrong.

"Persy," more than one person whispered with a knowing nod.

Jake prowled about the Dusty Rose, walking endlessly between the card room, barroom, kitchen, bedroom, and study. With his mind spiraling with images, he relived every second he had spent with Persy, rethinking every word she had uttered.

She had done nothing but lie to him from the very beginning. But he had chosen to ignore it, telling himself that soon he would learn the truth. That, however, had never happened. He knew virtually nothing more about her now—with the exception of the fact that she had given birth to no child, the bloodstain on his sheet was proof enough of that—than he had the day he walked into the kitchen and she pointed a fork at him. He nearly smiled in memory, but cursed instead.

"Oh, Persy," he whispered. "If that's really your name."

Turning away from his study desk, he glanced out the window at the crisp winter-swept streets. His protective armor of anger tried to slip and he pressed his eyes closed. But the anger melted away into despair. The day was nearly done, Persy was gone, and he was alone.

"Why?" he whispered to the empty room and the nameless faces that hurried through the streets below. "Why did you let me love you, then leave?"

But neither the room nor the hurrying masses below held the answer. The room remained silent and the people continued on their way, their footsteps never faltering, their glances never straying up to his window.

He jerked away with a curse, hating himself for the weakness he felt. He had survived and succeeded because he had never succumbed to the fatal flaw of weakness. Stronger men had spent years trying to exploit any crack in his armor, but had never succeeded. And now a little slip of a woman had done what others hadn't been able to do, bringing him shamefully to his knees. And with that thought, his anger surged once again and he sighed his relief. Anger he understood and could deal with. Emptiness he could not.

Persy's debut was only hours away. The house was abuzz with activity. Candles were everywhere, tied with white satin ribbons, encircled with wreaths of waxy green holly. And she had never been so depressed.

It was a relief when she finally managed to slip out of the house, walk the few blocks to the hack line, employ a cab, then ride through the streets to the Ladies Mile. Madame Gullierre was waiting.

"What is this!" the seamstress exclaimed. "Such a long face on one so pretty. And on such a day!"

Persy tried to smile. "I'm just tired."

"Then you should rest, *ma petite*. It will not do at all if you attend your own debut with dark circles under your eyes!"

But Persy knew she wouldn't be able to rest, in fact, she wondered if she'd ever sleep again. She had expected to feel something when she left the Dusty Rose and Jake Devlin, but she had been entirely unprepared for the stark loneliness she now felt.

She would never see him again. She had known that when she asked him to make love to her. Regardless, now the thought seemed impossible. But it was more than possible, it was reality and she needed to face up to it.

Pulling the small velvet bag from her reticule, Persy counted out ninety-six dollars.

"I hate having to charge you once again." Madame Gullierre shrugged her shoulders delicately. "But *alors,* what am I to do? I am not a rich woman."

"No need to explain, Madame Gullierre." Persy glanced

out the window. "Everyone has to do what they have to do, whether others understand or not."

Persy made it up to her room and had the dress hanging in the armoire with the help of Mrs. McFee, who no doubt was doubled over with gratitude.

"See, it all worked out fine, just fine," the cook babbled self-consciously as she smoothed the fine material.

"Yes, it has all worked out," Persy repeated emotionlessly, then escorted the cook out the door.

Left alone, Persy fell back onto her bed. Staring up at the plastered ceiling, she followed the swirls with her eyes, concentrating, trying to forget. But, of course, she could not.

Jake Devlin. Devilishly good-looking. Boyishly charming. Funny. Protective. Loving and caring. No, she would never forget.

She had the crazy desire to damn all else and run back to the Dusty Rose and say yes, shout yes, yes, yes, yes, she would marry him. But that was crazy indeed, for all the reasons that hadn't changed since the day her aunt and cousin regaled her with all the stories of his errant ways. She was here to make her debut into society. It was time to start leading the life of which she had dreamed. It was time to learn what this labor has been all about.

She flung her forearm across her eyes. Suddenly the "sophisticated life" held no appeal. She wanted only to be with Jake Devlin. She gave a derisive snort. What was she going to do? Become a dancing girl? Live in a saloon?

"Persephone!"

Persy jolted from her thoughts. Only seconds later Betty burst in, the door banging back against the wall. "There you are! I've been looking everywhere for you." Betty laughed, though it seemed to be a nervous laugh. "For a second I thought you had snuck off to wherever it is that you sneak off to every day."

"I don't sneak off, Betty." There was no heat or conviction in her words. She was too tired, and she didn't care if she was believed or not.

"Of course you do."

She shrugged her shoulders. "No different from you."

Betty eyed her cousin, then laughed. "Have you been seeing a man, cousin?"

"Yes," she said, refusing to lie any longer, regardless of the consequences.

A sly smile parted Betty's lips. "I knew it. That's why you were so calm when you found Thomas in my bedroom. You're no better than me."

The words were like a slap, hard and stinging, though they were true enough, Persy knew. But somehow, what she had shared with Jake seemed different. Different or not, however, she had ended her entanglement. Betty only seemed to be getting more deeply involved in a relationship that, based on Persy's little knowledge, was bound to end in heartache for her cousin.

Persy sighed. "Do you really think it's wise to be getting involved with him? Just the other day Nathan was saying—"

"Nathan? Nathan! That little peacock! He doesn't know anything!" Betty's voice rose an octave. "And of course it's wise. Thomas loves me!"

Common sense told Persy to let it go, but she had been letting it go for too long. "Has he told you that yet?"

"Certainly he has!"

"He's said, 'Betty, I love you,' has he?"

Betty shifted uncomfortably. "Not in so many words. But you'll see, Miss Priss! He *does* love me. And he'll prove it tonight when he—" Her words cut off and her eyes opened wide.

"When he what?" Persy persisted.

"Nothing," she quickly replied. "You'll just have to wait and see."

"Betty," Persy said, her tone warning. "He's no good. Don't do anything you'll regret."

"What do you know! Like I told you before, you're just jealous, just like everybody else!"

"Oh, Betty," Persy said, reaching over and squeezing her hand. "And just like I told you before, I'm not jealous. I'm just concerned that Mr. Weathersley . . . doesn't have your best interests at heart. I wish you would believe me."

Betty jerked her hand free. "You don't know the first thing about Thomas Weathersley, Persy. Just you wait and see."

The late-afternoon sun slanted through the curtains, casting the room in harsh golden light, and Persy thought that she knew a great deal more about Thomas Weathersley than her cousin imagined.

Velda came through the barroom door.

Howie looked up from his place at the end of the bar, clearly surprised. "I thought you'd already left town?"

"No, no, not yet. I convinced my father to stay another day." Her eyes were lit with anticipation.

Mr. Bills came up beside her. "Miss Velda, we didn't expect you this evening."

"I'm sure you didn't. But I couldn't pass up such a splendid opportunity."

"Opportunity?" Mr. Bills asked, sounding suspicious.

Velda didn't even bother to look at Mr. Bills as she scanned the room. "Yes, a grand opportunity."

Mr. Bills eyed her closely. "What are you up to, Velda?" His tone was firm and filled with warning.

Velda raised her eyebrows and looked down her nose at the tiny man. "You forget to whom you are speaking."

"I haven't forgotten anything. I just happen to have known you long enough to know when you're up to no good."

Laughing her delight, she simply turned away and continued to survey the room. "Where's your little cook?" she asked.

"What business is it of yours?"

"Testy, testy, testy."

Just then Jake came into the barroom from the opposite end of the room.

"Oh, Jake," Velda called.

"What are you doing here, Velda?" Jake didn't bother with pretenses. He was tired of pretending to like someone he clearly didn't like—regardless of what her father had done for him.

"My, aren't we in a huff this evening."

The Dusty Rose was filled with men waiting for the entertainment to start up at ten o'clock. Jake headed toward the bar.

"Jake, darling."

Jake didn't bother to glance her way.

"I was just asking Mr. Bills here where your little Persephone was."

This time Jake's step hesitated before he continued on.

Velda chuckled and sauntered closer, ignoring Mr. Bills's quiet warning. "Now, Jake love, why are you in such a nasty mood?"

Coming up to the end of the bar, Jake ordered a whiskey, straight up.

"Drowning yourself in drink?" Velda asked, coming up right next to him, her sly smile only faltering when she jerked her elbow away from Mr. Bills.

"Miss Harvey," Mr. Bills said firmly, "why don't you come with me."

"I don't want to come with you," she snapped suddenly before she forced her smile back on her face and turned back to Jake. "Don't you know where your little cook is, Jake?"

Jake slammed the empty glass down on the fine-grained bar and demanded another drink.

Velda laughed. "Yes, I guess I'd be drinking too if my fiancée was having an affair with the likes of Thomas Weathersley."

Mr. Bills cursed. Jake's hand stopped halfway to his mouth, the amber liquid sloshing over the side at the sudden movement.

All was quiet and Jake turned deadly eyes on Velda. "What are you talking about?" he demanded in a hard, cold voice.

Velda's smile wavered, though she pulled back her shoulders. "I happened to see your little paramour slinking out of here last night."

Mr. Bills looked startled. Jake's eyes narrowed. "Go on."

"Well, I followed her."

His eyes bored into her. "To where?"

Velda's confidence returned. "*Up* Fifth Avenue."

With a practiced nonchalance that hid the sudden burning anger, he took a swallow of whiskey. At length he set the glass down. "Go on."

"She had a hansom drop her off a good two blocks away from the *mansion* she entered—from the back, mind you. She was sneaking around if ever I saw sneaking."

Jake's mind careened with thoughts as he tried to make sense of these revelations. What had Persy been doing at a Fifth Avenue mansion? Was she a maid? Or a cook for some wealthy matron? He didn't understand.

"What does Thomas Weathersley have to do with this?" he demanded.

Velda's confidence swelled. "Not five minutes after Persephone snuck around the side of the house, along came Mr. Weathersley, who glanced around to see if anyone was looking, then followed your little cook around back."

Fury riddled his body. Jealousy snaked through his

mind and heart like a raging fire. He remembered the day Weathersley had arrived unexpectedly. He had dismissed Persy's odd behavior at the time. But now it all came back to him in a rush. She and Jake had been dancing. He had felt her sudden intake of breath. At the time he had questioned her response, but wrote it off as her being simply startled by the sudden appearance of someone clearly raging mad. Now he knew differently.

But then, as suddenly as it had come upon him, he discounted the jealousy. It was simply disgust that he felt. He wasn't a jealous man. She was a liar and a woman who without feeling any love for him had lain in his arms, all the while cavorting with Weathersley on the side. The blood on the sheets was probably fake, just like everything else about her.

Unbidden, the image of her innocent ways loomed in his mind, telling him Persy had never *cavorted* with anyone before him. But quickly he scoffed. She was an actress, a good actress. And to think he loved her. No, he amended, *had* loved her.

"So what do you think of your simple bride-to-be now, Jake?" Velda asked, breaking into his tormented thoughts.

Jake didn't bother to answer, he simply asked, "Where did she go?"

Velda's eyes widened. "What do you mean, where?"

"Which house? At what cross street?"

"Well, Jake, really—"

"Unless you're lying about what you saw you should have no trouble telling me where the house is."

"Well, umm . . ." she stammered and stuttered, clearly not having expected this turn of events. But finally she told him.

Mr. Bills and Velda stood very still, watching as Jake stormed out of the Dusty Rose.

"Oh, my!" Velda whispered.

Mr. Bills grabbed her arm and turned her toward him. "Oh, my! That's all you have to say?"

Velda tried to wrench her arm free. "I'm just surprised. This isn't what I had planned."

"Surprised that he stormed out of here, clearly intent on confronting Miss Daltry?"

"Well, yes, I suppose."

Mr. Bills sneered. "What did you expect him to do? Fall into your arms and beg you to take Persy's place?"

Velda glanced down at her shoes.

"Answer me!"

"Well, I didn't think that far ahead."

"You didn't think! You never think, Velda!" He took hold of both of her arms and forced her to look at him. "You are a beautiful woman with a lot to offer. But you are so caught up in punishing Jake for not loving you that you're letting your life pass you by." His tone softened. "Forget Jake Devlin, Velda. Get on with your life."

Jake galloped his horse straight up the narrow length of Fifth Avenue. He had given no thought to what he planned to do when he got there, much less what he planned to say. He only knew he finally had to know the truth. He needed the answers to who she was, what she did—why she had lied.

When he careened to a halt in front of the house Velda had described, streams of finely dressed New York society types streamed into the house. Silk-stockinged footmen held doors and directed guests into the towering mansion glistening in the night like a precious jewel. He nearly smiled at the realization that the crush of guests made it possible for him to slip into the house—to find Persy and confront her. Anticipation made him warm, as if he had drunk fine brandy too quickly. Would she be in the kitchen? he wondered. In the parlor serving hors d'oeuvres, perhaps? Scrubbing a bathroom floor?

Or in some back room in the arms of Thomas Weathersley?

Blood pounded in his temples. Rage flowed through his veins. And before he could think better of it, he tossed the reins of his fine thoroughbred to a startled footman and burst into the house. He would find her, and expose her, and make her suffer just as he had suffered since she fled from his bed in the wee hours of the morning.

But all thought came to a deadly halt only seconds after he stepped through the massive front door when he saw her.

At first he forgot that he was angry, that he was furious. She was more beautiful than he imagined. She floated down the stairs in a cloud of white, her hair pulled up and back in an elaborate design of twists and curls. He wanted suddenly to slip his fingers through the mass as he had done last night and revel in the softness. He wanted to run his palms gently against her naked skin and come into her in one hard, driving thrust. But then she gasped, as if indeed he had done just that, breaking the spell, and he remembered how she had lied. And he realized then why her hands were so soft and her sensibilities were so pure. She was no working-class woman in need of money to support herself. She was a New York society debutante with more money than she knew what to do with.

His hand gripped the banister, his knuckles turning white from the force. A debutante. Not in need of money. Or the job he had given her. So what did it mean? he wondered.

"Jake," she breathed.

She was just returning downstairs after freshening up. She had never danced so much in her life. Everyone it seemed vied for her attention.

Stopping halfway down the staircase, her hand clutched the banister much as Jake's did, only her knuckles were covered by pristine white gloves.

People turned to stare. Uneasy murmurs rippled through the room as Jake was recognized.

"How dare he!" someone hissed.

"Surely he wasn't invited!"

"Well, if he was, then I think it's time we leave."

Jake turned around, his cold hard stare making them step back.

His anger sizzled through the foyer, and the guests backed farther away into the huge ballroom. But Persy hardly noticed. Persy hardly cared. For seeing him, standing there, so unexpectedly, understanding came clear like a bright sunny day.

She loved him. She did. She could deny it no longer.

Why hadn't she accepted it before? she wondered. But she knew. She hadn't allowed herself to know. She had wanted the sophisticated life for so long, and had put so much importance on it, she hadn't allowed coherent thought to seep through her protective armor. But her armor was gone, shed like a snake's skin, leaving her with the undeniable truth.

She loved him.

She loved this dark, dangerous devil man who owned a tawdry saloon, and had loved him since the day she saw him in the streets wearing a purple waistcoat. He was kind and good, and more real than anyone she had met so far. Someone who would fit in perfectly in Paradise.

Take the devil home to Paradise.

The words wafted through her head like a tiny ray of hope. They seemed so real. And so perfect.

"Jake, how did you find me?" she whispered, thankful that he had.

Jake laughed though the sound held no mirth. "Don't waste any more dramatics on me. I've seen enough to last me a lifetime."

Surprise washed over her face. "Dramatics?"

"Yes, did you enjoy yourself? Did you and Weathersley spend your nights laughing about how gullible I was?"

"What?" Her brow furrowed in question.

"You don't have to pretend anymore. I know all about you and Weathersley."

"What are you talking about, Jake?"

"Do us both a favor," he said derisively, "don't playact anymore. You're not particularly good at it."

"Jake! What are you talking about? What does any of this have to do with Thomas Weathersley?"

Jake glared at her. "Velda followed you home last night. She saw your loverboy follow you inside. Do you meet him every night? Is it an illicit affair, or is it an arranged marriage and both of you decided to get your kicks elsewhere?"

Persy gasped.

"Enough, Persephone. That is your name, isn't it? Or did you lie about that, too?"

"Jake, please, let me explain."

"So you can come up with some new lies? No, thank you. I've had enough of your stories." He gave her a look that should have turned her to stone. "Just tell me one thing, was it worth it, did you have as much fun fooling a group of people who had come to truly, sincerely care about you as you thought you would? Did loverboy enjoy the tales?"

"Jake, stop! It's not what it seems! Please, let me explain."

"I don't need anyone to explain what slinking into back doors of grand houses in the middle of the night means. I already know."

"But you *don't* know! I didn't know Thomas came here last night. And he certainly didn't come for—"

"Oh, dear Lord!"

Persy nearly tumbled down the stairs when she whipped around at the sound of her aunt's distressed voice. Jake stiffened, ready to be castigated further by this society matron.

Margaret Daltry stood at the top of the stairs, tears streaking her powdered face.

"What is it, Aunt Margaret?"

"I can't believe it. It can't be," she cried, taking the steps like a drunkard.

"What? What's wrong."

Margaret didn't seem to care that she was making a scene as she continued down the staircase, or that people began to poke their heads back out of the ballroom. It looked to be the most scandalous night of the season.

"Aunt Margaret!" Persy demanded. "Tell me what's wrong!"

"She's gone," she wailed. "Gone!"

Sixteen

To think, Persy murmured to herself, she had come to New York to experience the most wonderful night of her life. In reality, it was the worst.

Aunt Margaret cried and sniffed as she descended the stairs. Just when she reached the last step, she moaned, then began a headlong swoon straight for the black and white marble floor. Before she hit, Jake reached out and caught her in his arms.

"What the hell is going on around here?" he grumbled as he staggered under Aunt Margaret's considerable weight.

"Hurry, in here." Persephone motioned toward a side room that would afford them some privacy. Whatever was wrong, or whoever was gone, though she had a sinking feeling it wasn't one of the maids, was no business of the large crowd of partygoers strewn throughout the house.

Jake lowered his burden onto a small settee. Persy fell to her knees at her aunt's side without regard for the dress that had given her nothing but trouble since she laid eyes on it, forgetting for the moment her own dilemma.

"Aunt Margaret, what's wrong?" she demanded gently, patting her hand.

Margaret's eyes fluttered before they opened. At length she seemed to remember what had transpired, and with the return of memory, her face distorted and she began to cry once again. Jake groaned.

Persy scowled at Jake before turning back to her aunt. "Aunt Margaret, please, tell me what has happened."

"She's gone. Gone."

"We know that. But who, Aunt Margaret? Who is gone?" Persy asked, her heart at a standstill as she waited for the inevitable.

"Betty. My sweet Betty is gone." Margaret pulled a single sheet of paper from the folds of her dress and thrust it at Persy.

A childish scrawl that Persy instantly recognized as Betty's announced that she was in love and going away to get married.

"Oh, dear," Persy breathed. "She didn't."

Jake stepped forward and took the note. "Who didn't?"

"My cousin, Betty."

"How could she do this to me?" her aunt wailed.

Persy began to pace, sickened that Betty could do such a thing, while Jake read the missive. But she had little time to be sickened. They had to find Betty and bring her home before it was too late—if it wasn't too late already. She whirled around to face Jake. "Didn't you say that Velda saw Thomas Weathersley sneaking around here last night?"

Jake was still angry, and he looked it. "Yes, to meet you, she said."

Persy rolled her eyes. "To meet someone all right, but not me." She stepped farther away from her aunt who still cried on the settee. "My cousin Betty has been secretly seeing Thomas Weathersley for some time."

"Not you?" he asked, his eyes intense.

Persy stopped. For the moment she forgot her cousin. "Oh, Jake, I'm so sorry about everything. You see . . ." Her words trailed off. Where to begin? What should she say? What could she say to put things right?

"What's happened?" Uncle John flew through the doors, the tails of his cutaway coat trailing behind him. But at the sight of Jake he careened to a halt. "What the hell are you doing here?" His panic was replaced by anger. "What have you done?"

Persy gasped. Her uncle, without knowing what had transpired, blamed Jake at the mere sight of him. "Uncle, Mr. Devlin has nothing to do with this. Thomas Weathersley has run off with Betty."

Uncle John stiffened. "How do you know that?"

She took the note from Jake and handed it to her uncle. John read the missive quickly. "This doesn't mention Weathersley."

Persy cringed. "No, but Betty has been seeing him for some time."

Margaret wailed louder. "Why didn't you tell us?" she demanded through her tears.

Why indeed? Persy wondered. But of course she knew. She had been in no position to tell anyone anything. But it was Uncle John who came to her defense.

"Don't blame Persephone," he said quietly. "Betty told us herself that she loved Thomas. If we are truthful, deep down we suspected something, but we chose to ignore it, hoping it would go away. There's no use in laying blame at anyone's feet but our own. We have to find her and bring her back before irreparable damage can be done."

"But where do we look?" Margaret cried.

Persy clasped her hands together and was near to tears of her own. Where indeed would they look in a place as big as New York? she wondered.

Uncle John sighed. "I don't know."

Jake glanced between Margaret and Persy before he uttered a curse, then said, "I do."

All heads turned toward Jake.

"I'll be back, hopefully with your daughter."

Jake headed for the door. Persy ran forward and grabbed his arm. He turned back but the look he gave her was so cold and hard that she flinched away. They stared at each other, until finally Jake shook free of her hold and slammed out the door.

Jake rode through the streets. He knew where he was going, he just didn't know why. Cursing into the bitter cold, he shook his head. What had made him offer his help? Stupidity. That was it. Plain and simple, he was stupid over Persephone Daltry, and had been since the day he met her. And between that pathetic, surely contrived look of despair on her face, and his absurd relief that she wasn't having an affair with Weathersley, he forgot for a moment that she still wasn't exonerated from her other crimes.

Jake sneered his laughter. Crimes, ha! The only crime had been that he had been taken in—by a society miss! And now he was trying to help her. More the fool he.

But he continued on down Fifth Avenue, knowing that no matter how he felt about Persy, he couldn't sit back and let someone like Thomas Weathersley get away with ruining another innocent, no matter how foolish the girl obviously was.

Mel's Saloon was alive with men from the rougher side of the city and women who under brighter lights would look old and ill. It was places like this that gave all saloons a bad name. But that was the least of Jake's problems just then. Locating Persy's cousin and extracting her from the bowels of the building where he was certain he would find her was.

"Well, well, well," a short man with a paunch said.

"Mel," Jake said simply.

"Come to see what your betters are about?" he asked with a nasty laugh.

"That would be hard to do here."

The man's smile hardened into an angry line. "What do ya want, Devlin?"

"Thomas Weathersley."

"What ya want with him?"

"That is none of your business."

"Then I don't know where he is."

"You better start thinking fast. I doubt that keeping safe scum like Weathersley is worth it if I have to summon the authorities to extract one hopefully still innocent society miss from the bowels of your establishment. I don't think the authorities will look kindly on finding her here."

"A society miss!"

"Yes, a society miss."

Mel ran an agitated hand through his greasy hair. "I knew she looked too prissed up to be a gutter doxy. Damn his hide for getting me involved."

"Now, if you'd like to tell me where I can find Weathersley, I'll get the girl and be on my way."

"Top floor, last door," he muttered and cursed.

Jake took the stairs two at a time, up and around, until he reached the top floor. The stench and grime sickened him, reminded him of days he wished he could forget. For a second he was forced back to long ago. A child fending for himself. No love. No family. Stealing food to take the edge off his hunger.

All of his success vanished and he was once again that boy. It hit him hard. And he realized that the memories had as much to do with Persephone's desertion as the stench in this tawdry saloon.

He pushed it all from his mind. His life was at the Dusty Rose, doing what he knew best with his kind of people.

Good, hardworking, working-class people. He realized now that Persy had done him a favor in leaving, because when he had finally found out from where she came, he would have had to leave her himself.

He found the door and after no more than a cursory knock, he smashed it in.

What he found didn't surprise him, though it sickened him much as the stench and grime had moments before. Weathersley, dressed in nothing more than his white shirt, the tails of which fluttered over stark-white buttocks, pinned a young woman against the wall, her clothes gone already as she whimpered and cried.

After no more than a few bold strides, Jake had Thomas by the back of his shirt. Thomas didn't know what hit him as he crashed into the opposite wall. Betty fell to the floor, huddling there, whimpering.

"What the hell are you doing?" Thomas roared suddenly, lunging for Jake.

"I have to wonder that myself," Jake muttered as he quickly sidestepped Thomas's headlong flight.

Crashing into the other wall, Thomas slumped to the rough-hewn floorboards. He shook his head like a wet dog, as if trying to clear his head. This apparently accomplished, he found Jake, then charged again. This time, however, Jake sighed and was forced to render the man unconscious. With that, Jake turned his attention to the infamous cousin, Betty. He noticed she had stopped whimpering, was trying ineffectually to cover her nudity, and looked at him as if she wasn't sure if she should be relieved or concerned.

"What now?" she whispered, her voice trembling.

"Get dressed, I'm taking you home."

Jake secured a hansom for Betty, then followed the carriage up Fifth Avenue to ensure that she reached her destination safe and sound. It was late when they arrived, though not late enough apparently, since the gala event was still going strong.

When Betty would have simply walked to the front door, clearly in a daze, Jake guided her around back. As long as he had managed to find her and save her from being ruined by Weathersley, he might as well not undo his hard work by allowing her to waltz in the front door, clearly not dressed for a ball.

Once he had her safely in the kitchen, he turned to leave, but was stopped when Persy flew through the door, her aunt and uncle close behind her.

Everyone came to a stop, staring. Betty looked uncertainly at her parents before tears streamed down her cheeks once again and she ran to her mother.

"Oh, Mother, I'm so sorry," she cried.

Margaret stood stiffly, angry at what her daughter had done, her hysterics of earlier magically gone. "What were you thinking?"

"Margaret," John said softly.

"No, John, she has to learn. She has risked this family's reputation over a man we warned her was no good. But no, she knew better, and look what happened."

"Nothing happened." Betty hesitated and glanced down at the floor. "At least not what you think."

"Nothing happened?" Margaret nearly shouted, wrenching free of her daughter's grip. "You flee from your debut, a grand ball I painstakingly planned in your and Persephone's honor. You leave a note and risk all that I have worked so hard to achieve!"

"Yes!" Betty unexpectedly shouted back, dashing her tears away. "It's always what you want to achieve, without ever giving any thought or consideration to what I want!"

"What, like Thomas Weathersley? Or did you simply want to hurt me?"

Betty turned away. "I just wanted to be me. Not what you expected me to be."

"What I wanted you to be?" Aunt Margaret demanded.

"Yes, a replica of you. So I gave you what you wanted. Someone only concerned with lineage charts and money."

Margaret gasped, as did Persy. How many times had Betty gone on about how much she loved Thomas Weathersley? she wondered. Had it all been an act? Or was Betty simply flinging accusations around in the hope that some would stick on someone else besides her?

"Don't blame this on me, daughter. You have been willful since the day you were born, and when things went wrong you blamed the nearest person. This time I'm convenient. And this time you aren't going to get away with it."

With that Margaret Olson turned and left the kitchen and Betty fled up the servants' stairs. John sighed and followed his wife.

Persy and Jake stood quietly.

"Thank you," Persy said at length, embarrassed by her relatives. These people were shallow and selfish. Just as she had been for the last several months. And she was ashamed. "Where did you find her?"

"At Mel's."

"How did you know to go there?"

"If you'll recall, the day Weathersley barged in he boasted of Mel's and the rooms the bar had to take women. Perhaps you had already slipped out by then. I don't remember."

Persy cringed but wouldn't turn away.

"Knowing Weathersley's penchant for ruining innocents I took a chance that he'd go there." He shrugged. "I was right."

"To think, I assumed that supposed gentlemen were supposed to be good and decent, while saloon owners were supposed to be . . ." Her words trailed off.

"Corrupt and amoral?"

Persy sighed, embarrassed and mortified that he was

right. "But I've been proven wrong!" She glanced at the doorway through which her relatives had fled. "Even my own flesh and blood have proven me wrong."

"Not in the way you think. Corruption and morality isn't determined by genealogy charts or addresses. It is determined by the makeup of the man—be he rich or poor, related to presidents or pickpockets. That is what you failed to realize."

"I feel so ashamed. I should know that." Suddenly her expression grew fierce. "I do know that!"

Jake looked at her in disbelief.

"But I do! I learned that at home."

Jake looked at the door through which her aunt and uncle had fled. "I find it hard to believe that you learned anything like that in a place like this."

"But that's just it!" she said triumphantly, excitement and hope bubbling up inside her. "I wasn't raised in a place like this! I was raised in a place where I was taught right from wrong, and to be fair and equitable. But, foolishly, I had never given those ideas much thought. I had longed for the sophisticated life for so long that I disregarded my upbringing. And it took someone that a great many society tomes taught me I should . . . look down upon to remind me of what I had learned—to teach me firsthand about honorability."

His look was still hard and cold. "No charge for the lesson." He started to leave.

Her eyes grew wide. She had to make him understand. But what else could she say? "You're not leaving, are you?"

"Of course I am. I've done my good deed for the day, now I'm going back to where I belong."

He pulled open the door. A gust of late winter wind rushed in to wrap around her. Dried brown leaves left over from summer tumbled across the flagstone walkway, pushed on by the winter breeze. "I don't want you to go."

Though she whispered the words, they rang loud and true in her head. She didn't want him to go—ever. And she knew then, not only that he was a far better man than the likes of Thomas Weathersley, but that she had to come up with some way to convince him to forgive her, or at least to give her a second chance. She couldn't let him go.

But Jake seemed to think differently. His hand still grasped the gleaming brass handle of the door. He stared out into the darkened night. And he didn't speak.

So Persy persevered. "You asked me to marry you."

"Foolishly."

She pressed her eyes closed and told herself that he couldn't have just stopped loving her. He was angry and hurt, and lashing out. "Well, now I'm saying yes."

She heard his intake of breath and hope burgeoned. But hope was dashed when he looked back at her and said, "The offer has already been rescinded."

This time it was Persy who sucked in her breath. And before she could train her thoughts and string together a response, he was gone, leaving her alone in the very room where her problems had first begun.

Persy sank down onto a hard bench in the kitchen, having no idea what to do. The fire popped and crackled in the grate, music and dancing wafted down to her from the ballroom, one floor above. She'd had her debut, and her taste of the sophisticated life. And now all she wanted was Jake Devlin. But he had made it clear he no longer wanted her.

She ran her finger along the edge of the hardwood table. A vast emptiness began to fill her. She missed Paradise desperately, along with her parents and grandmother and siblings. What she would give right that second to have them gather around her and tease her and love her until she felt better! And she wanted suddenly, desperately, to go home.

But she also realized that, yes, she wanted to go home, but she wanted Jake to go with her. She remembered the small ray of hope that had flickered in her heart earlier. *Take the devil home to Paradise.* And this time hope burst forth. Suddenly she knew what she had to do.

With that she raced up the back stairs as fast as the hobbled skirt would allow her to go and changed into a warm velvet gown. Only minutes later she was on her way down Fifth Avenue to Prince Street to confront her perfect prince.

The massive side door through which Persy had always entered was locked. When she knocked no one answered. She had no choice but to turn around and go home or enter through the front door blazing the name Dusty Rose to all who cared to look. And she wasn't going home.

No sooner did she step inside than she was noticed. The whistles and indecent shouts made her blush. The girls, however, were busy talking and laughing with some of the patrons. Howie was busy making sure none of those patrons stepped out of line. Mr. Bills was nowhere to be seen and neither was Jake. But this was just fine with Persy. She preferred to confront Jake in private.

She headed for his office, assuming he was there, but didn't get much past her first step when Jake appeared at the top of the stairs, a woman she had never seen before on his arm. Her heart plummeted to her feet.

He didn't see her and the laughter that floated down to her sounded forced and hollow. Encouragement surged— little encouragement, granted, but she would take what she could get. But then he saw her. He stood poised, one foot on the step below, his countenance a mask of hard, unrelenting anger.

Cowering seemed appropriate. The little encouragement she had experienced deserted her. Suddenly the masses of men throwing back drinks and tossing out profanity like there was no tomorrow seemed safer than Jake Devlin. But she refused to be a coward. She got herself into this mess. She'd get herself out.

She shrugged her shoulders and forced a smile. "Surprise, surprise."

And a surprise was indeed what she received when a man yelled, "Hey, sister," then slapped her on the rear end.

Persy yelped. And Jake took the stairs two at a time until he had the perpetrator bowed over the bar before anyone knew what had happened.

"Don't you ever touch her again," he said in a voice of barely controlled fury.

Men moved away, and it was Howie who finally pried Jake off the other man. Mr. Bills appeared then. "Excitement's over. A round of drinks on the house."

The crowd, with the exception of the man who had slapped Persy, and who was now banished from the Dusty Rose, let out a cheer of approval.

"What are you doing here?" Jake demanded of Persy, turning back to her with a vicious look.

Her chin tilted and she pulled back her shoulders. "I came for you."

All conversation in the barroom trailed off. There was not an ear in the place not suddenly tuned to the little drama that unfolded before them. Only the dancing girls on the stage could have gotten their attention at that point, and maybe not even them.

Jake ran his hand through his hair and cursed. "I already told you, I don't want anything to do with you. I don't need any lying society miss in my life."

Persy sighed. "I'm sorry that I deceived you."

Jake scoffed.

And Persy stiffened. Anger to match Jake's surfaced. "I don't think you're in any position to cast stones, Mr. Devlin. As I recall you're not above deceiving loved ones yourself."

This time, Jake stiffened. "I hardly think—"

"You hardly think, nothing. You're no better than me whether you admit it or not. We're two of a kind." She took a step closer. "We both lied to extricate ourselves from difficult situations. We both should be ashamed. And I am. But I've apologized. Now I deserve a second chance!"

"Like hell you do."

"Why not?" she demanded, unaware of the crowd that was looking on with great interest. "I said I was sorry. I didn't set out to deceive you, just as I didn't set out to care for you either."

The words he was about to speak died on his lips.

"I know you care for me, too, Jake Devlin, you told me so last night." She took another step closer. "And I don't believe that such caring just disappears. You'll remember that fact once you get over being so angry at me."

"Get out of here, Persephone," he said through clenched teeth.

She only stepped closer, until she was standing no more than a few inches in front of him.

"If you don't leave," he said tightly, "then I will."

"You can run, Jake Devlin, but you can't hide. You love me," she stated, her chin tilted defiantly. "Admit it."

He grabbed her by the arms then. "It doesn't matter what I feel. There's no future for us. Don't you understand that? Things can't work out between us."

The force of his words mixed with his tone startled the bravado from her mind. Her brow furrowed. "What do you mean? Why can't this work out between us?"

Jake stared at her long and hard. At length he sighed, then leaned down and kissed her on the forehead. "This can never work because I'm from the gaming hells of life, and you're from the upper crust. Our worlds don't meet, they just collide every once in a while. Just as we collided."

"But you love me! You wanted to make a life with me! How could that have changed?"

"I know nothing about family and commitment, or permanence that your kind of life requires."

"How can you say that?" She looked at him with eyes wide with incredulity. "You have made a family out of the Dusty Rose," she said, her arm sweeping over the crowd that gathered round. "You have been committed to this place and all the people in it for years. You defend and protect those around you. I've never met anyone so loyal in all my life. Good heavens! Because of your loyalty to Harold you nearly succumbed to marriage to his daughter. *That,* Jake Devlin, is family and commitment and permanence."

"That's different."

"Why?" she practically screeched.

He started to turn away.

She grabbed his arm. "You were willing to marry me before."

"That's when I thought you were like me—working class."

Her eyes widened with outrage. "And what does that mean? Did you assume that as working class I didn't need family and commitment and permanence?"

Jake shifted uncomfortably. "Well, no, not exactly." As if it took every ounce of willpower he possessed, he shook free of her grasp and set her at arm's length. "But since we are from two so different worlds, there's no future for us here in New York. I'll never be accepted by your relatives and their friends. And I could never take you away from your family."

Excitement grew in her eyes. "You're right!"

Jake was taken aback.

Persy laughed. "You are absolutely correct! There *is* no

future for us here in New York. But neither one of us belongs in this huge bustling place. We both belong in wide-open spaces where you can see forever—where I know you have longed to go. The first time I saw you I was struck by the longing in your eyes."

"It was indigestion," he grumbled.

But Persy only laughed even louder. "Call it what you like, but I know a place that will cure you of whatever it is. Like I started to tell you before, I wasn't raised here! My family isn't here. They are there. Out West. Out West, where there is a place for us. Out West where a man can be whoever he wants to be. A place where no one asks questions and no questions are asked. A place like I told you about when we first met, where a man's past is his own business and his future is only what he can make it. A place called Paradise. The place I have always called home."

"What are you talking about, Persy?" His voice was low and dangerous.

"I'm not from the upper crust! I'm not even from New York! Until last December I'd never been anywhere near New York. I'm from Paradise Plains, Texas!"

He looked at her hard. "Paradise," he stated finally, the hard edge on his voice softening.

"Yes, Jake, Paradise."

This time when she took his arm he didn't pull away.

"I really am sorry that I deceived you," she said, her voice soft, insistent.

She saw emotions pass through his eyes and she felt a glimmer of hope. "And though you have no reason to believe anything I say, could you try to forget the past and believe me when I say I love you?"

She felt the muscles in his arm stiffen, but he didn't speak.

"I love you, Jake Devlin," she repeated. He had to believe. He had to give her a second chance. "I love you, and I have since the day I saw you in the distance."

The muscles in his jaw worked.

"I've loved you since the day I saw your purple waistcoat flash in the sunshine."

He looked away.

"Then I loved you even more when you stepped out of the kitchen shadows—"

"And you pointed that scrawny little fork at me," he finished for her, his voice like sandpaper.

Tears sprang to her eyes, and she pressed them closed, hoping, praying. When she finally looked up, Jake was watching her. "I'm sorry, Jake," she whispered, "so very sorry."

And then he pulled her to him, and pressed her head to his heart. "Oh, God," he groaned, "you foolish woman. You don't know who you're getting yourself mixed up with."

Persy smiled into his chest. "I'm getting mixed up with the man I love."

He set her at arm's length and looked at her for an eternity. "Are you sure?"

"Very sure." She glanced away, then back. "And perhaps you would reconsider reissuing that marriage proposal."

A hint of a smile flickered on his lips. "You want to marry me, do you?"

"Jake," she said, her tone warning.

"All right, all right," he said with a laugh, before his smile vanished and he grew serious. He took her hand. "Will you marry me, Persephone Daltry?"

"Yes, oh, yes," she cried, before she fell into his arms, and a resounding cheer exploded in the brass and polished wood hall, as friends and patrons alike cheered them on.

Music started up, and everyone began to sing and dance, up on the stage, up on tables, around the hardwood floor. But Persy and Jake were oblivious to the crowd, aware only of each other, cherishing this moment that both had been certain would never happen.

"Will you come home with me?" Persy asked hesitantly amid the noise.

Jake tightened his hold as images of gutters and loveless pasts spun through his mind. But suddenly, without warning, they were banished, and his mind filled with sunshine and laughter, and his sweet Persy. "Home," Jake murmured against her hair. "I like the sound of that."

Seventeen

THE COACH ROCKED AND SWAYED ALONG THE FLAT-PLAINS trail. Butterflies jumbled altogether in Persy's stomach. She was married now. A married woman. It had all happened so quickly she could hardly believe it was true. But the sight of the delicate band of woven gold strands on her finger and Jake Devlin on the bench before her brought the truth home quick enough.

Mrs. Jake Devlin. Persephone Devlin.

She shook her head and smiled.

"What are you smiling about now?"

Jake's deep voice washed over her, bringing her out of her reverie. "I can't wait for you to see Paradise Plains. And my family."

Jake shifted his weight uncomfortably. Every time she mentioned her family Jake grew uneasy. She knew he was nervous because her family didn't know she had married. All she wrote in her letter was that she was coming home —with a surprise. She wanted to tell them about her husband in person, not in a letter. And Jake said he wouldn't travel clear across a good portion of the country unless she was married to him. When she teased him that he was surprisingly prudish and old-fashioned for an ex-saloon owner, he had pulled her close and told her he wasn't about to take the chance that he might lose her once again. And that was fine with her. She couldn't stand the thought that they had come so close to never seeing each other again.

What would have happened had Velda not jealously told Jake that story about Thomas Weathersley? And what would have happened had Jake's pride not demanded that he stalk into her aunt and uncle's home to confront her? Tongues were still wagging about the shock and outrage of the notorious Jake Devlin storming into the Olsons' home as if he owned the place. Fortunately, that was all they were talking about. Not a word of Betty's near disastrous marriage attempts had been uttered. Jake had seen to that. Thomas Weathersley, Persy had heard, had traveled to the Caribbean to oversee the family's investments there. She suspected Jake had seen to that as well.

And what, she wondered, would have happened had she not followed him back to the saloon? He would have stayed at the Dusty Rose, she would have stayed at her debut, and they never would have seen each other again. She pressed her eyes closed at the thought. She had come so close to being irrevocably stupid. But when she opened her eyes, he was there, until death them do part. She had only been stupid for a finite period of time—not irrevocably so.

She reached over and took his hand. "Have I told you today how much I love you?"

He pulled her over to his side of the otherwise empty stagecoach. "Yes, but tell me again." He nuzzled her cheek as he whispered the words against her skin.

"I love you." She laughed, the sound rumbling deep in her throat.

Suddenly he stilled. He looked in her eyes and she saw

the teasing had fled. In its place was that stark look that made her heart break into a million tiny little pieces—that look that said he could hardly believe she was his. It was the look of the lonely child who had been abandoned in the streets, and raised from the gutters by sheer wit and determination.

"Oh, Jake," she whispered, "I love you more than you could think possible."

For one fleeting moment he pressed his eyes closed. When he opened them again, he looked not into her eyes but at her body. Without saying a word, he brushed his fingers along the skin at her throat, before they trailed down, over her collarbone, slowly, down farther, grazing the fullness of one breast. Persephone sucked in her breath as sensation coursed through her body. And it was always the same. His reverence of her body, her amazement that anything in life could be so good. How could she ever have doubted that they were meant to be together?

His finger lingered at her nipple, circling slowly over the silk of her gown, until she could feel the rosebud rise with desire.

"Sweet, sweet Persy. You want me." He seemed amazed.

"Yes, you devil man," she breathed, "and I'll always want you."

The backs of his fingers crossed over to her other breast. "Forever?" he whispered, his fingers circling.

"Forever," she replied, her head falling back.

He pulled her into his lap, so that she faced him.

"Jake," she half giggled, half moaned, when he pulled up her skirt and forced her to straddle his thighs, her knees pressing into the soft cushion.

"Yes, love?" he murmured against her neck.

She held on tight to his shoulders as the stagecoach

rocked along toward Paradise. "What if someone were to see?"

Jake chuckled. "Short of a long-eared, bony-legged jackrabbit, there's not a soul to see what's going on in here."

"What about the driver?" she asked, though she could hardly think for the feel of Jake's fingers cupping her buttock, slipping so far down that she felt the tips caress her most intimate spot. He pressed her against the evidence of his desire, again and again, in cadence with the rhythmic sway of the coach.

"If the driver looks down here," he said, "we'll be in a lot worse trouble than getting caught making love. We'll be riding off the road and no doubt perish from the speed at which we would hurtle into the boulders."

He slipped his finger inside her and she cried out with pleasure. She thought about possible detection no longer.

It had been the same every day since that night before her debut—the night she thought would be her last with Jake. Thank goodness, she had been wrong.

With a boldness she didn't know she possessed, Persy reached down between their bodies and fumbled with the fastening when her body craved so much more. In one driving thrust, he came into her, and they became one.

"Heart of my heart," he whispered, his throat tight with emotion.

"Yes," she agreed, "heart of my heart."

Wanting to touch his skin, she ripped at his shirt until his black curling hair on his hard, muscled chest was revealed. He held her hips, moving her on him, faster and harder, her head flung back, until she collapsed against him, each spent.

When their hearts had slowed, she smiled and circled her finger against his chest. "I don't know how I'm going to stand not sleeping with you for who knows how long."

His body tensed. "What are you talking about, Persy?"

"Well, the house where I grew up is kind of full."

"Full?"

"I told you I have a large family. Before I went to New York I slept in the attic with my sisters, in a narrow bed that folds away into the wall."

"Fold-away beds?"

"Yes." She giggled, still not having moved. "My father is something of an inventor. No telling what he has built in my absence."

"How long have you been gone?"

"About six months."

"Surely not much could have been done in such a short time."

"You don't know my father."

Jake groaned. "But I'm about to meet him. And as far as us not sleeping together, you can forget that, even if we have to sleep on the hard dirt with nothing more than the moon and stars for a ceiling. Your father is just going to have to understand."

Persy pulled back, thinking of how much her father loved her mother. Very gently she traced his chiseled jaw. "I suspect he'll understand. And he'll love you. So will everyone else."

"How do you know that?" he grumbled. "I'm not so sure how I'd feel about my daughter showing up with a saloon owner as a husband."

"Ex-saloon owner."

"Yeah," he said, his voice far away. After a moment he looked out at the passing scenery. "I wonder how they're doing?"

"Who? Everyone back at the Dusty Rose?"

"Yes," he said. "It still amazes me how it all worked out."

"Do you regret selling it?" she asked, suddenly pensive.

Jake gave a sad laugh. "Regret, no. Relieved, yes. And

it's hard to imagine Harold and Mr. Bills owning and running the Dusty Rose together."

"I think it's perfect."

He shook his head in disbelief. "You're right."

"And Velda and Mr. Bills getting married was perfect, too."

"Who would have ever thought it?"

"Me," she stated proudly. "When I first met them."

He looked at her, then smiled. "And did you predict Harold and Lilly, as well?"

"No." She laughed. "That marriage caught me completely by surprise."

"But marriage seems to agree with Harold."

"He looks a good twenty years younger."

"A good wife will do that to a man," he teased.

"I wondered why you had started looking like a babe in its mother's arms."

"And now I have to face your family."

This time Persy groaned.

"If that was supposed to fill me with confidence," Jake said, his voice laced with sarcasm, "it failed."

"Sorry," she replied distractedly. "I was thinking more of *my* reception than yours."

"What do you mean?"

Persy sighed. "I'll be the first Daltry not to complete their labor."

"Ah, yes. The infamous labor." Jake smiled and reached across and took her hand. "Why do you think you've failed?"

"Well, I've obviously failed. As I told you, I was sent away to become the belle of the ball, to have my grand debut." She shrugged her shoulders and shook her head in resignation. "And here I am, returning six months early, wanting nothing more than to get home."

Suddenly she stopped, her breath held. "Wanting nothing more than to get home," she repeated breathlessly. "That's it! That has to be it!"

"What is it? What are you talking about?"

"Don't you see?" she cried with growing excitement. "My grandmother sent me away because she must have realized that I was desperate to get away."

Jake seemed to consider. "After initially hearing your story, and with all you've told me since about how close your family is, it didn't seem to make sense that they would willingly send you away to start a new life."

"You're right! Absolutely right! It didn't make any sense to me either. I never thought it did, especially when I saw how upset everyone was by my departure, including my grandmother—the very woman responsible for the journey. But Grandma must have known! She must have figured that if I was ever to be happy in Paradise, I had to learn to appreciate it."

Jake smiled and squeezed her hand. "And do you appreciate your home now?"

"Yes! Oh, yes! I've missed Paradise terribly. And I can't wait to tell my family that."

Suddenly she looked worried. "Do you think they'll believe me?"

"Why wouldn't they?"

"Because I'm returning six months early. They might think things didn't go well, and that I returned not because I wanted to but because I had to."

"You were anything but a failure," Jake said dryly, "if that Lewis fellow and his friend Nathan are any indication. I thought I was going to have to resort to violence to keep them away from you."

Persy giggled. "They certainly weren't pleased that I married you."

"I don't think I had much to do with it. You marrying anyone other than either one of them would have gained the same reaction. Besides, even if you didn't have the undying love of two society fops—"

"They weren't fops," she said, feeling the need to defend two people who had been so kind to her.

"They were fops. And as I was saying, if you didn't have the undying love of those two society fops to use as proof, you have the fact that you convinced me to follow you to such a place you love so well."

"I did, didn't I?" she whispered.

"Yes, Persy love, you did."

The stagecoach pulled up and came to a rambling halt. Persy took a deep breath. For all her words of encouragement to herself and Jake, she had no idea what to expect when she stepped out the door. She hoped she was right and that she was sent away to learn how to appreciate Paradise Plains. If so, she hadn't failed. But if not, arriving six months early, married to a saloon owner—former saloon owner, she revised—she very possibly could be in deep trouble. But there was no other way to learn the answer than to step out of the carriage and confront her family.

"You can't sit in here all day," Jake said.

"You're one to talk."

Jake chuckled. "And to think I used you as an example of a sweet, abiding woman who knew her place."

She smacked him playfully. "I know my place all right."

"Yes, love." He pulled her close. "In my arms." Before she could respond, he pushed her toward the door. "Can't put this off forever."

With no help for it, she stepped out of the carriage, and at the sight of the entire Daltry clan, her concerns were replaced by the sheer joy of her homecoming.

"Persy!" they cheered.

In seconds, she was wrapped in the arms of her family, with everyone talking at once.

"You're home!"

"We missed you!"

"We thought you'd never return!"

Persy pulled back. "How could I not," she said, her voice choked with emotions.

And then she saw her grandmother, the woman whom she most resembled, the woman who had sent her on the journey.

They stood at least ten feet apart. Their eyes locked and Persy's heart pounded. What would her grandmother say? Her countenance gave no clue. But just when Persy thought she could take it no longer, Minerva's gentle face broke with a radiant smile and she opened her arms.

Persy flew into her embrace and held tight. No words were spoken at first, until in Persy's ear, so no one else could hear, Minerva whispered, "I was so afraid we had lost you."

Tears burned in Persy's eyes. She had been right. "Oh, Grandmother, I've never wanted to be anywhere more than I want to be in Paradise right now."

Minerva held her granddaughter at arm's length but before she could speak Persy added, "I realize now that you sent me away so I could actually experience the life I had longed for. Only then could I return home and be happy."

"Oh, darlin' girl, I'm so proud of you. There were times when I wondered if you'd ever understand what I had done and why. There were times when I was afraid that you would end up loving that life as much as you thought you would and stay." Her voice cracked. "But I had to believe that we raised you to love your family and would see the goodness of your home."

Minerva stepped back. "Now," she announced, "one more Daltry has completed their labor."

"Yes," Odie said, "she completed her labor by coming back to us."

A cheer went up.

"In record time," Lee added with a smile to his closest sibling.

"And now for Persy's prize," Minerva stated, a smile curved on her face.

"Oh, no!" Persy suddenly cried. "You don't need to do anything else for me. Sending me away was enough."

The family looked confused.

"Yes, by sending me away, I found my prize."

"You found your prize in New York?" C.J. asked.

"What are you talking about?" Allie demanded.

"Uh humm."

The entire Daltry family turned toward the stagecoach. Jake stood on the threshold, before stepping down. Persy's heart burgeoned with love at the sight of him, his dark hair tousled in the breeze.

"Can I help you, young man?" Odie Daltry said, forgetting prizes for the moment.

"Need directions?" Lee asked, stepping forward.

"Who are you here to see?" Venus asked with her lips tilted in a flirtatious smile.

"Venus!" Jane reprimanded.

"What?" she instantly demanded.

And then suddenly everyone was talking at once. Odie was admonishing his daughter not to talk back to her mother. Allie was adding her two bits, while everyone else joined in for nothing more than good measure. Only Jake, Persy, and Minerva seemed oblivious to the noise.

"Who is this?" Minerva asked Persy overloud, gaining everyone's attention.

Jake stepped forward and placed his arm around Persy's shoulder.

"This," Persy said, a smile slashing across her face as she gazed up into Jake's green eyes, "is my prize."

Silence. Even Jake seemed taken aback by her bold statement, before he offered her a teasing smile. But moments later, the teasing was gone, and Persy could feel the tension in Jake's body, matched only by her own. She wasn't sure if her family was simply shocked or angry. Minutes ticked by and still no one uttered a word.

But then Bub stepped forward, his hands on his hips, and looked Jake in the eye, a look of intense scrutiny on his thirteen-year-old face. "So you're the surprise Persy wrote to us about?"

A heartbeat passed before Jake said, "Yes, I suppose I am."

"Can you read?"

"Well, yes."

"Can you write?"

"I'd like to think so."

"Can you support my sister in the manner to which she is accustomed?"

Jake blinked, then blinked again. Never in his thirty years had he been grilled in such a manner, and never by someone who didn't even reach his chin.

"Can you?" Bub persisted.

"I think I can manage," Jake replied, amazed once again by the amount of money Harold Harvey and Mr. Bills had paid for the Dusty Rose. He could support Persy in a manner to which she wasn't accustomed and then some.

Bub's face grew fierce. "Manage?"

"Atlas," Odie admonished, though he stepped forward and took his son's place.

Persy cringed. Right in the middle of Paradise Plains, Texas, her new husband was being put through the wringer. "Had any of you thought to merely say welcome and save the rest for home?"

Lee stepped next to his father as if Persy hadn't said a word. But Jane, ever the voice of reason, bustled forward. "Persy's right. Let's go on home. We can talk then."

They rode in virtual silence all the way back to the ranch in a special carriage designed to carry them all. Jake would have loved the ride on any other occasion, but with multiple faces staring at him as if by just looking they could take his measure, he wasn't inclined to take note of the vast rolling plains over which they traveled.

Persy was equally uneasy. She had suspected many things, but this hostile welcome wasn't one of them. The short ride had never seemed so long. First the train ride, then the stagecoach ride, and both seemed short compared to this. Inwardly she groaned.

The sight of the house made her forget, at least for a fleeting moment, that all had gone awry. She was home. And Jake must have sensed her joy for he reached over and discreetly squeezed her hand. Their eyes met and held and Persy knew that no matter what happened, they would always have each other.

Everyone alighted and stood in front of the house, glares flying freely, and Jake nearly took the carriage and returned to town. But Persy held on like he was a lifeline, and from the ominous looks on her family's faces, maybe he was. So much for all Persy's words about how open and loving her family was. The gaming hells of New York were looking quite friendly just about now in comparison.

"Well, I suspect we had best go in," Odie said, his scowl stretching across his craggy face.

They trudged in unison up the front steps, Jake and Persy relegated to the back. And just after everyone had stepped through the front door, Jake and Persy nearly jumped out of their skin when every Daltry family member leapt around and yelled, "SURPRISE!"

And sure enough it was. A huge surprise with banners flying and everyone from the small town of Paradise Plains standing in the living room hollering their welcome, not solely to Persy, but to Jake as well.

As if they had known he was coming.

The thought hit Persy and Jake simultaneously. "They knew," Persy whispered.

"Yes, we knew," Minerva said, reaching out and taking Jake's hand. "And welcome."

"A Daltry welcome," Meredith said with a shake of her head. "Nothing is ever simple around here."

"How did you know?" Persy asked.

Minerva exchanged a glance with Jane before she said, "We had a nice little letter from someone named Lola."

"And a May," Venus added.

"And a Mr. Bills," Lee said.

"And a Howie," Odie offered.

"And a Lilly."

"And a Harold."

"And a Velda."

"Velda?" Persy asked.

"Yes, a Velda," Jane replied. "Even your Aunt Margaret wrote."

"I can't believe it," Persy breathed. "What did they say?"

Odie stepped forward. "Every one of them felt a need to express their gratitude to this man," he said, looking into Jake's eyes. "They all wrote praising your fine character, all seeming to think that we knew the two of you had gotten married." He looked at Persy with a raised eyebrow. "Which of course we didn't."

"I wanted to tell you in person."

Odie's gaze softened. "I figured as much." He looked back at Jake. "But what's important now is to let you know how happy we are that you're here, how happy we are that you and Persy came home."

The small crowd gave up a cheer. Jake stood nonplussed as this gaggle of Persy's family swarmed around him, talking all at once. He could hardly fathom the feeling. Truly they welcomed him—welcomed him home.

Minerva stepped away from the crowd to gain everyone's attention. "And even though Persephone seems to think she has brought home her prize, not to discount you,

Jake dear, but we have traditions, you know, and since Persephone has completed her labor early she gets a prize from us now . . . as well," she added, trying not to insult this new addition to the family.

"Probably a good thing," Jake teased. "I'm not sure what kind of a prize I will be. This city boy has never been on a ranch."

"You'll do fine," Minerva said.

"We'll teach you everything you need to know," Odie offered.

"It's easy," Lee replied.

"Now, now, now," Minerva cut in. "Before you all get off on something else, it's time for Persephone's prize!"

"Let's go, let's go," Bub demanded. "Let's go see Persy's prize."

Persy and Jake were pulled along in the tide until they were once again in the carriage, then driving to the west, along the river. And there it stood. A white clapboard house with a pitched roof, wraparound porch, and a white picket fence around the perimeter. It stood on a rise above the river, with a plethora of windows so a person could look out and see forever.

"I built it while you were away," Odie stated proudly.

"With my help," Lee added.

"And mine," C.J. and Bub wanted everyone to know.

"And now it is yours," Minerva said to Persy, "and your new husband's."

"A home of our own," Persy whispered.

Without waiting, Jake leaned over and kissed Minerva on the cheek, shook Odie's hand, then swept Persy up into his arms and carried her across the threshold. "Looks like we won't be sleeping under the stars after all."

Recipes from the heartland of America

THE HOMESPUN
❧ COOKBOOK ❧
Tamara Dubin Brown

Arranged by courses, this collection of wholesome family recipes includes tasty appetizers, sauces, and relishes, hearty main courses, and scrumptious desserts—all created from the popular *Homespun* series.

Features delicious easy-to-prepare dishes, such as:

Curried Crab and Shrimp en Casserole

1 large can crabmeat	1 pint milk
1 can shrimp	2 tablespoons butter
2 tablespoons flour	1 teaspoon curry powder
½ teaspoon salt	1 tablespoon chopped onion
1 tablespoon chopped green pepper	

Cream the butter and flour. Add milk. Cook over slow fire, stirring constantly until slightly thickened. Add salt and curry powder. Stir until smooth and remove from fire. Put onion and pepper into cream sauce and mix well. Shred crabmeat and clean the shrimp. Spread a layer of crabmeat in casserole and cover with a layer of cream sauce. Repeat with shrimp and cream sauce. Repeat this until all is in the casserole. Bake at 300 degrees for 30 minutes before serving.

A Berkley paperback coming February 1996

If you enjoyed this book,
take advantage
of this special offer.
Subscribe now and get a

FREE
Historical
Romance

No Obligation (a $4.50 value)

Each month the editors of True Value select the four *very best* novels from America's leading publishers of romantic fiction. Preview them in your home *Free* for 10 days. With the first four books you receive, we'll send you a FREE book as our introductory gift. No Obligation!

If for any reason you decide not to keep them, just return them and owe nothing. If you like them as much as we think you will, you'll pay just $4.00 each and save at *least* $.50 each off the cover price. (Your savings are *guaranteed* to be at least $2.00 each month.) There is NO postage and handling – or other hidden charges. There are no minimum number of books to buy and you may cancel at any time.

Send in the Coupon Below

To get your FREE historical romance fill out the coupon below and mail it today. As soon as we receive it we'll send you your FREE Book along with your first month's selections.
